A Month of Sundays
A Political Strip-Tease

Richard J. Sherry

ISBN: 9798836641078

Cover design: Kathleen Sherry

Contents

OCTOBER 2021

CHAPTER 1: BAKER

Tuesday, October 19, 2021
Eastern Montana

Baker mused on how he intended to upend American politics in the next six months. At the same time, because he was a man who loved landscapes, and felt the power of place, he was conscious at every moment of the road itself. He had driven it, after all, twice-yearly, out and back, for almost forty years. From the Midwest to his family home in Spokane, two days or three depending on whether he was with Jean or with her and the kids. Landscape familiar, powerful, always changing. And today, 750 miles of memory alone from Fargo to Bozeman. Somehow, deep down, he was relieved to be here, even though home for two decades had been Minnesota.

Baker's smile lingered as he drove west into Montana. After gassing up the Outback at Glendive at noon, he still had hours to go on I-94. *Big sky, empty range,* he thought. *My kind of country. Dry and open in October. Cool today, too.* Glendive petered out rapidly behind him. *Still,* he smiled, *you have to respect a town that could get four freeway exits for 2000 people.* Off to his left he could see the greenery still over the Yellowstone River, wide and shallow. The river would accompany him all the way to Livingston. *Bozeman tonight*, he thought. *Surrounded by mountains after months in the flatland.*

October 19, 2021, he mused. *Tonight, American politics changes.* He tapped the "Source" button on the steering wheel and brought up *All Things Considered* on Montana Public Radio. *This far out, it'll be Miles City*, he remembered. As the teaser for each story rolled over him, he considered how these stories might change in the next few months.

"Find out exactly what happened at the capitol on January 6th..... January 6th committee votes on holding Steve Bannon in contempt....Most of Texas' new districts are majority white, diluting power of voters of color....Black and Latino families are bearing the weight of the pandemic's economic toll..... Study abroad is coming back. But with more hurdles.... Rep. Jayapal on negotiations between Biden and House Democrats over Build Back Better...Trump shapes North Carolina's Republican Senate primary with an early endorsement....."

For a political science professor, NPR was like heaven.

In the end, it hadn't proved that hard to get the ball rolling. Setting up a private internet account outside the US, running it through overseas servers and back to the United States through a couple of different locations, and posting email messages a long way from where he lived, on private auto trips or even bus tours around the country, he nudged. The people he nudged, he suspected, would take it from there.

You have to be looking for it, he reminded himself. *It'll be on the news, if we're lucky. Or not so lucky,* he sighed. He had imagined how it *might* go, with some anxiety. Those were his nightmares. Over a space of three days, the governors of three states *might* be shot from ambush. One senator from Texas *could* be struck by a car and left with severe brain damage—*not that anyone would notice,* he thought. He shook his head, lips tight. The leaders of three think tanks *might* simply disappear while on a fishing trip together in Canada. Two federal legislators *might* be kidnapped and executed. It might be as bad as that.

And then he could imagine the shock. *Am I starting a flash-war between liberals and conservatives? If we get to violence, will innocent people get hurt?* He could imagine the reaction when someone who had shot a sitting governor brought in a pile of emails, corporate documents, spreadsheets, and said, "Governor So-and-So betrayed us. I'd do it again." And each would bring out evidence Baker had sent him.

It was going to be hard to get around that stuff, he thought. With help, Baker had hacked email and text message accounts, and then gone after internal documents from oil and coal companies and then even further, into the documents of international companies who had supported the government figures. Dumping it to the mailing lists of small radical organizations would mean that someone was bound to take action, and they would. Nudging people worked, but not always how or when you expected.

The results were likely going to be magnified, he thought, clicking into cruise control on the way to Miles City. *Easy,* he told himself. *Not quite ready for 80 yet.* After hours across North Dakota, even the small adjustment up from 75 to 80 fretted him a bit. Tonight, other documents he'd taken would be dumped as files to the New York Times, the Washington Post, two papers on the West Coast and one in Denver. And the Wall Street Journal. Over the next week, Republican "conservatism" and Democratic "liberalism" would be exposed in a way they hadn't ever been before.

And next week he'd arranged to start dumping, one Sunday at a time, material on every senator up for re-election next year, state after state, in alphabetical order. Thirty-four states, 14 Democrats and 20 Republicans, were about to find out about "transparency." *Announce it publicly,* he thought, a*nd send the materials to every voter in the state, gained from the finance files of the parties. That should do it,* he had thought. It'd be hard to estimate the response when every Kentucky voter, say, Republican or Democrat, got a copy of the file on "their" senator, showing where the contributions came from, letters suggesting how policies or laws might be written to favor one group or another, even "demand" letters from the senator's office to donors. And then there were the internal memos from the Party leaders to legislators. Even stuff from the White House. Well. That would put the voters inside the conversation. With just over a year until the 2022 midterms, voters were about to get an education in what was really going on in the federal government. *Some folks were going to shine like the stars in heaven,* he smiled, *and some will be in hell.*

Too bad FOX and CNN and MSNBC weren't on the distribution list, he smiled. *It will be fun to watch them play catch-up.*

The first challenge had been to ask "What-if," and then "How." "Why" or "Why not" weren't even on the table. "What-if" had been pretty darned attractive right out of the gate. "What if Americans had evidence in the words of their own legislators, their own 'Party' leaders, about what they wanted and about how things worked? What if the behind-the-scenes negotiations, complete with minutes or digital recordings, could actually be out there on the table?"

He was hoping that it wouldn't destroy democracy, but rather, that it would lead to a new affirmation of it. And that meant overturning the status quo of safe districts, safe senate seats. He didn't care about the Supreme Court—he wasn't "corporate," and this wasn't *The Pelican Brief.* It wasn't a Tom Clancy novel, either, though there were some similarities. He hoped it would be way less exciting. Baker still thought that Americans were decent enough to be revolted by the whole enterprise. And every night Baker, a praying man, prayed that he wasn't burning the house down.

At Miles City, he got off the freeway, turned right on Haynes, and drove down to the County Brew Coffeeshop, new since the last time he'd been through. As he swung his legs out of the Outback, he winced at the October chill, damp with rain to the west. The bank's time-and-temperature display as he'd driven in said it was 37 degrees. *Will I hit snow at Livingston?* he wondered. The drive from Fargo, begun at daybreak, was beginning to wear on him. He figured, though, that driving a two-year-old Subaru Outback across North Dakota and Montana made him pretty much invisible, even with Minnesota plates, and invisible was best, right now. Every tenth car out here was a Subaru, and the further west you went, the longer they seemed to last.

At the counter he ordered a grande Americano and a bacon ciabatta and two chocolate chunk cookies, paid with a twenty, and then stepped into the men's room while the barista got it ready. He glanced at himself in the mirror. No lunch crumbs on his shirt. A full head of dark hair, white at the temples, a little long right now. Slightly stooped, clean-shaven face neutral like a mask—he tried a smile on, and gave it up with a laugh—only a few wrinkles still. *Yes, but that's because you don't use your face very much,* he thought. Three minutes later, anonymous behind his sunglasses, jeans, low hiking boots, and a long-sleeved T-shirt and short-sleeved down vest, he was back in the car.

Let's see about the world, he thought, and tuned in NPR's *Here and Now.* Billings, Livingston, and Bozeman were waiting as he drove up the long ramp onto the interstate, away from the six casinos mixed in with the KFCs, Wendy's, McDonalds, and ever-present gas stations, high-canopied for the semis rolling through. *And then let's see if we can make it better.*

Besides, what did a PoliSci professor on terminal sabbatical have to do with his time, anyway, he asked himself. *And who'd suspect someone so innocuous?*

Mmm-hmm. Invisible and anonymous might be important for a while. A month of Sundays. He smiled at the phrase.

.

CHAPTER 2: WASHINGTON STUDY

November 2019
Washington, D.C.

The whole thing had started with some of his first Minnesota undergraduates. He discovered that if he built bridges to local politicians in the state capital, they'd take his students as summer interns. He'd signed them up for independent studies, debriefed them afterwards, and had the students present to his introductory classes. When one of his state senator friends had made the jump to Congress, serving as a representative in his district, he'd begun building a pipeline of fresh young students who could devote a semester to a "Washington Study Program" he'd devised.

Other state and federal representatives from surrounding districts saw these juniors or seniors from a local college—a *Christian* college, no less—and found they were dedicated, hard-working, didn't have to be told twice, and knew technology. Best of all, they were ethical: they kept their mouths shut, kept confidences. They were, generally speaking, politically neutral, and could work for a Republican or a Democrat and keep their own convictions out of it. The college loved it, featured it in all of their advertising, and after several years, word had begun to spread. From two students, he was up to thirty a year, and the program's enrollment was over a hundred. It had become a signature element for his department, and one of his colleagues began handling the "local" end, with interns in Minneapolis and St. Paul.

When Baker had started his career, it was rare enough to have a religious college with a business program; faculty thought they were betraying the liberal arts if they went beyond economics. But Baker's college was steadily different from other Protestant institutions: social work, business, nursing, elementary education, strong programs in the sciences. And they welcomed a political scientist. *Those darned Swedes,* he chuckled, *just want to bring Jesus quietly into everything. And love into everyone.*

Within two or three years, some of those PoliSci students were working in Congress full time, migrating to the offices of the Senators and House members from Minnesota. And then the program started placing interns more broadly in the House and Senate in Washington.

And because Washington is a place where knowing people is a key to getting a job—just like everywhere else—pretty soon his grads were working in a dozen offices in the House and Senate. They linked to the interns who were still undergraduates and there for a semester. And because they were who they were, young, active, attractive, smart, they were also gregarious. They made friends. Some of them, if so inclined, found churches together. Romances blossomed.

Because they'd all shared Baker's classes and their undergraduate years—though now, for some, it was a dozen years behind them—they networked.

One evening in November 2019, not in an election year, Baker had come to Washington to review how the program was going and to see if there were other opportunities. The usual flailing around was going on in Congress, but three weeks earlier impeachment hearings had begun against the president. It seemed as though landmines were going off daily in public, televised testimony. He'd been thinking in another direction, that the next step for the Washington program might be into some of the agencies, and if he could get some pre-law or accounting students interested, the Department of Justice. No one from the college had interned yet at the Supreme Court, but he thought it might be a possibility. He wasn't sure how the impeachment events would affect any of his plans, except that they would distract his students.

The students had been thrilled to see him at the "mid-semester review," with dinner, coffee, and conversation. He'd invited both the thirty current interns and the graduates of the program in the area, right up to Justin Ross, 30, working in a Senator's office full-time. In his quiet, unruffled way, Baker had shaped the beginnings of their careers, and he always asked what his next group of students needed to know. That night, meeting in a conference room at the Hotel Donaldson, three blocks from the White House, they began to unpack their experiences. The oldest was Ross, the youngest, 20, and the forty of them—and wasn't it a treat for Baker that almost everyone in the region had come!—finished dessert and coffee. He got up and stood in front of the podium, leaning on the table, jacket off, sleeves half rolled up. They'd seen him in Professor-mode for years.

"So, tell me how it's going. Newest people first," he smiled. He'd asked Luis, one of the current undergraduates, to take notes, and he sat on his right at the table, laptop ready.

Whenever he got in front of a group of students like this, Luis thought to himself, he radiated respect and interest. He treated all of them like grown-ups, and they returned the favor. *How do I get to be like this guy?* he thought.

They weren't slow to warm up. "Well, for one thing," one of the junior women began, "we're seeing a lot more partisanship than we expected. In our Minnesota delegation in Congress, I wasn't aware of how angry people are getting. Republicans and Democrats are finding it hard even to sit down together for coffee. It's like meeting with the enemy. You used to say that this was a 'Gingrich' legacy, but this is even worse. It's going to define a 'Trump' legacy. Some of the worst stuff is about this impeachment. Is it this bad in St. Paul?"

Baker nodded and smiled, that little lift of the right cheek that said, *"Yes, Gwen, we've been here before, and it's a little dismaying, isn't it?"* They'd laughed about it before. "How can I communicate this kind of tension and struggle to students? What should I be recommending? Keep their mouths shut? Keep their opinions to themselves?"

"No," the young woman laughed. *Gwen Rogers, Cedar Rapids*, Baker remembered. "You *already* do that. But I wasn't prepared, and I'm not the only one, for the kind of obsession about 'loyalty' and 'strategy' that's going on. It's at a whole different level. It's not just posturing, at least in our office."

Summer Morgan, sitting across the table from Gwen, another junior, nodded. *Denver*, Baker remembered. "It's insulting," she said. "I'm working with our two Senators and they're routinely getting threats in their official email. They can't hardly have a conversation with the outstate Republican reps in the House."

"Maybe I need to have you both talk to the class about this 'feature' when you come back at the end of the semester," Baker mused. "You're already scheduled for a session, but put this on your list. Bring examples, although be discreet." He glanced around, cataloguing them by name and hometown. "Who's next? How about you?" he pointed at another junior sitting next to Luis, Aiden Howard from Arden Hills.

Forty minutes went by with lots of ideas. Baker tried to keep them focused, and it was lively. Even those who didn't offer something were clearly engaged.

As Baker got to the most senior of the group, Ross, a full-time staffer in the Senate, he sensed something different. The atmosphere was shifting. Justin had been one of his earliest students in the Washington Study Program, the "WSP," and his excitement had inspired others after him. He'd been quiet all evening, although nodding occasionally. "What about you, Justin?" Baker began. "What can you point to that's important this year?"

Ross seemed suddenly ill at ease. He sat up in his chair, one forearm on the table, his other hand cupping his forehead. Suddenly, both hands were on the edge of the table. "I don't know that I can keep doing this, guys," he said, looking around the group. "I'm running into things that are dangerous to talk about, and even illegal. And if any of you says anything about this, I'm not just out of a job. It'll be worse than that. And it's worse than this impeachment stuff."

Silence. People leaned forward, riveted.

"I don't know how to manage some of the ethics and security issues I'm seeing—and not just in my office, but others as well."

"Luis," Baker said, "close the laptop. Everybody, turn your phones off. Right now. Put them on the table in front of you.

"Let's talk, and let's be careful."

CHAPTER 3: THE BALL ROLLING

Tuesday, October 19, 2021
Bozeman, Montana

What we are always afraid of, Baker thought, remembering that night, *is that democracy will die and that we will be responsible.* This was not the first time he'd considered the thought. He'd voiced it often enough in class.

He pulled off of I-90 at Bozeman at the Main Street exit, then down West Main to Seventh, and right two blocks to the Emerald Motel, which hadn't changed in years, except it wasn't called "The Crown on 7th" any longer. He remembered staying here with his wife when they went west, under the mountains on either side of the Gallatin Valley. *Well, don't go there,* he thought. He'd always remembered Bozeman as prettier than either Butte or Billings, and a welcome end to Bozeman Pass. The Pass always felt either claustrophobic or like a lumber mill log flume at full speed. *Mama's Mexican Food, Taco John's, or the Knife, Fork, and Spoon?* he asked himself, glancing at the signs outside the motel.

He checked in at the front desk, as anonymous as he could be, paying in cash tonight, and parked halfway down the long, one-story building. He pulled his suitcase and

14

laptop bag out, set them by the bed, and checked the Mama's Mexican menu on the laminated desk protector. He punched in the number on his cell phone, ordered take-out, and strolled out to North Seventh. Traffic was light after the rush, and he crossed the road toward the restaurant and then looked east to the Bridgers, the mountain range that ran for forty miles north and curving slightly west. Five thousand feet higher than Bozeman, they enclosed the long, wide Gallatin Valley. He would have them as company in the morning, all the way to the Wheat Montana Deli at Three Forks, a half-hour north and the right place for an enormous cinnamon roll, coffee, and mental preparation for the pass at Butte. Spokane tomorrow night.

He made a mental note to get several bags of flour for his sister-in-law at Wheat Montana, and then walked up to Mama's place, inhaling the texture of carnitas and black beans. *Not a bad night, still in the fifties. Jean jacket's fine.*

After supper, time to review where we are. He turned to go back to the Emerald, carrying the plastic bag and its styrofoam-trayed meal.

An hour later, he put the lid back on the plastic tray, stuffed all the paper goods and plastic into the carrying bag, and took it outside to the dumpster behind the building. *Not going to have that grease and hot sauce smell soaking into my clothes all night,* he thought. *As tasty as it was. How about a little reconnaissance and stretch my legs?*

He walked out on to North Seventh, for a half hour stretch after the long drive, and turned south. He'd left his sunglasses in the car, but had put on a western hat he'd had for years and seldom worn in Minnesota. He figured a jean-jacketed guy, even without cowboy boots, would be inconspicuous enough, and people didn't have to know it was a Minnetonka Moccasin foldup rather than a Stetson. It didn't take long to cool down in Bozeman, even though it'd finally warmed up after Billings, so he held a good pace. By the time he'd gotten to the Conoco station down at Main and Seventh, he figured that was enough, and crossed the street to walk against traffic on the way back.

He'd been careful all day, he thought. No car had followed him or stayed with him, easy to see on the flats outside Glendive, or between Billings and Livingston. He'd never bothered to activate the Starlink feature in the Outback, so as far as he could tell, the manufacturer, at least, didn't know where he was. He'd used a mix of cash and debit cards on the trip, so he hadn't been obviously trying to be invisible, but the debit cards were set up to accounts he'd had created a year ago and well away from where he lived in the Twin Cities, and under several names and addresses. His phones—multiple—were recent prepaid ones, and his normal network phone was stored, battery out, in his car. One of the burners was set up to start the mail-out sequence tonight, and once he'd done that he'd wipe it and get a new sim card.

When he was opposite the Emerald, with a quick glance at the parking lot, he kept walking all the way up to Peach Street. The Bridgers were lit up against the eastern horizon, the sun almost down. He waited for the light, an average-sized, late-middle-aged white guy with five o'clock shadow, unprepossessing, a little thicker in the middle than he likely wanted. Glasses, gold wedding ring, relaxed fit Levis. Crossing, he strolled back toward the motel, taking his time as the evening moved to full dark. Small businesses, small houses—one, he saw, was now a Women's Health center—the Papa John's on the corner, and then across the front drive, under the awning, down the walk, and into his room. No new cars since he'd arrived, and not a lot of travelers anyway as the pandemic resurged. Nice to walk in Bozeman, even with a mask. He'd felt like he was in disguise, standing out from all the Montanans--at least half the people visible, unmasked-- who didn't believe in the coronavirus. He still kept away from people, a legacy of months of the pandemic. *It is a college town,* he thought. *Everyone's from somewhere else, and no one recognizes me anyway.*

In his room, he pulled the burner phone from the laptop bag, powered up, caught the network, tapped the lone app to open it, and hit the "Enter" key. This one, programmed by a friend, added a text at the bottom: "Are you sure you want to do this?" He smiled, and said aloud, "Sho' nuff 'n' yes I do." *Will I ever get Captain Beefheart out of my head? Ah, seventies rock and roll.* He smiled. Then he hit "Enter" again, waited for the confirmation notice, powered down, opened the phone, pulled the battery and snapped the sim card and 32 gig memory card in half, and flushed them down the bathroom toilet.

And just like that, two years of planning started to unroll.

CHAPTER 4: PANDORA'S BOXLOAD

October 19-20
The Press

Within seconds after Baker hit the "Enter" key on his phone, an email regarding a certain Dropbox account appeared in six offices across the country. Editors at *the New York Times* US News desk, the *Wall Street Journal*, the *Washington Post* Politics desk ("WaPo," in the trade), the *Seattle Post-Intelligencer* "Washington" desk (the "P-I"), the editor of the *Los Angeles Times*, and the editor of the *Denver Post* began downloads as soon as they read the cover memo, with software scanning for viruses the only slowdown. Within minutes, they had their senior reporters on the phone.

And they began calling each other, something which would have surprised those outside the profession.

Almost as one, the editors had realized that this was the news story of the decade, if not the century. And for a change, each of them was at the edge of greed and horror. Greed, lust, desire to be the first on the street, to break the story, to win the advertisers, to get the Pulitzer. And horror not at losing out to someone else, but at getting the story either wrong or disastrously wrong.

Within an hour, every newspaper on the list was holding meetings, reporters breaking down each package by state, while the editors themselves were on a private video call consulting with each other. Since they were more or less competitors, such things happened rarely if at all. But since even national papers like the *Times*, the *Post* and the *Journal* were also regional in circulation, the editors ignored convention. The *Times* and *WaPo* editors had agreed, and had the others on board, that this meeting was not to be recorded *anywhere*, by *anyone*, and that no electronic records of the conversation would be permitted. The *WaPo* editor ruefully acknowledged to herself that the NSA was probably going to record the whole thing, at least if you believed some of her conservative family members.

Baker had sent them a Pandora's boxload, in the form of Adobe portable document format reports, minutes of meetings, internal memoranda from Congressional offices, correspondence between think-tanks like the Heritage Foundation or the Brookings Institution and legislators, and state-level minutes, correspondence, and memos from the Republican and Democratic party offices to legislators and to donors. The document dump included politicians from five states.

A cover memo laid out a plan to provide documents to voters beginning the next Sunday, with one state per week featured. The memo was blunt, and it was, for journalists, exhilarating and terrifying.

To: Journalists and Editors
From: The Month of Sundays Group
Subject: Scheduled mailings
Date: October 20, 2021

Enclosed is a package of documents at the Congressional and state levels regarding the influence of donors and lobbyists on legislators. You will find correspondence from the individual legislators and their staff members to "influencers," as well as memoranda and directives from these organizations. We have provided documents from the state-level political parties, corporate correspondence to legislators, and documents from the White House to legislators regarding policies, strategies, and legislation.

This package is organized by individual states, including Michigan, Texas, West Virginia, New Jersey, and Minnesota.

Beginning next Sunday, registered voters in every state in which a Senate seat is contested in 2022 will receive a similar set of records and documents. We anticipate sending out one packet per week, for 34 weeks. We will conclude this distribution by July 3, 2022.

These documents may be verified to be authentic, although it may take subpoenas to produce the originals. As someone once wrote about a similar document, "It is profusely illustrated and you will not find a dull page in it."

A note: delivery of this stuff is already arranged. This letter triggers a cascade that is pre-programmed. Redundant servers and avenues of distribution have been prepared. You Post people say that "Democracy dies in darkness." Let's see if you can light it up for growth.

Copies: Seattle Post-Intelligencer, Los Angeles Times, Denver Morning Post, Washington Post, New York Times, Wall Street Journal

"Some of this stuff has to have been obtained illegally," the editor of The *New York Times* said from his video box on the screen. The impact of his comment may have been reduced, since he looked like a *Hollywood Squares* character on the computer screen. "Maybe all of it. It purports to come directly from Senate and Congressional offices. And some of the corporate or donor stuff—including lists of donors with amounts given—will get us pretty close to lawsuits, won't they? Legal is already looking at this—a full staff in at midnight, just like the reporters."

"I don't know if you looked this far," the editor from Denver spoke up, "but we've got documents in here that relate to protecting drug production and distribution, like oxycodone, opioids. And it's not just West Virginia, where the lawsuit is. Some of it suggests legislators in Colorado were involved. When you get a corporate letter suggesting changes in proposed legislation, and addressed to a sitting representative *and* a sitting Senator, it makes my hands shake. And…it also makes my mouth water," she finished with a smile.

"You know, we're used to getting things like this and turning them into stories," the *WaPo* editor mused quietly, sitting back in her chair and steepling her hands. She was a little pleased that the note had cited her paper's motto. "But what will the country do when it gets this information directly? It's not a matter of us shaping it, assembling it, finding what's relevant and telling people what it means. *Everyone* will see *everything at the same time*, this group says. This is going to be extraordinary, and probably we'll get some violent responses when people find out they've been lied to."

The *LA Times* editor leaned in to respond. "What alarms me is that *we* won't see this until everyone else does. We're going to be right there with them, week after week, figuring out who's been naughty or nice. And my bet is on naughty." He hesitated. "I don't want to get philosophical about this, or ignore the mess sitting in our lap. How will this 'cascade' affect everything else—not just politics, but the economy, every social issue that depends on people working together to solve problems? Will it bring us together, or drive us apart?"

From Seattle, the *Post-Intelligencer* editor spoke up. "I have a couple of questions. Why us? I mean, explicitly, why the P-I? We're the only one of you that doesn't publish a *paper*. We're exclusively online, and have been since 2009. I wonder why this Month of Sundays outfit picked us—this group? I mean, where's Atlanta? Where's Pittsburgh? Where's Chicago? Where's New Orleans, or Dallas? And had we better get them on the phone, or what? No one likes to share a scoop, but this isn't a scoop. When you find out that a major corporation has been funneling money to both white nationalists and left-wing anarchists, we have a damned dump truck full of manure, or a trainload of dynamite. And where's CNN or FOX or MSNBC, or even NPR? We *have* to report it, but my God, what's going on here?"

The *WaPo* editor visibly took a note from someone off-camera, looked at it, and paused. Her forehead wrinkled as her eyebrows went up. "Did you notice that while several of these states are pretty important, in terms of electoral votes, none of them has a Senate seat contested next year? Pretty cagey. This group is teasing us, and isn't giving anything away until Sunday.   And by the way, the Dropbox account just disappeared," she said. She looked into the camera. "Like it never existed. I wonder who did *that*. We'd all better secure these files offline. And right the hell now."

Through all of this, the *Wall Street Journal* editor had been silent. "I know all of you are asking yourselves the questions the P-I editor did a minute ago. Doesn't it seem clear to you that by including us in the mix, this group is also looking at what news like this does to American business? And what is that going to mean? The LA Times folks are right—this could set off a cascade of panic in finance.

"And could I just observe here that this Month of Sundays group is either really, really confident or just plain stupid about this schedule? They tell us they're going to string delivery out so every state can just savor or anticipate what is, frankly, undemocratic corruption—but they've also told us implicitly that they don't think anyone can stop them. They're taking a huge risk with this plan—if the government finds out how they're doing it, they'll stop them cold. Or someone else will." He paused. "Oh....and stopping them will show how corrupt the system really is, won't it? Mmmm. Maybe not so stupid," he mused. "People who try to stop them have to decide which is the greater risk, letting the package go to press or trying to stop it."

The *Times* editor, not the most senior among them, but perhaps with the longest public reach, responded. He'd called the meeting in the first place. "Okay. I agree with all of your concerns. Can I suggest that we meet with our teams for a couple of hours and then reassemble by video at 2 a.m. Eastern for an hour? And if we can, let's keep this away from everybody—including the White House, the Parties, and the broadcast media, at least until we figure out what's going on. And if you're corporate—Seattle, WaPo—can we agree that the bosses don't get to see this stuff for a couple of hours? Of course, they'll have to, but we'd better have a good idea of what's here, first." With nods from everyone, some with rather grim expressions, the meeting ended.

The *Seattle P-I* editor, once she'd signed off, turned to her assistant, who'd been taking notes on an old-fashioned legal pad. "Get those files secured on drives that aren't connected to the net. I don't want them tampered with. If someone can erase an account like that, what could he do to our stuff? Get me our best IT guy, and have him here as quick as you can. Tell him it's an emergency." She was pretty sure everyone else was doing the same thing, but as an internet-only company in the middle of Microsoft country, she thought she might have an edge. "We need to know a bunch of things about this. I'm not even sure what we need to know. For sure, we need to review what we know about privacy laws and some of this material."

The P-I's tech lead, thirty-ish, sandy-haired, earring in his right lobe, black wire-rims firmly in place, sat at a conference table with the editor.

Will morning ever get here? she wondered.

He began. "Okay, I assume from the beginning that this is so confidential that I'm out of a job if I breathe a word, right?" At her nod, he continued. He'd had an hour with the files.

"Yes, at least for the next three or four days." He'd seen the cover memo.

"Right. Well, the first thing I can tell you is that this whole package, when you break it down, came from probably fifty or sixty different sources. You can see that from the file headers. That means there are probably a lot of people involved in this, or some smaller number had unbelievable access. The total number of documents is over 500, distributed among five states."

"Okay, I know all that. Is it authentic? That's what's important."

"I'll get to that. There's stuff related to each of the sitting senators, Democrats and Republicans. Like you said, none of them is up for election this year. This package might change this. For many of them, there's communication from their party headquarters. From the headquarters, we've got lists of donors, affiliations if they're corporate, and amounts. Now some of this is public, but some of it is not. From both the officeholders and a range of lobbying groups, including outfits like ALEC—I *did not say* ALEC itself—there are memos and reports suggesting legislative language, together with the rationale underlying it. There's a prominent one, the USCC."

The editor cringed when the tech had mentioned the American Legislative Exchange Council, funded by a range of conservative groups, and responsible for drafting and promoting legislation that was anti-immigrant, pro-business, anti-environmentalist, and generally socially conservative.

Let's hope they're not in here, she thought, sitting back. *They've got some serious money behind them.* And when he mentioned the United States Conservative Conference, she knew this would be challenging. *They play as rough as anybody.*

"Whoever sent us this also sent parallel documents that show where that language was included in the bills that came out of committee. Material that comes out from the USCC is usually confidential, because they don't like the public to know someone else is writing their laws for them."

"I know that," the editor said, with some exasperation. *I'm too tired,* she thought. "Move on."

He looked up from his screen. "A lot of that should be public, and probably is, in other sources. So, there's no doubt that a lot of this will be verified as authentic. Whoever sent it knows we can check it out. But there's something else going on. Some of this material is almost certainly not on the 'official' computers or in records that will go to the National Archives, where you could get it with a Freedom of Information Act request. It's on peoples' personal computers."

"How do you know that?"

"Because the things that they're discussing would send them to jail or get them thrown out of office if they ever became public. They're actively talking about *quid pro quo* stuff. And I have no doubt that it's authentic, and that if you put in a FOIA, a Freedom of Information Act request, you'd never find it. Look at this."

He pulled a document up on the screen, and turned the computer so she could read it. "The jackass actually signed this thing?" she asked. "I *know* this guy. *How did we end up with copies of this?*" She was almost shouting. The editor leaned in, visibly angry, finger stabbing at his laptop screen.

"I have no idea. But that's not the biggest issue here. The biggest issue is that we have donor files from a couple of organizations that specialize in *not* revealing their donors. They're the original Dark Money sites. They don't have to disclose. But we have donor lists, and more than that, we have donor letters directing where contributions should go. And they look to be as authentic as everything else."

The *P-I* editor could feel a prickling on the back of her neck, and decided right then that this needed to go

27

upstairs. *Just not yet,* she thought, remembering her promise.

"Two last things," the tech added. "First, just to state the obvious. These files go back at least ten years, and at the same time the package is up to date. Some of this happened as late as April or May, from the date stamps on the files. So, we maybe go from the Bush administration through Obama, Trump, and the first months of the current presidency. I don't know how they did that, right now. Second, none of this, as far as I can see—and whoever did this went the extra mile to make the whole bloody thing *searchable,* so you can find stuff easily—none of it has to do with national security or defense or anything like that. You'll have to look at this, but I wonder if someone out there has a conscience about that." He stopped.

"And what the *hell* is the meaning of that name? 'Month of Sundays'?" he muttered.

"That's one of those old expressions you're too young for." She leaned back again. "If you told someone you couldn't find something in 'a month of Sundays,' you'd mean 'so long a time you might as well forget it.' In this case, it's almost strictly accurate. They're going to release the data every Sunday for 30-plus weeks." Something struck her, and she laughed out loud. "It's a strip-tease! *It's a political strip-tease!*"

The tech looked at her, surprise clear on his face. Then he smiled, too. "Somehow, I don't think we'll get tired of it," the tech said, as he closed the laptop and stood up.

"No, me neither," the editor said. "But you *can* get tired if it lasts too long. Keep working. Keep what you find quiet. Bring it to me, and nobody else."

CHAPTER 5: NUDGING

"Uh, hello? Can I speak to Morris Watson? This is Adam Hill, calling from Gillette, Wyoming."

"How did you get this number?" a woman's voice answered, irritation evident in the tone.

Standing next to the pay phone in the Wal-Mart, Hill tipped his hat back and leaned closer to the phone. "Fella named Ed King suggested I call you, and from this number. If you want, I can call back from somewhere else." He glanced off toward the entrance, casually sweeping the space to see if anyone appeared to be watching.

"King, huh. Okay. In ten minutes, call the number I'll give you. What's your cell number, and I'll text you. Be away from where you are. Don't call this number again. Ever."

Hill gave her the cell number, then hung up the phone and walked to his pickup, off in a corner of the parking lot. He pulled the Dodge Ram out onto Wyoming Highway 59, heading south, and was quickly out into open country, low rocky mounds on either side, flat highway, and nothing to disturb the view but a few billboards for a motel in town and the vaping shop. He'd just gone by the Oilfield Services sign and was almost to 4 Corners Road when the ten minutes were up. He pulled off onto the dirt road and picked up his cellphone. The text number was waiting.

When a quiet "Hello?" came from the earpiece, he launched in. "This is Adam Hill, calling from Wyoming. I'm a rancher out here. A fellow named Ed King said I should call you about some things I got in my email. Do you know anything about this 'Month of Sundays' outfit?"

"You too, huh? Since neither of us knows the other one, what exactly do you do out there near Gillette, Wyoming?"

"Well, to begin with, I don't live in Gillette. I'm from a much smaller town away from here. But I'm sort of the contact person and organizer for a social group we call the Northern Patriots. And that's about all I'm going to tell you right now. What about you?"

Morris Watson, on the other end of the line, was silent. "I'm in upstate Wisconsin. I do something similar out here for a similar social group, the Iron County Rangers. So, you got something from the Month of Sundays, huh? What was in it?"

Hill pulled out a sheet of paper from a folder on the seat next to him. "Well, what I got was focused just on Wyoming. There were letters from some of our politicians in DC—we've got damned few, just two senators and one guy in the House—to the coal and oil companies out here. And then there were letters to the environmentalists which said almost exactly the opposite. Put that together with ...."

Watson interrupted him. "Mm, sounds a lot like what I got, but mine's all about Wisconsin iron mining."

Hill began again, picking up speed and volume. "You know, what pisses me off the most is that my county went about 90% for Trump and the Republicans. My governor's a Republican, and so is most of the state senate and the house. Democrats might have five seats. And it's the damned Republicans that are selling us down the river."

Watson waited for a second till he thought Hill was done. "Same here. But have you wondered if there's more that we aren't seeing?"

"Well, yeah," Hill admitted. "But what I am seeing is bad enough. Is there anything we can do about this?"

"As much as I hate to say this, I'd say take it to the newspapers. Maybe—just maybe—FOX would pick it up." Watson started again. "You know, Wisconsin's pretty heavily divided—big cities all go Democrat, but most of the state is small towns and farms, and we pretty much all go Republican. Our county's swung Republican since the unions collapsed. Of course, there's Madison, which is looney-tunes all the time. But the stuff I got in the mail is so obvious, and so bad, I'm going to share it around with people like me up here."

"Okay, I've thought about that, too. But I've got some hotheads out here—maybe you do, too. You know, some of them are still hiding out from the DC thing back first part of the year." He suddenly realized he ought to be a little more guarded. That damned ECHELON program from the NSA was probably all over this conversation. "I don't know what they'll do if they see this."

"Well, people gotta make their own choices on this stuff. I'm a little provoked, myself."

"Tell you what," Hill said, looking up into the open sky and hoping no satellites were looking at the big, black Dodge Ram just then, "can we get a bunch of us social group coordinators together to talk about this? Somebody maybe needs to do something about this."

The voice on the other end came back slowly. "I might know some people, some other coordinators. I'll talk with them. Can I call you back on this number?"

"Only for a couple of days," Hill responded. "After that, I'm dumping this phone."

"The Northern Patriots" wasn't a conspiracy-based group. Oh, they had a couple of folks a half a bubble out of plumb, but most of them weren't, and didn't listen much to those who were. Ed King wasn't a member of the group, but a Wyoming state senator representing five counties in the north central part of the state. King was in his early 60's, a businessman, and independent, though a Republican. And he had connections to conservative groups across the country. And Hill had contacted Ed, because, for some reason, Hill was the one with the Month of Sundays digital package. King had been as startled as Hill.

Adam Hill was neither a radical nor ignorant. A graduate of the University of Wyoming, his background included range management and agricultural economics, and he had taken over his family ranch a few years ago, in his early 30's, as his parents moved to retirement. He read widely across politics and economics, and had a healthy appreciation for government and the law. Even as young as he was, his success in ranching made him respected in his county. He'd even thought about running for the state legislature, until the last election convinced him he wasn't conservative enough or crazy enough.

Baker had been busy on the "left" end of the political landscape, too. Massachusetts was a different animal from Wyoming. While no Senate seats were at stake, Massachusetts had Governor and Lieutenant Governor races open as well as all the House of Representatives. Both the state offices were held by Republicans, while the US Senate seats were held by Democrats. Every House seat was held by a Democrat.

About the same time Hill and Morris got their emailed packages, Lorraine Wilkins and Bruce Spenser got theirs. Lorraine lived in southern Massachusetts, just off Cape Cod, and Bruce lived in a western suburb of Boston. Both white, both in their fifties, they had heard of each other and were Facebook friends, but had never met in person. Each happened to know Amanda Ellis, a black attorney who lived in Dorchester, five miles south of the Boston city center. And she got the package, too.

Each would have self-described as "progressive," but as with "libertarians" each had a slightly different take on events and policies. None of them supported the violent side of "Antifa," for instance, and each took a more nuanced approach to "Black Lives Matter" than some of their progressive friends. Each of them, none more than

Amanda, could see that Boston and Massachusetts generally still had problems. Lorraine, the daughter of an Irish-heritage father, was particularly aware of the black-white tension that was strong in the city and stronger, but less visible, in the countryside. Each was, in his or her circle, a leader, a calm, critical voice, influential among friends.

And so they were each a little bemused to get an inside look at Massachusetts politics as it showed up at the federal level. Like their peers in Wyoming and Wisconsin, they found corporate fingerprints all over the work of their congresspeople. But they also found that lawmakers were getting letters from people the three of them would call radical, pressing and even threatening them to change their positions. "Antifa," and worse.

Like Hill in Wyoming, they began by calling people they thought they could trust. And in this case, they happened to call each other. Baker would have been pleased, if he'd known.

CHAPTER 6: FIRST REVEAL

Wednesday, October 20
Washington, D.C.

Before Baker had gone to sleep, he thought to himself, There's always a mole, always someone inside who works for someone else. It'll get out before they know it. He was sure of it.

And there was, someone working for The *Washington Post* who had a dual role with an alphabet agency, one of those three-letter outfits spread across the Virginia countryside or the big one in the ugly building just off the Mall. At noon, when the papers had had the files for more than twelve hours, she took a lunch break and walked a quick mile south down 13th Street Northwest, turned east on Pennsylvania Avenue, and crossed at 10th, walking into the Department of Justice. Walking between the barriers, her shoulder bag held tight, she glanced up to the motto over the door: "The Place of Justice is a Hallowed Place." Her contact, a mid-level staff member in the Office of Legislative Affairs, met her in the foyer and took her to her office. The Post staffer sat down.

"What's so 'hurry-up' today?" the staffer asked, handing her a cup of coffee and stepping back to her desk. "I was surprised you wanted a face-to-face."

"This," she said, passing a flash drive across the desk. "It's going to be explosive. You probably need to take this straight to the Attorney General. I will bet money that the President wants to see this before supper. I am absolutely serious. What's on this drive went to the Times, the WaPo, the Denver Post, the Seattle P-I and the LA Times at midnight. And the Wall Street Journal. It's straight political, and some people—right up to Senators—will lose their jobs. Some might go to jail."

The staffer put her hands on her desk, palms down. "I need to look at this before I take it anywhere," she said.

"Fine, and I need to get back to work before I'm missed. But I'm going to ask you for a receipt for this that we both sign. I want to make sure I'm not left holding the bag for something I gave you that didn't go anywhere. Write it out. Now."

That got the staffer's attention. Her WaPo contact had never made a demand like that. "No," she responded, tucking the drive into an envelope from her desk and sealing it. "If you're that concerned, it needs to go upstairs, and you with it. Come on."

An afternoon of explanations followed, covered by a note from "her doctor" explaining she'd gotten dizzy and had come in to see him.

The President, the Attorney General, and the NSA Director had dinner together, and then adjourned to the

Situation Room in the basement of the West Wing, with access to wall-mounted flatscreens and a computer scrolling through the documents. The NSA Director ran the computer, and the show didn't start until the room was cleared. The President had told them bluntly that he wasn't going to wait for a summary of the package and that he wanted to know both the scope and the likely impact. Despite his age, he kept up, drafting notes to himself and directing the others to prepare a presentation for the next day.

The Attorney General met with the Director of the FBI at 11 that evening. Weary, the AG described the situation to the Director, and handed him a copy of the USB drive. "The President is very concerned about this, and he'll be meeting with leaders of the Congress—and the party leaders—tomorrow morning. I'll have a formal request to you in the morning, but I want you to get your cyber people working on this as soon as possible. Start thinking about the team you'll need."

"How did the President respond when you saw this stuff?"

"He was alarmed, both by the hacking and by the potential damage to the country. On the other hand, when we read some of the files, he agreed that it was past time something like this might happen. The sweep of the hack is what took us all by surprise."

"Has he got enough bandwidth to handle this?"

The AG was surprised. "Actually, he knows enough to give this to us and get out of the way. I think he's got more important things on his plate, and he thinks so too."

"I meant, look, does he understand what's going on with this. Where it might lead?"

"Yes, I think he does. That 'old man' act of his is meant to be comforting and welcoming. He's plenty sharp."

In the Residence, the President reviewed his notes once before leaving his study. He figured he needed to know five things that might be "facts," and one that needed a legal opinion. The AG had the legal opinion piece, for tomorrow morning, and the FBI would work on the "facts" over the next days.

Who were the Month of Sundays group?

What did they have access to and what didn't they have?

How did they get it?

How could they distribute this material?

Should they be stopped? And if so, how?

CHAPTER 7: THE CAPITOL PAPERS

Thursday, October 21
The White House

On Thursday morning, the day after Baker left Bozeman for Spokane, the President of the United States hosted an unusual meeting. With him were the Vice-President, the Speaker of the House and the House Majority Leader, the House Minority Leader, the Senate Majority Leader and Minority Leader, the chairs of the Republican National Committee and Democratic National Committee, the Attorney General, the National Security Advisor, and the Director of the National Security Agency, which specializes in cybersecurity.

Most of the participants were surprised at the roster, as they had been at the note of urgency in the invitation. The legislators had been called by the President's chief of staff, the parties' national committee leaders by the President himself. The Vice President was the only other political figure whom the President had updated.

They'd all been escorted to the basement Situation Room, away from the Cabinet Room with its sunlit windows near the Oval Office. They realized that each had been seated across from his or her opposite number,

Speaker of the House and Majority Leader opposite the Minority Leader. Greetings were cordial but cool. They'd insulted each other repeatedly over the last few years, and the January 6th Insurrection Committee had had the effect of sand thrown into the legislative machine. The seating arrangements were odd in another way, too. Instead of sitting in the middle of the table, as he would in the Cabinet Room, the President's chair was at one end, then the political leaders on either side, and then administrators at the opposite end.

They stood as the President entered, then, at his gesture, sat down again. He began. "Good morning," he said. "Most of you have met each other, although I'm sure some of you are less familiar with the Director of the NSA. Something unprecedented happened yesterday, and we learned about it late in the day. It is related to national security, although not directly, but *directly* involves each of you in your political roles." *That got their attention,* he thought, noticing narrowed eyes and glances flickering across the table.

He grimaced faintly. "When the Attorney General and the NSA Director described it to me at dinner last night, I thought I was back in a Tom Clancy novel, something like *The Hunt for Red October* or *Clear and Present Danger.* Espionage, secrets, and danger." He smiled, but the smile stopped at his lips. A rustle ran through the room. Most of them knew that the President had been slated for a more formal dinner with several European leaders the previous evening. They didn't know that the Vice-President and her husband had hosted instead.

Around the table, people began almost to smile. Who knew this president read fiction to relax? And then they remembered where they were.

"I'm going to ask the Attorney General and the NSA Director to lay out what's happened. I have to tell you— none of you on the 'political side,' either legislators or national party leaders, has been informed of this. You're all on an even footing here—no one has an advantage. But I'm going to suggest you may want to keep this meeting confidential for a little bit. I can't be more definite than that. You'll see why. We'll talk about that at the end of the meeting." He gestured to the Attorney General.

"As the President said, something very unusual has happened. *Almost* unprecedented, I would say, and I'm not disagreeing with the President. The comparisons would be the Pentagon Papers in the seventies and the Clinton Democratic Party debacle in 2016. This is potentially worse. You could call it The Capitol Papers." The Attorney General had moved to a podium at the end of the table, and a screen emerged from the ceiling, the first image already projected. It was a set of logos, the mastheads of six newspapers. Several of the political leaders at the table seemed to pale. "Yesterday morning early, editors at these six papers got an urgent email that directed them to download files from a Dropbox account. Shortly after they did, the account disappeared. The files contained about 500 documents, representing five different states, and focused on the senators serving in those states who will *not* stand for re-election next year. The documents included information on campaign contributors, legislation and lobbying efforts to promote legislation, interaction with the national and state political parties, and correspondence with business leaders and other 'influencers.' Within all of this, a spreadsheet enumerated donors to 'dark money' organizations like PACS that normally don't report donations. Some of this data goes back as much as ten years, and some is as recent as last April or May. We're still analyzing it." As he spoke, a list of the categories appeared behind him. It concluded with a listing of the PACS contained in the spreadsheet. The Attorney General noted with satisfaction that his audience was leaning in.

"We're pretty confident that these documents are all authentic," he concluded. "At the direction of the President, we'll provide you with a hard-copy inventory of these materials at the end of the meeting. We'll also provide you with a digital file that contains the documents. I do not intend to tell you how we obtained this; it was, after all, directed only at the news organizations."

As the Attorney General looked around, he could sense the hair-on-fire tension in the room. The legislators were stunned, and the party leaders were looking at him in horror. Wide eyes, lips compressed, white-knuckled.

The President spoke, and heads swiveled to his end of the table. "I've read some of these documents, pointed out to me by the National Security Advisor and the Attorney General. I think you should know that some of them bear on the January 6th insurrection, and others make clear why some in Congress, strangely enough, are not voting for programs that would benefit the American people. Why is it that someone from a state with high levels of black lung disease won't vote for increased medical benefits? Who is lying to the Minnesota legislators about likely environmental damage from nickel mining above Lake Superior? You will see what I mean, and you'll see that I don't need to say anything further about these documents. They will speak for themselves." He paused and looked at both party leaders and legislators for a moment. Only a few looked back at him evenly.

The Attorney General continued. "There's more. Whoever sent this prefaced it with a cover memo. It says that this organization plans to release the same set of information on every state where there's a Senate contest, one per week for the next thirty-plus weeks." Heads jerked up and looked at him, eyes wide. "And that's because, as I said, the current data is for five states where no Senate seat is 'exposed' in 2022. Although," he added grimly, "that might change once you look at the files."

He stepped back from the podium. "Mr. President, that's our report so far. We have started to research the sources and methods used here, and we can't say anything more about them right now. We don't know enough."

The President looked around the room. "Are there questions for the Attorney General or the Director? Please ask them directly." He sat back.

The Senate Minority Leader, pale, asked, "Is there any way to prevent the release of this information? Do we know how it's going to arrive, or how it'll be used? My God, this is astonishing!"

The Attorney General nodded to the NSA director, who answered. "We're working on two fronts here. We don't know how this information was obtained—it clearly involves an enormous effort at hacking private as well as government communications—and we don't have a good idea yet of how it'll be distributed. The Attorney General may have hinted at this, but the range of communications comes from *private computers* as well as government ones. This is like another Hillary case, where business related to government operations and legislation was being carried on in such a way that it's not part of federal record keeping." He paused. "As far as distribution, the Attorney General hasn't released the cover memo to you yet, but"— he gestured at an image which appeared on the screen— "here's a relevant section." With a laser pointer, he circled a paragraph, and then underlined a sentence.

Beginning next Sunday, registered voters in every state in which a Senate seat is contested in 2022 will receive a similar set of records and documents. We anticipate sending out one packet per week, 34 weeks. We will conclude this distribution by July 3, 2022.

"This suggests," the NSA man pointed out, "that whoever did this has access to voter registration lists from some source. It might be at the state level or it might be a list compiled by the political parties. After all," he added, "if this group has correspondence from the parties to legislators, they might well have access to lists the parties maintain. And," he went on, "look at this comment on delivery."

A note: delivery of this stuff is already arranged. This letter triggers a cascade that is pre-programmed. Redundant servers and avenues of distribution have been prepared. You Post people say that "Democracy dies in darkness." Let's see if you can light it up for growth.

"I think that also says something about how the material will be used. It'll be informational. We don't know if that means it'll be balanced in terms of the political parties, and there's no way to know until it shows up. And we don't know if there'll be any contextual information provided that relates one document to another, for instance."

"Okay," the Minority Leader responded, "but can you stop it? I mean, stop at least the newspaper release? I think we'd all like to get ahead of this and discover how it affects us."

The NSA director shook his head. "We don't know exactly how it'll be delivered, except it's presumably electronic. You can't simply cut off all email or whatever. That's against the law. We're not China or Russia. And we think it likely that the MOS group has multiple email accounts or sites that we don't know about yet."

The Minority Leader almost cut him off. "All right, but what about the documents the newspapers got? What are they going to do with them?"

The Attorney General looked at the President, who nodded back to him. "We've discussed the newspaper issue with the President," the AG said, looking at each of the participants. "If we try to force them not to publish, it amounts to prior restraint, which is almost certainly unconstitutional, and as far as we can see, there's no cause for restraint. Nothing in here is related to national security, troop movements, and so forth. None of it, beyond the donor lists, concerns finances—so there's no case to be made for fraud. There are no logins or passwords of anyone. We don't see 'exceptional circumstances' here. Now, you can sue the publishers once it's printed, but Justice won't step in at this point." He paused. "And you might have trouble suing, if it's all true."

The Senate Minority leader raised a hand, and glanced at the President. The President nodded. "You know you say that about 'National Security," the Minority Leader began, "but isn't it the case that we have a violation of government computers? These are attacks on privileged communications within the government. If that's not national security, I don't know what is!"

The Attorney General replied, "Yes, and I understand your position. And we will attempt to locate and charge the individuals involved here. But what we won't do is attempt to suppress communications of this sort by shutting down whole sections of our electronic infrastructure. That's a cure worse than the cause.

"You might have noticed that there's not one single word about this in today's papers. I imagine they're as stunned by this as we are. They're probably trying to figure out what to do. We know they had a multi-site video call twice yesterday to discuss these materials. We haven't tried to get a recording of those meetings, and we'd likely be on pretty shaky ground if we did."

The President looked around. "Well, we've kept you waiting long enough. On the way out of the meeting, you'll get an inventory and a flash drive that has the files on it. I'm not going to tell you that you can't talk about it. The story will almost certainly be in the papers in the next day or so. But I will point out that if at some point Justice comes looking for these files, people would be wise not to have destroyed them or altered them. That would be obstruction. We have copies, too. We're not done looking at them, but like any whistleblowing incident, if they show laws have been broken, Justice will visit you. Thank you for coming." He rose, and the others rose with him. White House staff stepped into the room and escorted the legislators out. Smiling affably, the President watched them go, as the NSA Director and Attorney General moved down the table toward him.

In the hall outside the conference room, clumps formed immediately. The legislators stepped aside to meet with their aides, and in each case, handed them a flash drive and the inventory. The aides were sent back to their offices to print the contents of the drives. Moments later, the legislators were standing together, blocking the hallway. The Senate Minority leader spoke first, face to face with his counterpart. "Can we agree that we need to meet with our caucuses as soon as possible? We need to tell them what's coming, and at least advise them what's going on." The others nodded. The Speaker of the House cleared her throat and said, "Could I suggest that we as the leadership stay off the news shows or simply "No comment" inquiries for a day or so? I think we need to have a look at what's here. May we stay in communication about this?"

Her Republican counterpart nodded, but added with a grimace, "We've got House members—both of us—who find it hard to keep their mouths shut. How do we do that?"

The Speaker looked back coolly. "Well, we might ask them to think of any communication they've had with anybody that they'd be ashamed to see in public. Because in the next year, or even the next week, it might be. Criticizing someone else might feel sweet, but hypocrisy found out will be like pepper sauce in an open wound."

After a moment, the Republican nodded. "Yes, that might be the best way to play it."

They nodded to one another as they turned away. "Keep in touch," the Senate Minority Leader said, over his shoulder.

The Speaker and the Majority Leader walked upstairs to the assistant outside the Oval Office. "Can we get in to see the President?" the Majority Leader asked the assistant. The assistant handed the Majority Leader and the Speaker each a note, their names printed on the creamy White House notepaper. Both were somewhat taken aback, and then opened the envelopes.

The President was politely refusing to see them, as he regarded this a partisan issue he intended to avoid. And he had prepared his letter in advance for them, knowing they'd come to see him.

CHAPTER 8: PEND OREILLE &
PANDEMONIUM

Thursday, October 21
Eastern Washington

As the President finished his meeting, Baker was just about 2500 miles west-northwest, driving up Bead Lake Road, east of Newport, Washington, across the Thompson Memorial Bridge over the Pend Oreille River, and left on LeClerc Road.

Pend Oreille County nestled right up against the Idaho panhandle, with the river running through it, downstream from Lake Pend Oreille. *"Pend Oreille," "pond oray," the way the neighbors said it,* Baker thought, named for the "earloops," the dangling earrings of the native Kalispel tribe. The north border was Canada, and the main road took you there through Cusick, Ione, Tiger, and Metaline Falls. About 9 people per square mile, and only 14,000 in the whole county.

Two miles up the road, at the middle gate of his property, he pulled in to the landing, stopped the Subaru, unlocked the padlock, opened the gate, and drove in. He carefully locked the gate after him, noticing that the "No

Trespassing" and security system warnings were still in place. Once beyond the landing, he stopped, tapped an app on his phone, and cycled through the security cameras at the gates and around the house. He drove up the middle gate road a few minutes later, through a forest of lodgepole pine, Douglas fir, and ponderosas. The single-lane dirt driveway eased up the long hillside, a little dusty and weedy this late in October, but not badly overgrown. Within fifty yards no one could see him from the road.

Years before, the land had come into the family, and Baker had bought it quietly from his brother-in-law's estate. A little less than two years ago, just as quietly—hard in a small town like Newport—he'd put up a small cabin, arranged to have power and fiberoptic run in, gotten a permit for the well and septic, and put up a garage big enough for a couple of vehicles and snow equipment if he needed it. It wasn't unusual to have three or four feet of snow for months, starting in January and lasting until March.

He wanted this whole thing kept as low key and inconspicuous as possible. It helped that he'd had the trucks delivering materials routed from the east, coming in from Sandpoint and Priest River, so they hadn't even gone through town. Since the whole operation was a quarter-mile uphill and off the road, almost no one knew about it beyond the county clerk. He'd splurged a bit, although no one would hear it from him: the solar panels on the garage roof couldn't be seen from the road, and the house was oriented to make the most of the sunlight once the sun cleared the hills to the east, just across the marsh. He had a diesel generator if he needed, behind the garage and heavily muffled. The satellite dish was camouflaged. Even the electric meter was on a post down by the road, and reported in wirelessly. The bills were paid electronically from his bank in Minnesota, and amounted to a few dollars a day. And since he'd electrified the fence and put up the cameras, he hadn't had any hunters trying to break through the gates.

He was pretty sure, though, that his neighbors were well aware of what he'd built and had looked around before he put the security system in. It was "neighborliness," in this part of the country.

From his car, he opened the garage door and drove the Subaru in. It had been a short drive from Spokane along familiar roads, and yet the house was new to him still. At just under 1200 square feet, it felt comfortable in the pines at the edge of the meadow, two bedrooms, a living room, kitchen, and bath. Less obvious was the fact that it had a full basement, poured concrete and insulated, and pretty much impermeable to electronics. The reinforcing rods in the concrete were supplemented by additional wiring that formed a Faraday cage in the walls, and the basement drywall ceiling hid a similar tight mesh of wiring below the main floor. *No electronic signals were going out from that room,* he mused. He thought it was overkill, but others had suggested it. *I am not Will Smith, and I am not an enemy of the state,* he smiled. *But some people might think so.*

He unloaded groceries, carrying them on the gravel walk into the back door and mud room, and then around the corner into the kitchen. He pretty well filled the refrigerator. A few things went to the small freezer next to the compact washer and dryer in the back hall. His security system had let him power up the appliances yesterday from Spokane, using the Wemo app on his phone. The app had also let him power up the pump and the small hot water heater, so settling in would be easy.

An hour later, household "opening up" chores finished, he sat down at the desk in the basement and started monitoring the internet.

Across the country, reporters and editors were holding their breaths. The six papers had agreed on something as unusual as the story itself: they'd break the story at the same time on their websites, each handling it however the paper thought best. Everyone had the scoop. At 5 p.m. EDT, the *Post*, the *Journal*, and the *Times* websites flashed for a moment and then brought up an entirely new set of pages. Simultaneously, the sites in Denver, Los Angeles, and Seattle did the same thing, the West Coast sites at 2 p.m. sharp. The headlines were different, but each included a scan of the "cover" email and several dozen stories with links to the documents. Each also contained a major story pointing out both the audacity of the theft of documents and at least a few snippets of what they showed.

The *Times* led with "Welcome to a Month of Sundays," followed by a story summarizing the release. In Washington, the *Post* led with "Political Laundry About to be Public." In Denver, it was "The Secrets Are Out: Political Documents in Your Mailbox." In Los Angeles, with a bow to *Sneakers*, it was "No More Secrets." Seattle, whimsically, and with an eye to its audience, used a Dylan title, "A Hard Rain's Gonna Fall." The Wall Street Journal editorial page opined on what effect "truth in politics" might have on the economy. The five print newspapers announced they'd follow the next morning with additional information and analysis.

From Denver:

Americans from five states are about to get an in-depth picture of American politics at work.

On Wednesday, an anonymous and unknown group calling itself "Month of Sundays" sent electronic documents to six major newspapers, and the papers are posting them on their websites. The "cover" email which introduced this project is included below. You can find the documents on our site. The files are linked to the offices of the ten senators in those five states, and they appear to be a "teaser" for the 2022 elections. The group promises to release one state's documents each Sunday for the next 34 Sundays, well into the primary season next summer, for the states with senatorial elections next year. They claim that their goal is to inform Americans about how their lawmakers actually make decisions.

Wednesday's "data dump" was for five states. Michigan, Texas, West Virginia, New Jersey, and Minnesota were chosen because none of their senators faces re-election in 2022. According to the "Month of Sundays" group, this coming Sunday will bring delivery of the first state where a senate seat is on the ballot. The "MOS" group has not specified the order.

As an example of what is likely to appear, in the "West Virginia" package our newspaper received are

--listings of the names of donors to the two West Virginia senators, including donations from "SuperPACs" that don't normally report donors.

--Letters to and from unions and corporations, as well as lobbyists and lobbying organizations. For instance, in West Virginia, a state where coal mining has dominated the economy, the senators received letters, including demands, both from major mining corporations and from the United Mine Workers. These included arguments both for and against legislation for increased health benefits, enforcement or laxity in safety regulations, and arguments for and against funding to provide education for miners displaced by shifts in energy policy.

--Memos that appear to be internal correspondence within corporations or lobbying organizations regarding legislation and financial support.

--Letters that appear to be between individual donors and the senators' offices on legislation the donors support, including promises of funding for campaigns.

--Both Republican and Democratic Party correspondence with the senators' offices is in the package, with letters both to and from the legislators.

--Minutes of meetings, including discussions of legislation and policy, have been included, although only a few of these are present.

--On three occasions, letters from the former President or White House staff members are included.

Our paper will cover these documents as a news story, and we have made a decision not to try to "interpret" them for readers. The Month of Sundays group has organized this material so that some things "comment" on others. They show how one group's preferences—or threats or ideas—influence the language of bills that become laws. To help readers get started, we have a set of links below that point out how some of these documents are related. All these documents can be downloaded from our website.

We want to make clear that we cannot verify the accuracy of most of these files. They appear to have been stolen from government computers and from private computers, as well, and so we suspect that the FBI is already at work looking at violations of several federal laws. Readers may want to read "Whistleblowing and Breaking the Law," an article listed below. Jen Williston, our Washington correspondent and an attorney, reviews the state and federal laws the Month of Sundays group is likely to have broken.

This coming Sunday, October 24, the "Month of Sundays" group has promised that they will somehow deliver a similar set of documents to the voters in one state. We don't know which state. We'll be watching along with you.

Washington has been silent about the "MOS" group and these papers. Neither the senators involved nor government officials have commented.

No one knows who the "Month of Sundays" group is, whether it's large or small, whether they're Americans or foreign actors. The notorious release of emails from the Democratic National Committee in 2016, which damaged Hillary Clinton's candidacy, originated overseas, probably with Russian hackers sponsored by their government.

Within a few minutes, tweets and Facebook posts and emails began to appear, with the papers' websites hit at levels that threatened to take them down. The *Times* and the *Post* had planned for this, and had established separate sites on different servers to act as repeaters.

Pandemonium erupted at the major television networks, not the least at CNN, FOX, and MSNBC. They'd been frozen out of the document dump, and were playing catch-up, downloading files from the *Times* and *Post* sites. Frantic calls went out to the party and legislative leaders, who had seen the files themselves only five hours earlier.

From now on, it was everyone for themselves, and devil take the hindmost. *Every man for himself, indeed.* Baker smiled, watching the news that evening

.

CHAPTER 9: HUNTERS

Thursday, October 21
Washington, D.C.

Baker had expected hunters would be on the trail as soon as the first mail drop happened. That was the whole point of being inconspicuous, of limiting contact, of setting up the cascade. *Try to get out of this without going to jail, eh?* he had challenged himself. Yet so far, silence until the papers' websites all changed at the same time, and the dam broke. He switched off the computer and went upstairs for a nap. *Won't know a thing until tomorrow, at least,* he thought as he closed his eyes. *Might light a fire tonight if it gets cool.*

Devon Cook, a cybercrime specialist, sat with her boss, Ed Collins, at FBI headquarters in Washington, D.C. The Attorney General and the Director of the FBI had spent the afternoon with Ed, reviewing the initial document package, and considering where the documents had come from and what this might tell them about the source. Ed had then been ushered out of the office and told to get answers. Devon was his first place to start. She had led teams before very successfully, and in a male-dominated law enforcement organization like the FBI, she'd earned respect and admiration. *She would need all her skills on this one*, he thought.

"Okay, you've had an hour to look at this package," he began. "What's your initial take?" He sat back, tipping the office chair just slightly. Fifty-ish, graying sandy hair, despite an exercise program widening around the middle, and tired. *Devon, don't put me to sleep with this*, he thought.

"It's pretty amazing," Devon began. The forty-year-old black woman was as animated as Collins had ever seen her, fidgeting, jerking, eyes alight, right index finger stabbing at individual sheets she'd laid on the desk. "Okay, several sets of documents here. Internal, things that could only come from a senator's office—memos, schedules, minutes of meetings. Quite a lot of people in any senate office might have access to them, so the pool of sources in any one office is huge. And because they extend for years, the pool is very deep.

"Second set," she stabbed at a second pile, "letters between the legislators involved and the national party offices. Policies, events, about fundraising. Some focus on coordinating messaging for particular audiences. You could imagine those coming from the party offices themselves, but since these all lead back to the senate offices, I'm guessing that the source is more likely there." She slowed down. "I don't know if you saw this," Devon pulled out a page and handed it to Collins, "but this *didn't* go to the senate office. It's a memo *internal* to the party office, which means somehow—if the source is in the senate office—they found a way to suck in correspondence *residing on outside computers.*"

Collins winced when he looked at the sheet, and gestured Cook to continue. A knock at the door interrupted her, and Devon glanced at her watch as an assistant handed a sheet to Collins. *Five o'clock,* she thought. *When will this come out?* As Cook began again, she could see Collins shrinking back into the big chair, almost as if the weight of the file was resting on him.

"And then we get to this stuff," she resumed, holding up pages with different letterhead. "Letters to legislators about policy and about funding. And then," she pulled out another, "here are two *internal memoranda* from the lobbyist's office that also *didn't* go to the senator. And just in case you didn't catch this," she put her hands flat on the desk, "the author lays out how they intend to screw the senator if he doesn't vote their way. And how they will blackmail him if he does.

"And last but not least, I've just isolated it because of the topic: these pages have to do with the 2020 election, reports of a strategy to overturn the election, and correspondence with the 'insurrectionists,' we might call them. When this comes to light—not *if*—this senator could plausibly be removed from office for conspiracy." She laid down a half dozen sheets clipped together.

"Here's what got me on the edge of my seat: this has to have been private correspondence on a personal computer that isn't government-issue. In fact, it's pretty clear that it isn't, including a private email address for the senator of which we have no record. We're back in Hillary-land, and whoever these people are, they've handed us somebody's safety-deposit box. Actually," she mused, "they've handed us *everybody's* safety-deposit box." Finally, she sat back.

"So, what do you want me to do? Find out who, and how? And how many people can you give me, because this is going to take a while."

Collins sat up straighter. He gestured to the door. "The note told me that the package has been released by the six papers. Now, here's what I'm thinking," he began.

Across the Potomac, in a building squeezed between the Pentagon, the Richmond Highway, and Reagan National, among other anonymous off-white dozen-story concrete-and-tinted-glass towers, Robin Myers, Elijah Flores, and Roger Gray drank coffee in a small conference room. They'd had a cookie each with the coffee, when Gray looked at his watch and suddenly got to business.

Myers thought to himself, *If you'd ever smile, Gray, you'd look like a scruffy Ned Ryerson, balding, open face, perpetually eager, narrow black hornrims. But you never smile.* Groundhog Day *with a frown.*

As if he were under restrictions about opening the sealed orders, Gray handed Myers and Flores each a manila envelope with folders and a lumpy flash drive inside. "If you don't know what this is," he said, "you'll be able to guess within the next half hour. Someone has done a "Capitol Papers" version of the Pentagon Papers. Robin, you're probably not old enough to know the reference, but Elijah certainly does."

He went on to outline what a senor legislative staffer had handed him.

"We don't know if the USCC has been penetrated—I've had this stuff for a half hour—but we need to know what's here and how it affects us. And if we find we've been hit, we need to find out how and who. And then we need recommendations about how to stop it. This has the potential of damaging organizations like us and impeding our mission for perhaps decades. I want you to answer those questions: what, how much, who, and how to stop them. I'd like a 'first look' report from you, in person, by tomorrow this time. This comes all the way down from the Chair of the Board and the CEO, and I'll be reporting back to them. Questions?"

Flores and Myers glanced at each other, and almost as one, shook their heads slightly. Gray stood. "For now, this is your office, and those papers don't leave here. You'll have secure computers in here within an hour. They're not connected to the internet, and they won't be. The tech who brings them in will also have information on security protocols. See you tomorrow." He picked up his coffee cup, left the cookie plate, and walked out.

They took seats opposite each other at the conference table, head and foot. Flores, longer dark hair streaked with white threads, fit but in his fifties like Gray, was the only Hispanic in the building other than the cleaning staff, and preferred being unnoticed by the whites who dominated the organization. If you'd looked at the directory, he wasn't there, but was part of an "Action" group housed off-site elsewhere in Arlington. Myers, "in" the directory, had the deliberately ambiguous title of "Information Officer," without the usual "Chief" or "Associate" rank attached. Dark-haired, thirties, tanned, *Must be a biker or a runner,* people would think. *Lean like a greyhound, loping like a runner.* They'd miss the long wolfish canines and the cold eyes. The outside and the inside man, both hunters and fixers.

Devon Cook had handed Collins her request for staffing at 7 p.m., just two hours after the papers broke the story. The news was all over the building, and she'd asked her admin to keep the calls away.

The Federal Bureau of Investigation had established a Cyber Division in 2002, and formed cybercrime investigative groups in each of 56 field offices across the country in 2003. Cook figured she needed some hotshots, and they weren't all in DC. Collins cleared her to call their supervisors.

Before she was done, she'd called four field offices and spoken to the Special Agent in Charge in Seattle and Denver and the Assistant Director in Charge in LA and New York. She had ten names, and the bodies to accompany those names would be with her by noon the next day.

She was pretty sure none of the folks she wanted would say no. This might be the highest-profile case of computer hacking in anyone's career, and everybody would want in. If you ever wanted to make a mark and get noticed, this'd be it.

Cook spent a few minutes that evening marshaling her thoughts about what they were looking at, and what the laws were. In practical terms, she knew the statute by heart, even though it ran on for several pages. Most of it, perhaps to add gravity, was about the consequences—fines, imprisonment, and so forth. *18 US Code Section 1030*, she breathed. Boiling it down, it came to this:

Whoever….accesses a computer without authorization or exceeding [their] authorized access…and gains information regarding national security…or financial records …or information from any department or agency of the United States; or …information from any protected computer….knowingly and with intent to defraud…." [From there, the law goes on to specify damage to computers or networks] [and then specifies stealing passwords or other information] "…and then returns to extortion or affecting interstate or foreign commerce or threatening to reveal confidential information" shall be punished.

Whoever the "Month of Sundays Group" was, they'd definitely broken the law by accessing governmental computers and networks, but they'd avoided complications like fraud, extortion, or seizing and revealing financial information. And as she'd seen herself, they stayed away from foreign relations documents and national security.

And she thought she could understand why the "MOS Group"—*Is that what we'll call them? Catchy enough?*—had done what they had threatened to do. She'd read some of the documents, even while thinking about how someone could get access like this. Whoever this was had some real computer skills, yes, but they'd also had a strategy in mind and an understanding of how this stuff would look in public.

When she'd read comments from corporate executives and from a senator quietly approving the January 6th riot, she'd broken out in a sweat. And when that same senator made some crude, racist comments about Eastern Washington rednecks back to the Democratic National Committee, Cook, raised in inner-city Seattle, had said things she wouldn't have wanted her daughters to hear. She had to hand it to the MOS people: they were steadily equal opportunity.

CHAPTER 10: PARTY LINES

Thursday, October 21
The Capitol

On Thursday evening, by arrangement, the Democratic members of the House and Senate met in the House chamber of the Capitol; the Republicans, in the Senate chamber. As Baker had scheduled this release for a week when both House and Senate were in session, nearly the full complement of men and women attended. This was the first in-person caucus for either party in more than a year, because of the pandemic. Both Republicans and Democrats had agreed to ignore guidance on the size of meetings.

In the Senate chamber, the minority leaders of the Senate and House stood behind the podium on the dais, conferring. The Senate minority leader knew that fewer than 75% of his colleagues were vaccinated, but was still surprised that only a half dozen had masked. *Well, wouldn't this be a disastrous super-spreader*, he thought.

As this was the Senate, he would open the session, and he and the House minority leader would welcome their colleagues and introduce the topic. A senior staff member representing each would actually present to the legislators, and then discussion would open. A representative from the party's national committee had a seat in one of the galleries, and would be available to answer questions.

The Capitol was beginning to fill by 7 p.m., as members returned from dinner, stunned by the revelations of the Month of Sundays group that were appearing on their telephones and on televisions in their restaurants. An undercurrent of uneasiness showed up in the low grumbles that reverberated across the room. Some of this was certainly because they'd been stripped of their cell phones, tablets, and laptops before they entered the Senate and House chambers, by agreement of the leadership on both sides. The devices went into a series of lockers in the cloakroom of each chamber. A few minutes before 8, members took seats—the Senators behind their accustomed desks, with House members filling in and taking seats outside the four rows of the semicircle.

He began. "Ladies and gentlemen of the Senate and House, thank you for attending tonight's meeting. And thank you for surrendering your electronic devices as you came in. I know, it's practically unprecedented, and I'll tell you why we've taken this step. News came to us today of a shocking invasion of our privacy when we met with the President this morning. The administration, through the Department of Justice, received this information last night, met with legislative and party leaders this morning, and released a number of documents to us at that time. We and the Democrats agreed to caucus with our members this evening. You will notice in the gallery the chair of the Republican National Committee, who will take questions if it is appropriate. Our colleague, the minority leader of the House, will speak next, followed by two senior staff. We anticipate this meeting will last several hours. For reasons which will become obvious, no press are invited here, and no recording devices."

A few minutes later, when the House minority leader had finished, the two staff members stepped to the desk below the dais. Behind them, at the gallery level, a large flatscreen slid out of the ceiling. The MOS cover memo was displayed. Within a minute, as the legislators finished reading it, the room was utterly quiet.

For the next hour, the staff members moved from an overview of the five-state package into the details of two or three states' documents. At one point, nearly every eye was on the chair of the national committee as a set of internal party memos appeared on the screen. Although she watched the screen impassively, she undoubtedly felt the contempt of the men and women below her. Several legislators on the floor, men and women, were in tears by the end of the presentation. A representative sitting near the back wall had fainted, and senior staff had been notified and quietly helped him into the Senate cloakroom.

The second staffer turned to the Senate minority leader, and stepped away from the platform, taking a seat at a desk below. The minority leader, on the dais but not seated, looked out at his colleagues. "I think we all have a sense of what this event means. As Mr. Jorgenson"—he nodded at the second staffer—"has indicated, we do not know much yet about the full contents of these documents. We don't know who has invaded our privacy, we don't know the extent of that invasion, and we cannot really imagine the effect this will have on individuals, the party, and the nation. We do not know, for instance, if the revelations will affect Democratic politicians to the same degree it affects us. I myself am having a hard time imagining what thirty separate disclosures over the next seven months will mean for the country. The Department of Justice has formed an FBI task force this evening to begin an investigation. I imagine that other organizations, including lobbyists, will do the same.

"The House minority leader and I and the national committee chair will take your questions at this time."

Immediately, there were men and women claiming microphones. "The representative from Ohio is recognized," the House leader gestured.

"Can you tell us what the President's response to this was? Is he going to exploit this in some way?" The two leaders glanced at each other. The senator responded. "The President had seen this information last night, and the first thing he did was call us together. We had a review of these documents just a few hours ago. He indicated that the Department of Justice would be examining this information for any criminal activity, and there will likely be investigations following as a result." He paused. "I spoke with the Speaker of the House and the Senate majority leader earlier in the evening. They told me they had attempted to meet separately with the President after our briefing—which is entirely expected—and that he had declined the meeting."

That got people's attention. "My sense is that he intends to stay out of this. It is not an Executive Branch responsibility. I think he expects us to deal with this and he will get on with governing. If there are legal issues, Justice is responsible here, not the President directly."

He paused again. "We must face the fact that a good deal of what we thought was private and privileged communication is about to be public. That will include, as you have heard and seen tonight, our interactions with lobbyists and donors. More than that, even things we didn't know about and could not expect to know about—internal documents of those donors and lobbyists—will also be displayed."

"Well, *shit*," the Ohio representative could be heard as she turned from the microphone and stalked to the back of the room.

A senator from Kansas rose, tilting his microphone up so he could be heard. "Is the government attempting to stop the release of this material?" The House leader took this one. "In the first place, we aren't sure how it's going to be released, which makes that difficult. As you heard from Mr. Jorgenson, nothing in these documents focuses on finance in a way that would demonstrate or encourage fraud, and nothing is present that is explicitly about national security. In the absence of those elements, the President does not believe that prior restraint of publication would be justified. Of course, they're trying to catch these people, and they hope that catching them would end the distribution, but they're not even sure of that."

The senator shook his head and sat down.

The leader of the House glanced sidelong at his colleague, and stepped forward to the microphone again. "There's something else we should talk about here. As you saw, information from the Republican National Committee is also being released, including documents between staffers and between the party leaders and the former President. Those materials make pretty clear that some of our number were being pressured to support the President's contention that he won the election, and that some of us in fact have complied and some have complied enthusiastically. More than that, the letters between RNC staff members privately show that they knew the election had been fair and that the President had lost.

"Did you hear me on that?" he asked again. "Voters will know that we knew from the beginning that the election was fair, and some of us have lied about it, and a lot of us have exploited that lie.

"Now, I don't know how you are going to square that with the voters, if these materials show up in your state's distribution of documents. But you'd better give it some thought. Because we could be watching the total discrediting of the Republican Party here. At a minimum, we are probably looking at a complete change in national leadership." He looked at the gallery, where the RNC chair sat stone-faced and defiant.

"Don't think you can do a 'what-about-the-Democrats' here. Let them solve their own problems. They have them, too. But the fact is, they won the election and we lost. *And we knew it and lied about it.* And unless we address our issues, we will lose the next election, too. Doubling down on calling them socialists and communists will bounce back in our faces, apart from the fact that the people using those labels will smell like they've come out of a dumpster. I'd encourage you to lay that strategy aside. It's outlived its usefulness."

The Senate minority leader stepped forward, shoulder to shoulder with his colleague. "Now, we'd like to hear something more than whining or bitching about this. It's out there, and more of it will be out there. We'd like to know what you think about how we should respond. Sunday's coming, and so are the talk shows. Talk radio is always on, and so is talk TV."

After five minutes of silence, people began to move to microphones in the aisles. The Senate Minority Leader noticed that none of them were from Minnesota, New Jersey, West Virginia, Michigan, or Texas. *Damn right you'd better be quiet*, he thought. *I'll talk with you tomorrow.*

On the other side of the building, the Speaker and the Majority Leader were having their own problems.

A progressive House member had the microphone, and was highlighting information on West Virginia's affiliation with coal companies—part of the West Virginia package— and the way companies seemed to be shaping federal policies. This lasted until a "centrist" Democrat spoke up about how the progressive who had just spoken appeared to be in bed with several violence-proclaiming groups linked to Antifa.

The Speaker of the House gaveled the clash to an end. "Look at this," she said, pointing to the projection screen behind her. The document on the screen was linked to an "environment-friendly" lobbying firm, directed to one of the House members in the room. "Then look at this," she gestured. On the screen appeared a second document, from the same lobbyist, in which he described how he was manipulating the legislator and the appeals he was using, including the hint of financial compensation. "Just tell me how you think the American people are going to feel about you when they read this?"

"Now, some of us have been arguing that we need to push back against systemic oppression in the system, but how are we supposed to do this when some of you are selling stock and making enormous gains on the basis of insider trading? We look like we're part of the problem! And we *are.*

"And this whole 'Antifa' thing. We *cannot* be linked to this, and if any of you is in fact supportive of Antifa, you will not have my support for re-election. Look at this 'Antifa' letter, signed by one of its core people, directed to the senator from New Jersey. It suggests that Antifa is willing to work for his election, if he will lay off them for a while. Did you notice the paired letter from that founder to an associate, boasting of his threat—and how he would blackmail the Senator *no matter which way the Senator reacted?*"

The progressive House member abruptly left the microphone and sat down.

"May I remind you that Minnesota isn't the only state that had Antifa problems last year?" She looked out over the chamber, eyes sweeping the crowd for individuals she knew. "Hadn't we better be asking ourselves what will happen if there are letters like this in the Oregon, Washington, California, and Georgia files, whenever they come out? As much as I hate to even mention him, we had better be in O'Reilly's 'no-spin zone', because the American people are going to be angry enough to throw all of us out of here if they find we're part of this."

"Who will speak for us? Who has the credibility and the temperament for it?"

In the end, they settled on a reluctant senator from Minnesota and a House member from Tennessee.

CHAPTER 11: PRESIDENT'S PRESS CONFERENCE

Friday, October 22
The White House

The President's press conference on Friday afternoon, October 22nd, was, of course, live across all the networks and carried on National Public Radio. He stepped into the Brady Press Briefing Room, down the hall and around the corner from the Oval Office, on the first floor of the West Wing. Thin, fit, a slight squint from the bright television lights, he smiled slightly at correspondents he'd known for years. Following him in were three vaguely familiar faces, including the Director of the National Security Agency, the Director of the FBI, and the Attorney General.

He stepped to the podium at exactly 2:00 p.m., unusual enough for any president, on time, opening the briefing book his press secretary had placed there moments earlier. He began.

"Welcome, everyone, and welcome, my fellow Americans at home and around the world. There are a number of items I'd like to speak about before I address the elephant in the room, the 'Month of Sundays' group."

From there, he summarized several initiatives the administration was pursuing, emphasizing as he did how legislation was currently stalled in the Senate, despite ongoing negotiations, on the Build Back Better Agenda and Bipartisan Infrastructure Deal. After fifteen minutes of review, he paused, turned the page in his briefing book, and looked out at the reporters.

"In the last three days, a group calling itself the 'Month of Sundays' has announced that it would begin a campaign of the release of information regarding the actions of legislators in the federal government. On Wednesday, we became aware of this campaign after some American newspapers received emailed documents from this group. I met with several executive branch officials on Wednesday night, and met on Thursday with the leadership of Congress and representatives of the Democratic and Republican National Committees. I gave them copies of these documents, as they had not yet been released to the general public. Thursday evening, last night, the newspapers either published them or gave links to those documents online.

"You all know the result, because we've seen it on television and heard it on radio this morning. I understand that the networks are seeking a number of senators and representatives to speak on weekend television programs. This seems entirely appropriate. I was informed this morning that Democratic legislators have selected a senator and a representative to speak on their behalf; I expect we will hear that Republican legislators have done the same.

"Let me say at the beginning that the 'Month of Sundays' group has broken several federal laws, and undoubtedly state laws are in play here as well. Access to government computers—and that means those used in all branches, legislative, executive, judicial—is restricted, and taking documents from those computers breaks the law. We also have laws against taking documents from private computers or networks, and those appear to have been broken as well.

"The Department of Justice has already formed a task force through the Federal Bureau of Investigation to examine the documents we've received. Their mandate is to discover the sources of these documents, how they came to be collected and released, and who is responsible. The FBI is not the only agency of the government involved, I will add.

"It is still not clear how the 'Month of Sundays' group intends to distribute information to the American people, which they have promised to do. Indeed, we may have to wait until Sunday, when documents are sent to the voters in one state. We don't even know for sure which state at this point." The President paused for a moment, and then rested his hands on either side of the podium, and leaned in slightly before he began again. His eyes were level with the onlookers.

"It is not improper to speculate that agents outside the United States may have been responsible for the release of these documents, much like what happened in 2016 with emails from the Democratic National Committee. At the same time, we have no evidence that this is the case.

American citizens, frustrated by what they perceive as corrupt behavior, may be responsible, and are acting as whistleblowers. In any event, the proposed scale of this operation is startling, and has led us initially to see it as the work of an organization, one about which we know nothing right now. I and my administration are concerned that the net effect of these documents may be to undermine the credibility of our democratic institutions, precisely at a time when autocrats overseas have done the same—we can cite Venezuela, Hungary, Russia, China and elsewhere.

"There is one element of this situation I wish to emphasize here. It is possible that these documents may reveal actions which are illegal, and which can be laid at the feet of specific individuals either in elected office or outside the government. The Department of Justice is examining these materials for such actions, and will pursue further investigations if the circumstances warrant. I think we would all be disappointed if we found that representatives of the people had acted against their interests or in the interest of profiting from elected office." The President's voice, measured until the last sentence, was suddenly very cold indeed. He paused for a few seconds, and then began again.

"In my meeting with the leaders of Congress yesterday, I attempted to make it clear that I will take no role in the investigation of these leaked documents beyond hearing appropriate reports from the investigators. I will not step in to favor my own party, and I will not seek to publicize or capitalize on what is revealed about our Republican colleagues. Reporting is the role of the news media, and investigation the role of the Justice Department and others. My role as president is to execute the laws of this nation and uphold the Constitution.

"We intend to provide additional information to the American people in the next few days, as our investigation continues."

With that, he stepped back, nodded slightly, picked up the briefing book, and walked away. Shouted questions behind him bounced off the closed door of the briefing room, and a Secret Service officer stepped in front of the door to emphasize the finality of the President's departure.

CHAPTER 12: ORDINARY PEOPLE

Saturday, October 23
Arvada, Wyoming

Adam Hill had driven away from his Gillette-area phone call with Morris Watson on Wednesday, October 20th. At home, an hour away near Arvada, he spent the rest of the day on ranch work. Winter was coming, and he and his family needed to move the Herefords and Angus into better pastures. It might be 58 today, but frost was forecast for the next three nights. The ranch had 300-plus cow-calf pairs, and it was a day's job moving them between pastures. Someone in the East or Midwest might think the ranch's 9,000 acres was enormous—14 square miles—but in the semi-arid region of Wyoming, it was enough and not too much. He could add as many as 100 head more, but the math on what it would take did not pencil out well. No reserves, and Hill was cautious.

He had given a lot of thought to the conversation with Watson in between paperwork and a brief spell feeding the horses, a chore more pleasant than doing the bookkeeping. When his wife called him in for supper, they had talked through the call and what he ought to do next.

"So, what do you think?" he had ended.

Allison looked him straight in the eye. "Well, I don't
think you ought to be in a huge hurry. But I think it'd be a
good idea to make some copies of the things that most
bothered you, and then get the Patriots together and talk
about them. You can show them what you have. And you
might want to be selective about who hears this, and make
it unofficial, a game night, or something. We could do it
Saturday."

"Tell me why you feel that way."

"I haven't seen any of these files, and I can tell already
that you're steamed up about it. And if you're steamed,
Red and Jake and Charlie are likely to be ready to break
things. And maybe hurt people. Get people to talk sensibly
about what this stuff shows you, and then take it up the
line, down to Cheyenne. Get Ed King and a couple of the
group to go with you, and sit down with the governor or
with the Senate president. If necessary, ask for the attorney
general to see this stuff. Let the governor confront the
elected officials. If it's as bad as you say, he can ask for
their resignations, or he can have the attorney general
begin an investigation." So far, as the sunlight faded
outside, she had been quiet, and he had appreciated
looking at her with the view of the straw-colored prairie
behind her out the window.

She had stopped, and reached across the table to hold
his wrist. "I want you to be deliberate about this. You
have credibility with people, and I want you to keep that."

That had been Wednesday. By Saturday morning, he'd
lost some of his hesitancy. The news coming out from all

over the country—the closest, Denver—seemed to confirm that this Month of Sundays group was a real thing, and the President's press conference on Friday seemed to imply that what he'd received was trustworthy. And Allison had read the files, too.

Allison had called a group of couples they got together with for fun, and some had driven 20 miles to get to the ranch for chili and homemade bread for supper, pie for dessert, and anticipation of games. The Hills moved around the dining room table, scooping up plates and clearing things as the other four couples talked about the news of the week. Several had spent time on the files showing up on the internet, and most were laughing at the consternation in Atlanta and New York as CNN and FOX struggled to keep up. It had been pretty amusing to see some of the "brand-name" broadcasters wide-eyed and shaken when their own letters to legislators showed up on the opposing network.

Adam put a pile of stapled papers down on the table in front of his seat, and Allison came in with a full coffee cup from the kitchen. She smiled down the table as her husband sat down.

"We got you here tonight on false pretenses," he said, with that half-smile they knew. Heads turned back and forth between Adam and Allison as people got quiet. "All of you know about this Month of Sundays stuff that came out on Thursday night, right?" Small nods or head-shakes all along the table—but even the shaking heads meant "Can you believe it?" and not "No."

"Well, on Monday, even before this happened, I got a similar package in my email, but it was for Wyoming. Only two other people have seen it so far, Ed King, our state senator, and Allison. I called somebody in another state like me—got the name from Ed—and he got something similar for his state, and that state's stuff isn't out yet, either."

The room was very quiet.

"Here's a packet for each of you. It's not everything, but I'd like to talk you through what I see in what I've given you. And I'd like you to advise me on what you think we ought to do.

"Let's look at it together."

An hour later, the five couples were ready for another slice of pie and another cup of coffee each. Adam had led them through the papers he'd assembled, and steered the discussion around three issues that had jumped out at him.

First, in a state where coal and oil production, along with agriculture, dominated the economy, he'd shown them three sets of emails or letters. In one, the Republican National Committee had recommended an approach to and language for attacking the "Green New Deal," language that Adam could show them had been picked up by Wyoming's legislators at the state and federal level. They he showed them an internal memo from the Party that acknowledged that a number of the major talking points the Party recommended using were absolutely false, for instance those by a Senator from Wyoming who argued that "There's another victim of the Green New Deal, it's ice cream. Livestock will be banned. Say goodbye to dairy, to beef, to family farms to ranches. American favorites like cheeseburgers and milkshakes will become a thing of the past." Adam had stapled the Senator's remarks to the actual proposal from House Democrats.

He showed them discussions at both the state and national levels about increasing the use of terms like "socialist," and "radical" in messaging about Democrats, and the recommendation the Party was making about support for President Trump. And finally, he showed them RNC materials surrounding the January 6th riot, with notes from the White House that indicated that the administration knew they had lost the election, but were prepared to fight anyway. Tucked away in a corner of that document was a party proposal to repudiate any Republican officeholder who questioned the President's version of events.

"There's more about some corporate stuff in there, too—lobbying against renewable energy, offers to support them for re-election if they'll turn it down."

"So, here's what I need to know," Hill said. "I think there's enough really questionable stuff here to take it to the governor and maybe the attorney general. The fact that almost everyone in office is Republican shouldn't matter. They're also ethical people. Should I take it to Cheyenne?"

The vote was unanimous. Adam drafted an email just before midnight, Allison reviewed it and tuned it up, and they sent it, asking the governor for a meeting on Tuesday morning. Adam had included mention of the Month of

Sundays group and included one sample. They figured that ought to get someone's attention.

CHAPTER 13: ALASKA

Saturday-Sunday, October 23-24
Alaska

Talk-radio on Saturday, whether it was conservative or more centrist "news," ignored college football (Illinois upset Penn State, Iowa State upset Oklahoma State), ignored the last games of the Major League Championship Series (Astros 5, Red Sox 0; Braves 4, Dodgers 2), and nearly overlooked the Supreme Court's refusal to block a Texas abortion law. Instead, listeners and callers-in were quoting from Baker's email package, courtesy of the internet and the newspapers. The tone was more than a little fed-up, heading toward hostile.

Sitting on the porch of his mountain meadow home in the afternoon sunset, listening in online, Baker was both glad and a little nervous.

A few hours later, at midnight, Sunday morning, October 24th, about half the registered voters in Alaska, Republican and Democrat alike, received a brief email with a website link. About a quarter more had a five-megabyte attachment to their email. And the other quarter got a notice that something was waiting for them in a Dropbox account on line. Almost immediately, law enforcement was notified—after all, they were voters, too—and reported the "drop" to the FBI, which was already aware of it. The emails all were identified as from the "Month of Sundays Group," with a subject line of "How Alaska's Legislators Make Decisions."

All three sources, apart from the downloadable files, led to dead ends. The Dropbox account was registered to an email address in Europe. The email account and the website were new, had only been accessed to get them registered and established, and couldn't be linked in any obvious way to anyone. By 6 a.m., about 200,000 voters from the Alaska Independence Party and the Republican and Democratic parties had gone to the website, about 50,000 had opened the email attachment, and about 50,000 had claimed their Dropbox file. Since this represented about half of all registered voters, and since the files could be shared between voters, it looked like pretty good coverage.

A good start, Baker thought as he had another cup of coffee after breakfast, leaning against a support column on his front porch and looking across the meadow. He had a radio playing in the background, and was listening through the screened window into the living room. NPR was reporting in about Alaskans' reactions, courtesy of *Weekend Edition.* Later in the day, he expected he'd hear more on *All Things Considered,* limited to only an hour because it was Sunday. He was curious about what the Sunday television talk shows might have on, and if the Democrats and Republicans would be able to control their messaging as he'd heard from the President. It seemed unlikely that one Senator and one Representative from each party would be able to manage the firehose of questions coming at them.

Off to the north and south, he'd occasionally hear the sound of a deer rifle, because it was most of the way through the white-tailed deer season. Another week, and it'd be quieter.

Almost immediately, stringers for the major media had begun sending the files to their papers and broadcast outlets in the lower 48. Everyone knew it would take a while to find out what was in the package, but once again Baker had helped out his readers by clustering related letters and papers together, and making them all searchable. Some things came to light immediately.

Legislators were watching, but so were Flores and Myers and their employers.

CHAPTER 14: SUNDAY TALK

Sunday, October 24
Newport, Washington

Baker was down in the basement of his cabin, with three separate computers, Leroy, Eunice, and Dave, handling separate internet feeds of the Sunday morning talk shows. It was still only 8 a.m., and Baker was in jeans, sweatshirt, and moccasins, coffee in hand. He had *This Week, Meet the Press,* and *State of the Union* on the screen, live in the Eastern time zone, and it all brought back memories of Lyndon Johnson and his famous three-screens to see how the news was playing. He figured that if necessary, he'd catch them on the satellite replay when they finally came out for the West Coast audience.

Right now, the feed was two Democrats and a Republican, one each per show, and the second Republican, a senator from the Midwest, would be on *Face the Nation* later. He had closed captioning on for all of them, so that even live, he had a good sense of what they were saying.

As a Minnesotan, he was most interested in what his Senator had to say, and how she'd respond. He'd always considered her one of the most temperate, straightforward people in politics, and was ashamed of the Democratic Party for not selecting her in 2020 at least as the Vice-Presidential candidate.

The host, white, white-shirt-and-tie-dark-jacket proper, was starting soft. Baker thought of Warren Zevon, and hummed to himself, *'I saw a werewolf drinkin' a piña colada at Trader Vic's. His hair was perfect.'* Watch yourself, Senator. *This guy's a predator.*

"Senator, I expect that you've seen the 'Month of Sundays' materials this last week. What's your impression? Are they authentic?"

"I'm not in a position to judge that, you know. I do trust the President on this, and I expect that the FBI will confirm this if one of my committees hears a report from them. I will say that I've gotten letters from donors and from constituents that sound a lot like the ones that showed up in these files. I actually have a couple of staff members looking through our own correspondence—there's a lot—to see if we've gotten something similar. And," she added with a smile that looked a little forced, "how *we* responded."

The interviewer glanced down at his notes. "Apart from the release of these documents—a federal felony—that is in itself surprising, did anything else surprise you in what you read?"

The senator, seated at a desk facing the interviewer, seemed to settle herself a bit. "Yes, I'd say so. I'm not happy to admit that some of my Democratic colleagues appear to have adopted political positions in support of extremists, and that some of my Republican colleagues appear to have done the same thing at the other end of the spectrum. I haven't read all the files yet.

"I think one thing that surprised me a lot was the influence of some of the big-name 'foundations' in shaping political choices. I won't name names here, but I realized that behind some of the arguments legislators use is a whole agenda and scripts developed by others."

"Have you reviewed some of the PAC documents in what was released?"

"Yes, I have." The senator stopped right there.

The interviewer seemed surprised. "Are you willing to comment on them?"

"Let me say this," she said, and looked right at the camera. "When I realized who was funding Antifa, and who was at the same time funding groups like the Proud Boys, I was very, very angry. Someone has written that the core strategy of both groups is violence, and we've seen that from both groups in Minnesota. My husband will tell you I don't swear a lot, but I said a lot of ugly things for about ten minutes straight. When men at the top of the income pyramid are funding anarchists—both left and right—you have to ask why. And trust me, a bunch of us will be asking why. In public."

"Do you think 'whistleblowing' like this is good for the country, and for democracy? It seems like there's a lot of 'pot-stirring' going on here."

"Let's hold on a minute there. The first thing to say is that this release is illegal. It's a crime. But that's often been the case with whistleblowing—someone wants something kept under cover, and so you find a way to criminalize its release. But do I think it's good for democracy? Only *maybe*, right now.

"We are becoming aware—and if these releases keep going on we'll be *very* aware—that government hasn't always worked for 'the people' at large. Instead, it's often worked for the people who contributed the most, or who could promise the most—like a commitment to establish a manufacturing plant in someone's district. Or who could promise someone votes. Or who could offer a trade-off, like 'you support my bill, I'll support yours.'

"But these letters and memos and reports are hinting at something more than that. They suggest—and, by God, I hope we get more evidence—that there's a whole group of people out there with wealth and power who are looking to impoverish the rest of us. I'll be more direct: they intend to screw us, and you can take that as a synonym for forcible rape."

The interviewer's eyes were darting everywhere, and the senator's measured tone, every word bitten off, seemed to alarm him.

"How do you think Congress will respond?" he asked hurriedly, clearly being fed something through his earpiece.

The Senator paused a moment. "There will be consequences, no matter what. I think, in terms of legislation, we might well see a new mandated openness about lobbying, about communication with donors. We might even see that the PAC contributors won't be allowed to be invisible any more. I think there'll be a lot more scrutiny of extremists. We *might—*" she smiled and drew out the pause—"we *might* see some senators and representatives resign, be recalled, or go to jail. It might take that to get our credibility back again."

On another station's *News Sunday*, a Republican congressman was highlighting what he saw as Democratic failures shown up in the documents from the first group of releases and then Alaska. A panel of contributors, two from the network, one a former government policy expert, and one a White House correspondent, waited until he was finished.

The first network contributor smiled disarmingly. "So what's your take on the President here? Is he doing the right thing to let this go on? Should he have stepped in to stop these documents being released?"

Now, Baker thought, *the smart thing to do would be to point out that the President wasn't releasing them. And that if he had tried to stop their release, he might have been up against the Constitution.*

The congressman took the low road. He immediately jumped in with an answer. "Well, I think he'll regret letting this stuff out in the open, because it's for-sure going to cause division. And I think, when you look at everything carefully, there's much more damaging material from and about Democrats than Republicans. I think it's a political mistake that shows how out of touch he is with the American people."

The White House correspondent practically sneered. "You honestly believe that, Congressman? Because from where I sit, the releases from your party's headquarters, together with the documents regarding the election, make me ashamed to be a Republican! And the party leaders' internal discussion of the kind of rhetoric to use against Democrats is simply disgusting. *Did you even read the documents, congressman?"*

By the last sentence she was practically shouting, leaning forward across the panelist's table, bracing herself on her elbows, looking like she was ready to stand up or jump over the table to reach him.

He shrank back in his seat, and the network cut to a commercial.

By Monday evening, questions were being raised among members of the Alaska legislature. House Bill 186, calling for all coronavirus mandates to be laid aside, was itself laid aside for floor discussion about the performance of Alaska's two senators and one representative. All were Republicans, but of various flavors from moderate to very conservative, and all heavily funded by corporate interest Political Action Committees. All three, Baker knew, were exemplary individuals, although some of their positions were a little incoherent. They wouldn't raise controversy, reasonable people that they were. It was the detail about the financial interests behind them that might raise eyebrows.

Baker, listening to NPR on Monday afternoon, was hoping that those details might be putting the fear of God into legislators from other states. He was pretty sure they were watching this trainwreck coming at them.

CHAPTER 15: HUNTERS 2

Sunday, October 24
Washington, D.C.

By Sunday afternoon, Cook and her team had met twice. They'd started on Friday afternoon, had spent much of the day on Saturday working together, and had prepped a report to the Director and the Attorney General by Saturday evening. They'd outlined what they knew and where they were still hunting. They admitted they would find out a lot more from the Sunday distribution. But they'd taken time to watch the senator from Minnesota, and most of them smiled when the interviewer cringed.

Cook's team was a mix of older and younger, men and women. All were under fifty, some just into their thirties, all had been agents for at least five years, and several had broken major cybercrime cases in their region. Technical skills trumped length of service, in cybercrime, and these were standouts. Some of them looked to be young, but they were all excellent. Two or three were genuinely creative and innovative, capable of turning a problem on its head and finding alternative ways to connect things. *I wonder if I can keep up,* Cook thought, as she looked at them.

She looked at the list on her pad.

Reed Price—New York
Michael Life—New York
Patrick Adams—Chicago
Adrian Davis—Seattle
James Reznik--Seattle
Angela Hall—Los Angeles
Nicole Watson—Washington DC
Fritz Elder--Denver
David Harstad--Denver

"Okay," she began. "Adrian Davis, summarize what we have up until this last drop of files this morning."

The trim, short-haired black man from Seattle looked up at the group, glancing down at his laptop occasionally to make sure he got everything. "First, we outlined what it is we need to know—the who, what, why, when, how, and how much—where isn't as important, because it's all on the net. Patrick pointed out that 'where' matters in terms of source." He glanced over at his Chicago colleague, a lean, tall black man resting one arm on the table. "Second, we agreed that we're up against some significant handicaps. It's pretty clear that what's been released is only a selection of what the MOS group actually has, and that these pieces were chosen deliberately to make a point. Because we don't know all that's in the collection, we can't make good guesses about where they got everything. Whoever did this changed the 'properties' tags on the document that shows when they were created."

To make his point, he pulled up a letter from a lobbyist to a senator from Texas. He looked at the 'properties' of the file, and showed it blanked. "Further, because the file formats have, in some ways, been anonymized, we'll have a hard time looking for embedded identifiers in the documents. The papers themselves might be dated, but that doesn't tell us when they were taken or copied. The act of copying itself confuses the 'creation date' tag attached to the file. We think we *can* make some guesses about 'who' and 'how' by examining the offices from which the files might have come." He looked up.

"Good start, and thank you," Cook responded when he finished. "We'll take some time on that next. But let's talk about what happened today. Michael and Angela, can we hear from you?"

Angela Hall looked at Michael Life, who nodded, and then she began. "Well, we all know pretty much that the delivery started this morning, right at midnight Alaska time. That's one hour earlier than Pacific Daylight Time, or four hours earlier than we are here on the East Coast. Delivery was in three modes. The first was an email to registered Republican, Democratic, and Independent voters—there are three large parties in Alaska, and actually, the Independent party looks bigger than the Democrats—with a website link. The link was to 'monthofsundaysgroup.com,' and the only page on the website invited people to download a five-megabyte file, which was a highly compressed set of pdfs. The second delivery method was an email with the same file attached to the email. The third was a link to a Dropbox account, again with directions to download the same file. Gmail was used for all the email.

"We immediately requested information from the web hosting service about who had registered the MOS.com website. At the same time, following Rule 41 Search and Seizure provisions, we requested a warrant from a federal judge that would permit us to search the hosting service computers and determine what we can find out about the source. The email was sent from a Gmail account, and we've filed the same request to search Google computers about the storage of the file and the owner of the Gmail account. We did the same thing with the Dropbox version.

"Here's where the fun begins. Each Gmail account was set up about fifteen minutes before midnight." She paused. "Oh, I didn't mention that whoever did this actually used six different Gmail accounts, two for each method of delivery. And the Dropbox account had been set up about an hour earlier. The Gmail accounts were one-shots, and the files on the Dropbox account were deleted about an hour ago, so just about eight hours after setup. Our warrant should give us access to them before the account is permanently deleted."

"And, by the way, the commands to delete the account came in through a TOR server based in Germany," Michael Life added. Angela nodded. "We might or might not be able to backtrack it."

Heads were nodding around the table, and faces showed wry smiles. The summary was clear, and certainly commendable, but Cook thought that the nods were likely propers given to whatever outfit this was. Very professional, it was feeling.

"Okay, thanks. Good summary. Now, what do we have on contents? Jim Reznik, David Harstad, what have you got so far on the earlier distribution?"

Harstad, with a glance at Reznik next to him, began. Harstad had covered the papers coming from congressional offices out to constituents and correspondence coming in. Reznik had looked at all internal documents, including those between other congressional offices. Their first take: no illegal acts from the congressional offices, but lots of discussion about the external forces, including the Republican National Committee, on legislation, on policy statements, and internal alliances. "One thread caught my eye," Reznik said, "and Dave saw it, too, in what he looked at. There's a lot of what you might call 'Trump-centric' language and perspectives. Beginning in fall 2020, the language of conspiracy and election fraud ramps up, and it continues right through the spring of 2021, with strong encouragement from the Party to keep in line in public statements. And mind you, these are *internal* documents between congressional offices."

Harstad added, "We both think it's relevant to note that this is not a surprise, and it's actually a feature of everything the party did in its fund-raising all year long. The difference—and we both thought this was important—is that the people composing this stuff from the RNC appear to believe it's true, rather than just a matter of rhetoric for the public. In other words, they're 'true believers' who want legislators to go along with them. They don't appear to be posing. The legislators and their staff seem a little reluctant, at least privately. At the same time, when we look at letters from the leaders in the RNC, it's clear *they* know the claims of election fraud are manufactured."

"Anyone, comment here," Cook said. "How do you think this is going to play with the public? The reason I'm asking, and the reason I think that's a useful question, is that we need to ask ourselves *why* these documents are out there. How will this show Alaskans something useful about Congress—useful from the point of view of the MOS group? This goes to motive, which might help us work back to source."

Discussion went on for ten or fifteen minutes, but Cook wasn't listening for sentiments so much as for her team's thinking. Did anyone have a handle they hadn't tried on this first go-round?

Fritz Elder said something that stopped the conversation. Cook looked up from her notes. "What was that, Fritz?"

Elder, ironically one of the younger team members, mid-thirties, dark-haired, toyed with his pen for a moment, then looked directly at Cook. "I asked who are the people in these offices most likely not to be suspected of anything? Who are the folks with limited access but who might almost be overlooked because of it? And I think it's interns. College interns, those generally warm, cuddly, bright, naive, wet-behind-the-ears interns. That's where I'd start looking."

"Keep going," said Cook. "I can see why. 'Start' how?"

Elder was leaning forward, starting to gesture, voice a little more confident. "Do we have a personnel list of staff who have worked in Senate and House offices over the last several years or longer? How are we sorting them out? We know there were background checks at the beginning. Are we looking at all at their electronics? And I wonder if it's worth asking whose names appear and *don't appear* in the files?"

Reed Price leaned in and waved at Elder. "I like the idea, but aren't the interns pretty much semester-at-a-time people? The documents stretch out a long time. Shouldn't we be keeping a look at the permanent staff, too? And this is across a host of offices—if the MOS group is telling us the truth, more than forty Senate offices, at a minimum. How could interns do that?" His voice wasn't combative, but Price had a point, and it reinforced Cook's sense that the scope of the problem was growing, not shrinking. The closer you looked, the more complicated it was.

Cook knew that another part of the investigation team was doing the personnel work, but thought Elder might be on to something. She made a note on her pad, then looked at Elder and Nicole Watson, who hadn't spoken yet. "Fritz and Nicole, there's another group looking at staff personnel right now. Interface with them, find out how they're approaching this, and let us know tomorrow what you find out.

"Okay, right now let's turn to the 'how' of 'how did whoever it was get all this information, including stuff on external computers.' I want to hear ideas. What do we know, what can we guess?"

CHAPTER 16: STARTUP

November 2019-present
Minneapolis, Minnesota

Baker had faced two immediate questions when he'd awakened the morning after Ross's revelation in fall 2019. *Is there anything I can do about this?* He had thought about that quite a while. Coupled with it was, *Will anything make a difference?* As an optimist, a historian, and a political scientist, he could see several possibilities. If it had been possible, he'd have tried to talk it out with Jean, who could have cut to the heart of the second set of issues, the ethical ones, the ones that balanced likely damage over unlikely positive change.

Wide awake in his hotel bed, early, early in the morning, he had missed her, and he had remembered. Of course, the more he remembered, the less likely he was to step back and let this go. She'd been gone six months, and he still felt wounded.

He had shut the door on that, and got up and made coffee in the small French press he'd brought along, moving automatically between the microwave, the press, and the refrigerator for the half and half he'd bought yesterday. He kept thinking about it the whole time. The issue was clearer: members of Congress were steadily making choices that benefited some citizens and not others. The "some" were well equipped, well-funded, persistent, and determined. They were Republicans and Democrats alike. The "others" were unorganized, relatively less wealthy, less focused on how decisions were made, and included more than nine in ten Americans. They didn't know what was going on under the table or behind the closed door. In some cases, the national party apparatus was pushing—even enforcing—compliance. Was it possible to show the nine in ten the depth of manipulation going on, in ways that were inescapable? And as he thought about it, he realized that Jean's death, unavenged, and even silenced, was an example of this. For all his academic degrees and tenure and relative security, he was one of the nine.

So, the two big questions were, *How could he manage to get the data*, first, and then *How could he distribute it?*

The central problem was access, he had decided. How do you get into the emails and letters that would be evidence? What about using the people he already had on the inside, his interns and former students who were literally on the ground?

He could almost hear Jean, feel her tapping on the side of his head. *"Ethical problem: people could go to jail for this,"* she'd have said. *"You are involving your students, trusted to be in your care, in a conspiracy that breaks the law."* He didn't want to ask students to help him break into their office computers, because when they were caught—he had to think in those terms—their lives would be ruined. He didn't want to compromise them without their knowledge, either. It wasn't just that they'd despise him for what he'd done, and his shoulders sort of itched at that thought, but that in some way the trust they had in institutions and people would be lost, maybe for good.

That thought had sat with him for several days. Finally, he decided a) that the problem was so great that it called for him to act (and he knew he was making a bad choice here, and Jean's imagined voice was echoing in his head) and b) he had to find a way not only to keep the interns "out of it" even while exploiting their access, but c) he needed to find a way to erase his footprints, if he could.

The next step was a consultation. No one seems to recognize that you can be a computer science professor at a Christian college and understand perfectly well how to accomplish shady or questionable things. His friend Eric Bailey, in the next college building over from his, taught computer security and computer forensics as well as programming (C++, Python, Javascript and, God be praised, COBOL, Unix, and Linux). Bailey was old enough to be a grandfather and to have programmed in every version of Fortran since Fortran II. Baker had stopped programming when he quit his Commodore 64. Even then, he hadn't known what he was doing when he typed in the *Speedscript* word processing program from *Compute's Gazette*. But that had been what he could afford.

And he and Baker had run together at noon for years, until their knees gave out. They still got together for coffee.

The conversation had begun in Bailey's office over good Caribou coffee Baker brought from the marketplace food cart next to the Dining Center. "Eric, I want to tell you about a project, and I'd like your help," he'd begun.

Bailey had looked at the coffee and smiled. "This must be good, if the bribe comes up front."

Baker sat down, his smile thinning a bit. "Well, maybe it is, and maybe I'll go to jail."

Bailey's hand hovered over the coffee cup, his palm resting in the steam coming up through the lid. Looking straight at Baker, he let his hand enclose the coffee like a carnival claw machine reaching for a plush teddy bear. "I owe you a lot, you know. Let's hear it. Start at the beginning."

"Here's what I want to do. What will it take to do it?"

Bailey had explained the elements he'd need. First, he needed a custom program that would upload itself onto other computers. There were a jillion of them, Bailey said, the work of hackers everywhere. The problem was, security companies knew about them and helped people defend against them. So he needed a way to get that program onto those computers that wouldn't trip the security fence. Second, the uploaded program needed to be something that spread itself anonymously, could lie dormant, and then at a command could aggregate documents and then send them back to the end-user. Third, that program had to erase itself to the point that it couldn't be detected afterward. "What's the point of having the stuff you want if your target knows you have it? Bailey'd asked. "And what's the point of getting caught?"

Then he went on to talk about the second half, how to deliver it. Bailey had actually thought that might be a lot easier, given the internet's status as a swamp. Baker had learned more than he'd thought possible about TOR servers and about VPNs. It took several more sessions and more Caribou. He'd even sprung for the big cranberry muffins, the consumption of which Eric would have to conceal from his wife.

And in the end, Bailey'd said he'd help. The Baileys had loved Jean, too. Within two months, Bailey had handed him the programs on a flash drive, shaken his hand, and taken early retirement at the end of the semester. They moved to their farm in Hayward, Wisconsin, closer to the grandchildren, out in the country, and well away from trouble. They even closed out their Facebook account. Electronically, they disappeared, beyond electronic bill paying.

First, Baker used his interns, over the two years he had, and he "used" them without telling them. He still cringed when he thought about it.

All he needed to do was send them all an email update, once a week, with a photo or two or three from home. In each of the documents, thanks to Bailey, was a bit of code that wrote itself into a file that was slowly building on each of their computers or phones. By the end of the term, the program now built was "sending itself" with every email to whoever was the addressee. And so on. At some point over the Christmas holidays or just after spring finals, all those "addressed" computers reported in, sending every email in the user's inbox and every document in the documents file to one of two dozen computers Baker had set up around the country. Every couple of days, Baker would set up an email account somewhere and download the whole batch.

Within a month, he was buying 1-terabyte drives, gutting them out of computers he'd pay cash for on craigslist or Facebook Marketplace and then recycling the computers as scrap. It'd be easier to get them from the Micro store in St. Louis Park, but there were cameras. Sometimes for a couple of days a month he sorted and arranged the information he'd gotten.

And then at a command from Baker, the programs erased themselves. Including the programs on his interns' computers. It was as though nothing had happened at all. Next semester, do it again, only this time, reporting emails and documents just since the last batch.

Baker had three semesters, he figured, to get what he could. Maybe only two. The big haul was in spring of 2020, updates in fall 2020 and spring 2021. He needed to begin "Month of Sundays" by late October to have any effect on the 2022 midterms.

Ironically, the coronavirus pandemic made it easier and harder. While his interns were in D.C., masked, they did everything online. A few gigabits here and there were practically untraceable as the nation transitioned to Zoom, Teams, Duo, and heavier and heavier email. It continued through fall 2020, and then eased up during spring 2021. By then, he was using all his spare time to organize what he had, linking documents together and updating the state files.

The last data dump had been at the end of May 2021. No trace of his work remained on any active computer, and his interns' computers and their accounts had been scrubbed as well.

The sorting process was, of course, enormous. He began by excluding whole categories of email, focusing on the Senate offices and the senators themselves standing for re-election. While the House might still be in play, it was the Senate that, by its very nature, held things up. And if "safe" Senate seats could be contested because of corrupt or malign influences, the House, he knew, would follow suit. It didn't even matter to him whether it was a Republican or a Democrat in office; by the time he was done, people would know what clues to look for about integrity and honesty.

Distribution, he had realized, would be equally challenging. He knew from the start that he wanted to organize the data by state, and he wanted to send information to voters in the state, so it meant he'd either need to send a link to every voter or to have their email addresses. Fortunately, in scavenging data he ended up with the list of every registered voter known to the party offices. He could, if he wanted, email every voter in a particular state.

But should I do that? He asked. *And if I could, what would be the consequences?* Should he "park" the documents at a particular web address and have people download them? Should he just email the whole package to every state? Based on what he'd seen, the "package" would be awfully big, even compressed. Should he send it as if it was from their political party? Should he send it from the *other* political party? Should he send it from the "Month of Sundays Group"?

For more than a month, he'd batted the possibilities around, trying to weigh the advantages and the consequences of the choices. He knew someone would try to stop him. Would it be smarter to develop multiple approaches, so if one failed or was compromised, he'd have another? *Not just smarter,* he mused, *essential.* So that's where he left it. *Full-court press,* he concluded. As Gladwell had written once, *That's how David beats Goliath.* Do the unexpected, and never quit doing it. Maybe it'd keep him out of jail, and maybe not.

Eight years earlier, in 2013, Baker had been a tenured late-career academic in a college with stable to declining enrollment. He could see the crash coming, even if the alumni, some of the administration, some of the Trustees, and some of his colleagues couldn't. Minnesota, like most of the upper Midwest, was skidding toward enrollment numbers of the 1980's. The hope of capturing a stable, consistent percentage of the state's high school graduates was a way of saying two hard things: "We're the prisoners of demography," and "We don't believe we can expand our reach." Baker recognized these underlying assumptions, even if he didn't believe them. The Political Science program he'd built, centered around the Washington Study Program and hands-on engagement with state and federal legislators, not-for-profits, and industry connections, had tripled the number of undergraduate majors in his department. He and his Business Department colleagues had collaborated with the Communication Department to build a "Sales" emphasis in business that had ballooned to over a hundred majors in the emphasis, echoing an initiative from another university, down the road.

He was optimistic, and he was a contrarian who looked for innovative, collaborative approaches. But in 2018, as a new college president took office, he had seen the writing on the wall. He and Jean had decided on phased retirement, running the Washington Study Program and preparing it for a hand-off, teaching one course a semester with a finish date of spring 2021. The college offered him a one-year full-pay "terminal sabbatical" that started in June 2021, with a project to come out of it. Jean's death, in May 2019, at the hands of a drunken driver who happened to be related to a Western Minnesota congressperson, just made it easier than ever.

And with that sabbatical in place, he had a research project to end all others. With her death, he had every reason in the world and not a shred of restraint beyond "Do no harm."

Baker had faced the likelihood that he'd be discovered, and the real possibility that he'd go to jail. Although he'd done his best to minimize his own exposure, he could calculate the cost. But he did not intend to expose anyone he might have accidentally compromised.

From the beginning, he'd been weighing the moral and ethical issues of this project. Working in Washington was inherently morally ambiguous, he'd realized from the start. You represented an aggregate of citizens, whose own interests were divided. Republican, Democratic, or Independent, you swore an oath to defend the Constitution, first.

"I do solemnly swear that I will support and defend the Constitution of the United States against all enemies, foreign and domestic; that I will bear true faith and allegiance to the same; that I take this obligation freely, without any mental reservation or purpose of evasion; and that I will well and faithfully discharge the duties of the office on which I am about to enter. So help me God."

It became challenging to recognize and gauge who were the "domestic enemies" and how to respond to them. One person's domestic enemies might include corporations seeking to mine in your state, or leveraging jobs for tax advantages. Some projects might enrich the state's citizens, and some might impoverish them. Some bills might expand the franchise, and some might narrow it in the interest of "election security." "True faith and allegiance" was a minefield a legislator had to negotiate every day, and

A Month of Sundays

loyalty to one's party—"dancing with the one who brought you"—was no safe standard.

It wasn't so different in St. Paul, either, but when a state senator went home during a session or afterward, the neighbors pretty much knew what she'd said or voted on. In outstate Minnesota, that meant your neighbors, right in front of your face, were your constituents. Minnesota might be famous for mildness, indirection, and passive-aggressive communication—*thank you very much, Garrison Keillor!*—but your ice-fishing buddies or bridge club or women's circle at church wouldn't be shy about asking you hard questions. Someone at the coffee shop would sit down with you, uninvited, and tell you straight if you were being a jackass. It wasn't New York, so they'd be polite about it, but a white-haired grandmother smiling like Betty White would have the skin off you over coffee and a poppyseed muffin.

He remembered a story told by a friend about the first academic dean he'd worked for, a calm, quiet Dutchman from western Minnesota, who'd memorably asked one of his subordinates sitting at the conference table, "And just what *kind* of shit were you using for brains on that decision?" Oh, yeah—a lot harder to be corrupted when your friends would call you on it in a heartbeat.

But the farther away you were from home, the harder it was to maintain your integrity. You found yourself weighing competing goods, and sometimes competing evils and not recognizing them for what they were. He remembered the detective Miller talking to Holden:

"There's a right thing to do," Holden said.

114

"You don't have a right thing, friend," Miller said. *"You've got a whole plateful of maybe a little less wrong."*

Sitting on his front porch on this fine Sunday October afternoon in 2021, looking west across the meadow, Baker hoped he was more clear-eyed than Holden, the central character in *The Expanse*, although just as hopeful. And so Baker was breaking the law, and hoping against unintended consequences.

Baker had never served in the military, or in public office, but like every one of his generation he was raised, hand over heart, on the pledge of allegiance: *"I pledge allegiance to the flag of the United States of America, and to the republic for which it stands, one nation, under God, indivisible, with liberty and justice for all."* The last set of phrases had moved him more and more: "one nation, under God, indivisible, with liberty and justice for all." His career teaching in a religious college had been all about those phrases, helping students to understand their significance and their consequences. He shied away from thinking of it as his "calling," in some Protestant sense, but he acknowledged his responsibility. Maybe it went back to Teddy Roosevelt's "The Duties of American Citizenship," an 1883 speech some were just recently re-discovering. Even though Baker could lay aside some of Roosevelt's comments, it was easy to admire the common sense and even idealism that ran throughout the speech.

Roosevelt's sentiment was pretty clear. "The first duty of an American citizen, then, is that he shall work in politics; his second duty is that he shall do that work in a practical manner; and his third is that it shall be done in accord with the highest principles of honor and justice."

CHAPTER 17: REPORT TO THE PRESIDENT

Monday, October 25
The White House

The Monday morning news was, as expected, full of commentary—and some actual facts—about the Alaska documents. Devon Cook had the emailed reports from her team up on her laptop, and was reviewing them as she sat in an alcove in the White House. This would be her first Presidential briefing, and even though Collins sat across from her, killing email, she was nervous. She wished they'd had more to say.

Cook and Collins had wondered if the President would be alone for this meeting. He wasn't, and the Vice President, the Director of Central Intelligence, the Director of the NSA, and the Director of Homeland Security flanked him as a Secret Service agent ushered the FBI agents in. They sat across the Cabinet Room table from Cook and Collins, and Collins hoped they'd planned for Cook to demonstrate some computer graphics for them. For a first briefing, she wanted no hiccups.

She needn't have worried. At a gesture from the President, a large concealed flatscreen slid down from the ceiling, along the wall at the end of the table. A technician stepped into the room at the same time, leaned over Cook's shoulder with a whispered apology, and connected a USB dongle keyed to the room's system to a port on Cook's laptop.

The President smiled, and asked Cook if she was ready. "Yes, sir," Cook responded, and opened the laptop, flipping open a file folder next to the computer. Collins noted that Cook's habitual jittery energy settled down immediately when she was about to present.

Cook began. "Mr. President, our team is reviewing the materials sent out to Alaskans yesterday, and we are still reviewing what MOS sent to the media on Wednesday. Three things to begin with: first, there's still no financial information being released, and there are no threats to national security in any of these documents. Second, the pattern of including both congressional office correspondence and files from computers outside the government has also continued. Some of these 'outside' documents are from lobbyists or other funders, some are from private individuals. The FBI is looking at everyone who's been named as an author. Finally, it's clear that the MOS only sent us part of what they might have. They've selected documents to comment on one another.

"This means that the size of the leak is still unknown, and its extent still in doubt. Further, we have no immediate answers about who's responsible." She stopped. "Sir, we are looking carefully at all digital evidence to see what we can find out."

"We also have some indications, Mr. President, that MOS has sent similar state-oriented materials out to leaders of libertarian and progressive groups around the country. We monitored a conversation from someone in Wyoming talking to someone in Michigan or Wisconsin, and that means there may be more. This hasn't been reported anywhere. The purpose of those mailings isn't immediately clear."

The President looked across the table at her. "Thank you, Agent Cook. Please thank your team for me. Now, I'd like to ask a couple of questions, and I realize you may not have any answers about this yet. Does this show any sign of foreign involvement? You heard me on Friday. I'm thinking about whether this has parallels to the DNC server break-in back in 2016."

"While we don't know the source for sure, sir," Cook replied, hands on the table on either side of her laptop, "I don't think this is from overseas. If it is, it's a whole new level of sophistication that we haven't seen from the Russians. Back in 2016, the Russians attacked servers, but they limited their "take" to one set of documents. This is enormously bigger than that, and seems to demonstrate inside access initially, but then a very sophisticated trawling scheme that branched out to computers outside the government. I'll add that we don't even know if the 'inside-outside' was one computer program or two, right now. But it doesn't feel like the Russians. I'll add that we don't really know what the Chinese might be able to do in this area."

Cook paused for a minute. "Mr. President, I used the word 'trawling' there—do you fish much?"

With a smile, the President shook his head slightly. "Not since I was a kid. But I think I know what you mean by 'trawling'—explain it to me. 'Trolling' is moving slowly over the water trying to catch a fish with a moving bait. I think of 'trawling' in reference to commercial fishing, and we're actually trying to get a ban on that in some protected areas."

Cook nodded. "Well, sir, this data hack is like trawling. It looks like it scooped up everything, and then the MOS group decided to keep only some things, those related to particular states and particular actions by Senators and Representatives and the political parties. Oh, and the lobbyists. But in the process of trawling, they've actually stirred things up so much it's hard to isolate how they might have done it. Think of us as trying to swim through a lot of silt and mud right now."

The President looked back at her, still with a faint smile. "I get it," he said. "Now, how do you think you're going to proceed?"

"Here's what we've done already. We've sorted the files from Wednesday—my team is doing the same with the Alaska files from yesterday—by date, by addressee, by author, by topic. Because this is all digital, we can do this kind of sorting and organizing in multiple ways at once, and then filter however we want. We're looking for patterns of authorship, patterns of timing. But we're still groping in the fog.

"Mr. President, I think you'll understand the image I'm going to use next. If this had been a hack like the DNC email intrusion, you'd see a snapshot taken at a particular time. Because any hard drive or email account will have one set of data on it, it's like looking at a thread that goes on over time. That thread might look like it's linked to other threads, because other people have written to people on the main account, and, let's say, the primary users will have written to them. But you can see the thread—those contacts are one-time, or limited. The apparent 'branches' don't go anywhere. It's like the way we see our individual lives, full of memories that touch the lives of others."

"This isn't like this. It's like getting the whole woven cloth presented to us. It's everybody's hard drive, it looks like, whoever was in touch with anybody else. It's like God's view of the world, and not that of a single human being. It's all the threads at once in a tapestry that stretches over years. What that means is that the 'intruder' might be in the government, or might not.

"Somebody wrote once that what you see depends on where you stand, and also what sort of person you are. One person standing in the same place as another might notice different things. Well, when we go at this we can't be sure where this person is standing, in the first place. So, we're looking at the documents, but we're also looking at the people who might have had access in the first place."

The President leaned back, considering. "Okay," he said slowly. "I think I get that. I'd like you to have a written update for me, maybe once a week, on your progress. If you make a big breakthrough, I'd like to know as soon as you figure what it means. I won't micromanage, and I don't want Ed, here, to do that either." He smiled at Collins. "But keep me updated, okay? I think this is pretty important, and not just for the issues of security or law enforcement. We are likely to see significant, immediate political changes which can hurt or help us, nationally. It's not just about the political parties. I don't want to see us get to destabilization because people don't trust us. And yes, you might say *more* destabilization because people *already* don't trust us. Let's see if we can change that."

CHAPTER 18: WHOLE CLOTH

Monday, October 25
Washington, D.C.

Cook didn't know that her civilian counterparts had even a little bit less to report. Myers and Flores' Friday meeting with executives at the US Conservative Conference had been embarrassingly brief.

And now on Monday, things weren't looking a lot better, although they had some ideas and one real breakthrough. They'd played out the same possible avenues Cook's team had, and had begun looking from the other end, the documents released, to get some sense of their firm's exposure. They knew that they likely didn't have a full set of what MOS had retrieved, but they thought it was their best shot.

Neither looked well. After an all-night Thursday into Friday, they'd separated, gotten some time at "home," and spent Saturday meditating on the project. Myers was married, and Flores was married with grandchildren, and they'd both deliberately done a "family" weekend to come back with fresh eyes. It was while Flores had been sitting with his wife he'd had a revelation. She was wrapped up in a loosely woven shawl, sitting in the shade on their patio, and he'd felt that *snap* in his head that turned the problem inside out. He'd called Myers, and they'd spent the early evening tracing through the Texas documents.

Myers and Flores had an edge, they thought, on the FBI. Everything Cook and Collins knew or thought they knew was going to Myers and Flores, thanks to a well-paid but low-status staffer who was busy typing minutes, archiving photos, and keeping track of telephone calls for the task force. Myers and Flores weren't getting them in real time, but usually within a couple of hours. They didn't have the resources or the brainpower the FBI could muster. But they did have money, and money bought discreet access.

They were well aware of the sorting Cook's team was doing, and thought they might try to approach this from another angle. They went after a limited slice, those documents that clearly derived from someone in their organization, or the ideas that might have come from interaction. They could see the fingerprints of their people, sometimes a little smudged as a conference-goer went home and paraphrased an idea from their shop and fed it into public circulation.

But they had the conference programs and registrations, and so could pick out when an idea had gotten promoted, and when somebody had turned that around and sent it to a congressman or senator. And they could then get a handle on the "somebodies" in their own organization.

Myers and Flores met with Roger Gray on Monday afternoon. Flores explained it to a somewhat skeptical Gray, using his computer connected to a flatscreen on the wall. "Okay, here's what we have in mind. You see this." He circled several lines of text with a laser pointer. "It's in a letter to the representative from Texas, here, building a case for the congresswoman to consider some ideas that came out of the summer 2018 conference regarding expanded privacy for donors to non-profits. This turned out to be an important idea because it would mean that donors to *politically*-oriented nonprofits could also have their identities protected."

"Now, here's email over the next two months from the congresswoman, who sits on a couple of relevant committees, back down to her state-level colleagues in Texas urging them to adopt this proposal at the state level. I imagine that she agreed with us that if the proposal won enough support in the *states,* she could have more success at the *national* level. And here's a third instance: look at the emails sent to her Texas state legislature colleagues." Gray nodded. Once Flores pointed them out, they were clearly based on the initial letter. "And then all of a sudden," Flores brought up a split screen with a dozen different documents, "we have this. The Texas Republicans somehow are responding back to this proposal, or the general idea, and we suddenly have all their email around this idea."

He pointed to the screen image. "So we have....."

July 2018—we send a letter to Rep. Diaz, congresswoman from Texas

August—she sends a letter to three Texas legislators

Sept. 1—they send letters out to other Texas legislators

125

Sept. 15—letters back to the original three from other Texas House members

"We think that something happened between the time the email left us and when Texas legislators suddenly began to undress in the living room with the drapes open. And that something is in the congresswoman's office. Probably something that got passed on to those folks in Texas." Gray held up a hand.

"You said 'something that got passed on to those folks in Texas.' Like a virus? And why do you think that?"

Flores flipped to another screen. "Thanks for asking— that made the transition easier," he smiled. "Look at this. Here's an email from a Texas state legislator to the governor. And here's the governor's answer back. There's absolutely no connection between the congresswoman and the governor, and yet these emails are in the Texas folder from the Month of Sundays. And that's the clue: we have to find out how these things can be connected. And the most logical way for that to happen is if you imagine this as a set of parallel threads that are linked by a set of threads that crosses those. In other words, *woven* like a piece of cloth." He held up a threadbare handkerchief from his coat pocket—so thin you could almost see through it, but still holding together.

Sept. 20—email from Rep. Adams to Governor
Sept. 23—email back from Governor

126

Myers took up the thread. "Whoever did this just gave us a clue about *how* they did it. Maybe they intended to, maybe not. It's like there's something in the water, and it's transparent, but it's there. Our normal virus scans don't catch it, but wherever an email goes that contains it, it'll spread from there. Now we have to find it."

Gray thought about this, and then his eyes got wider. Flores and Myers had a bet going on this one. Myers was waiting to see if Flores would get his money back. Gray sat up straighter in his power seat at the end of the table. "Do you mean that because a staffer from our office wrote something to a legislator—who undoubtedly wrote back—*our whole internal network might be compromised? And the contacts we have with donors and sponsors?!*"

Flores shrugged his shoulders. "We think it's entirely possible. And we're not going to know until we start getting more samples from the Month of Sundays outfit. I tell you, though, that senator from Minnesota made my blood run cold."

Myers closed the laptop in front of him. He smiled, and it was unpleasant. "To begin with, we think it'd be a good idea to back up everything we have, wipe the internal hard drives, reinstall the operating system and applications on every computer, and isolate the backups so they are never, ever, opened on a computer connected to the network. It means going back to paper, and telephone, and never, ever committing this sort of communication to digital until we hunt this down and wipe it out."

"*WHAT!*" Gray snapped.

"We don't know if they're done yet," Flores explained. "We can't find it, we can't see it, and for all we know it might still be there. Do you want to give them a roadmap of what our sponsors and donors have in mind?"

Gray closed the laptop in front of him, and picked up a pen. As he began writing notes, he was cursing vilely under his breath.

CHAPTER 19: CHEYENNE

Tuesday, October 26
Cheyenne, Wyoming

The Hills had a 300-mile drive ahead of them on Tuesday morning, for an eleven o'clock meeting with the Governor and, they hoped, the Attorney General. About four and a half hours, Allison figured, putting together some breakfast sandwiches, coffee, and water. Adam was finishing morning chores, and brought the pickup around to the side door, stopping long enough to change his boots, hit the bathroom one more time, and help carry things to the truck.

North to U.S. Highway 14, then east and southeast to Gillette, then state highway 59 down to Douglas, where they'd finally pick up I-25, which would take them south to Cheyenne. A long drive down, and they'd planned to stay overnight in Cheyenne, though they could easily have made it back. One of the couples from their Saturday night group would cover the evening chores for them. They thought they might well need to decompress afterward.

Allison loved the drive on 14, at least in the area around them. It was one of the earliest of the U.S. Highways, and though it had been worked on a lot since 1926, she still thought of it as a road to adventure. Behind them, 14 would take them to Yellowstone's East Gate, even though most of this country around them was grassland, and the hills were nothing at all. At night, you could be on Mars, she thought.

They were out the door at 5:30 a.m. They smiled at each other as they got into the crew-cab pickup, and once they got to 14 and turned east, she poured Adam a cup of coffee, put a lid on it, and set it in the console cup-holder between them. Then she unwrapped a good-sized sandwich, handed half to him wrapped in a napkin, and picked up her own. They enjoyed driving quietly together, especially watching the morning unfold from blackness. When Allison finished, she checked the lower glove box, verifying that the compact Ruger 9mm was in place. Reaching down under the seat, she confirmed that the lockbox of ammunition and spare magazines was there as well. Adam habitually carried his own handgun, and today was no different. *It's Wyoming, after all*, she thought.

They made the trip in good time, with a brief stop in Gillette for more coffee and then another at Douglas, where they gassed up and picked up I-25. Not for the first time Allison regretted the hundred-year-old decision to make the state capital Cheyenne, in the far southeast corner of the state, rather than Casper, a lot closer and a prettier town to boot.

Somewhere south of Gillette, they'd begun to talk about the meeting. They'd run an outline already, but this was a matter of just turning over how they felt about the issues in the Wyoming packet. They'd both compared the Alaska documents, and some of the "five-state" documents from the Wednesday before. Similar kinds of issues with lobbyists, and some similar evidence that state lawmakers were being hoodwinked or seduced. And it went higher, up to the party's national offices.

"So, what do we do if they ignore all of this, Adam?" Allison turned in her seat and looked at him across the cab, stretching a little as the ride went on. "We don't have a lot of leverage to do much, do we?"

"I don't know," he replied. "One thing we can do is simply release it to all of our friends. You know, just send the whole package out, now that this Month of Sundays stuff is public. I'm a little worried about that. I think some of our friends would be very unhappy, maybe unhappy enough to take direct action. I would *prefer* none of our friends end up in jail because of this. I like the people we know, even the ones who don't have things tightened down tight."

She laughed, counting those folks up in her mind.

They arrived by 10:00, as they'd planned, and turned off 25th street into the underground parking garage with access to the Capitol Building. As they drove up to the security gate, Adam pulled out his driver's license and a printed email from the governor's chief of staff. The guard told them they were expected and waved them through, directing them to the right, into spaces reserved for the governor's staff. They took the elevator up two levels, past the garden level to the first level, and turned left toward the marked suite of offices. Outside the suite, a state patrolman reluctantly asked Adam for his handgun, and stowed it in a lockbox that was one of several in a rack, handing him the key. Adam was a little surprised.

"When did this start?" he smiled.

"Just Friday," the trooper answered, shaking his head a bit. "Ever since the Month of Sundays stuff."

"What does that have to do with Wyoming?" he asked. Allison looked at Adam, surprised.

"I haven't seen anything, but the chief of staff said we'd better take some precautions about access. So here I am." The trooper shrugged and waved them through.

A few minutes later, they sat down with the governor, who was accompanied by Attorney General Dave Anderson. The governor welcomed them and introduced the attorney general, who waved a file folder of emails at them, and started in.

"Adam—first names okay?—can you tell me about this email package? You said a little bit about it, but I'd like to know more, as well as how you react to it."

"Mr. Anderson, I'm very concerned about what it says about state and federal politics. I wrote you a little bit about this, but here's the story. Last Monday, a week ago, I got this email from someone I don't know, labeled "The Month of Sundays Group," and a zipped file. Normally, I'd leave something like that alone, but the cover note assured me it was safe, and my software said so. So, I opened it up, read some of it, and then called Ed King, state representative for our county. I told him a little bit about it, and he gave me the name of someone in Wisconsin, and some directions on how to reach him. You know I sort of organized a social group up in our area, the "Northern Patriots," after the last election. We talk about politics and all, but we really are a social club. It's not like there are any Democrats in our area who might come gunning for us, and we don't believe that nonsense any way. So, I called this fellow in the Midwest, and he told me he'd gotten a similar package for Wisconsin. This was before anything went out to the papers. We agreed we needed to talk to some of our people to figure out what we ought to do.

"So last Saturday night Allison and I got several couples together, showed them some of the papers, and asked for suggestions. And they suggested we talk to the two of you." Adam noticed the glance between the two officials.

"Okay," the Governor commented. "Why us?"

"Well, first of all, some of the emails seemed to suggest that state legislators, and maybe even our senators and representative in Washington might be engaged in criminal activity. Either that, or that they weren't watching out for the interests of Wyoming. I sent you the ones from the coal lobbyist and the anti-environmental movement. But what really got my attention was the stuff from the Wyoming Republican Party, focusing on the 2020 election. The party—and I am a Republican, and proud of it—knew what the election's outcome really was, and yet kept urging the state legislators to overturn it. The Party officers knew that what they were doing was a lie."

He hesitated a minute. "Friends, when the President of the United States comes on the television and tells me a lot of this stuff is real, and true, then I don't think you can ignore it. I think you have to investigate the hell out of it, and hold people accountable if it's true."

The Governor looked at the Attorney General, then back to Adam and Allison. "Okay, as you can guess, we hadn't seen any of this until we got your note. How much more stuff do you have?"

Adam unbuttoned his shirt pocket, and pulled out a USB stick. "This is what I got, or at least a copy of it. I kept the original at home in my safe. It's several hundred pages long, when you unpack it." He handed it to the governor.

"You'd better keep it locked up tight," the Attorney General breathed. Adam noticed a few drops of moisture high up on his temples, and looked away.

The governor continued. "We'll review it today, and I'll ask the Attorney General to put staff on it today. Look for some word from us within two days," he finished. He stood up, and stretched out a hand. "You headed home?" The Hills stood up a little slowly.

"Not till tomorrow," Allison spoke for the first time. "We don't get to the big city all that often." She smiled, and her eyes lit up.

"I hear you," the governor laughed. "And pardon my language, but you just handed us some difficult shit we're going to have to deal with."

Allison smiled back. The four of them shook hands, and the Hills left, holding hands. Adam picked up his handgun at the lockbox rack, cleared it, and holstered it. They were quiet as they walked back to the pickup.

"What do you think?" Allison said, as they got in together. "I couldn't read them very well. They didn't seem surprised enough, did they?"

"I think we're going to check into our motel, and then we're going to go out for a late lunch, and then we'll just drive right on home. I don't know that this town is healthy. And I'm going to ask Bob to stay in the house with his shotgun until we get home." He looked over at her. "He *had* to have seen those documents from the state Republican party."

"Mm-hm. I thought as much, too," said Allison, reaching under the seat for the lockbox for a magazine, and then loading the Ruger from the glove box. She tucked it into the pocket of her coat. "It's Wyoming, after all."

They drove southwest away from the Capitol complex, and just a couple of miles away, off the I-25 interchange at Lincolnway, stopped at the Knight's Inn and registered. They spent a couple of minutes in their room, then got back in the car, onto I-25, and casually drove south to the Love's Truck Stop. Adam gassed up, and Allison put in a phone order at the Subway next door. She walked over and came back with a bag and two big drinks. Adam was taking his time, walking around the truck, holding his phone horizontally in one hand. Satisfied, he reached into the right rear wheel well and pulled out a box the size of a deck of cards. As she got in the car, she saw him casually flip it into the bed of a pickup at the next pump.

They drove north at a comfortable speed, and Allison smiled out the window as passed the governor's mansion just off the Central Avenue exit.

As they got into open country, Allison said, "No time like the present," and pulled out her laptop from the locked console area between their seats. "Go ahead," Adam said. "But do a quick check with that intrusion software before you do anything more."

By the time they'd gotten to Douglas, Allison had talked through an email with Adam, edited it, and attached the file from the MOS group. Adam took the exit off 25, then turned east into town, eventually zig-zagging to Walnut Street, where he pulled up outside the Converse County Library. Allison connected to their wifi without ever leaving the truck, opened her email, and sent the file to her in-state Christmas card list. Her subject line read, "Something Special from Adam and Me!" She had an email address in there for herself that didn't get used very often and didn't actually have her name on it. A few minutes later, the message showed up in her inbox. She smiled at Adam. "Looks like it went out okay."

And then it was back on to 59, now north and west, and headed for home. They'd be late arriving, but both of them were keyed up about what came next.

CHAPTER 20: OUT EAST

Tuesday, October 26
Lincoln, Massachusetts

Lorraine, Bruce, and Amanda decided to meet at Bruce's home in Lincoln, slightly north and west of Boston, on Bedford Road just off the Cambridge Turnpike. "Been in the family for seventy years," Bruce told them, adding that he hated to go into the city because of the parking. "It's quiet, and there's room for my truck." That seemed important to him, Lorraine thought.

And it was, she saw when she arrived. Bruce Spenser was a semi driver, nearing retirement, an owner-operator who traveled cross-country carrying freight for several Boston manufacturing firms. The Spensers ran their own business, which gave him flexibility to do things that mattered to him. He'd spent a week in Portland early in the year, trying both to protest and to cool things down from the anarchists.

They met on Tuesday night, more than a week after they'd gotten Baker's package, and unlike the Hills or Morris at the beginning, well aware of what they had. The question was what to do about it. No one knew that Massachusetts-related material was out. All three had been surprised about what they'd seen, and surprise had given way to disenchantment. They might have been committed to a progressive agenda that focused on justice for the poor and opposed white supremacy, but they found that some of their heroes had figured ways to make a good living out of "justice" causes.

Lorraine had read, years ago, Dr. Amos Wilson's brutal short warning: "If you want to understand any problem in America, you need to look at who profits from that problem, not at who suffers from that problem." As the three of them had looked at materials to and from their senators and representatives, it had been clearer and clearer that some people were not interested in problem-solving, but in 'problem maintenance.' Housing 'ghettos' in Boston, for instance, continued even after decades of anti-racist work. When Amanda had read letters from banks to legislators, she was furious. When the legislators themselves wrote back with proposals on legislation, she began shouting. Bruce poured her another glass of wine.

The worst moments were when they found the Antifa/Anarchist correspondence, a set of items all by itself, back and forth from various groups across the country and tied to several Massachusetts representatives through a local branch of a national protest movement.

And then they found letters from three different sets of foundations funding Antifa protests, white nationalist counter-protesters, and private security firms defending specific businesses in Boston. Amanda was the first to notice that the three foundations led back through a web to one single corporate source, and Bruce the first to point out that this appeared to orchestrate the clashes that had fueled Boston rioting in July and August. One foundation funded both sides of the conflict, as though the intention was simply to destabilize Boston and create distrust among Bostonians. It was Bruce who discovered that the foundation intended to build a new headquarters right on the ground where riots had occurred, and that the foundation had developed the plans for the building complex two years before the riots.

Like the Hills, they began to think about who they ought to call, and who should present it, and to whom it ought to be shown.

Wilson had also observed, near the end of his life, that American blacks were wrong to think that economic opportunity would continue to expand for them. Instead, he had argued that when American expansion slowed, or when whites believed that opportunities were increasingly limited, then black economic and social gains could actually be reversed. Lorraine and Amanda agreed they'd split up a section of the materials that had arrived together. They included materials from the Republican and Democratic National Committees, and served to highlight the kind of rhetoric each was using to describe the current economic situation.

Amanda the attorney had a much bigger contact list than either of the others, and had in fact been in law school with two of the current U.S. House members from Massachusetts. She was reasonably sure she could meet with them within a few days. While they'd been meeting, she pulled up the House's legislative calendar, and noted that the "legislative week" this week didn't include Friday, and that if she was pushy enough, maybe she could get several people together. While Lorraine and Bruce watched, she texted one of her friends, the House member from her district. She started with "We have MOS documents from Massachusetts. Would like to meet with you about them."

She had a text back within two minutes. Then it was just a matter of negotiating where and when. Friday it was.

CHAPTER 21: BAKER WATCHING

October 27, Wednesday
Eastern Washington

Baker was starting to wonder if his "nudging" was going to bear fruit. He didn't have any way to monitor what was happening with the several packages he'd sent around the country, and he tried not to be visible by searching for news on the various networks the fringe groups used. He imagined that the Massachusetts groups, simply because they were more likely intellectual (and he knew he was stereotyping) would take longer to respond. And he thought the Iron Rangers in Wisconsin might be the first. They were by reputation a hasty and feisty bunch, but he knew by reputation they were also careful and planned things meticulously. But the material had been out there ten days by now. He had tagged Arvada, Wyoming, in his newsfeed, and would check it this morning.

At his cabin, yesterday's rain had dropped the temperature down into the 40's overnight, and it wouldn't make 55 today. The leaves on the birches were gold now, and some had been beaten down by the rain and wind. And he'd have clouds all day, he figured. *Well, the weekend will be nice,* he thought, coffee mug in hand, as he looked west and southwest over the meadow. *And I have no lawn to mow and no leaves to rake,* he smiled. Living in the woods had real benefits for an introvert, and peace was one of them.

When he went to the basement and booted up the old desktop he'd nicknamed Leroy, there was clearly something going on in Wyoming, though. The local online, sheridanpress.com, had a report of an attempted break-in over in Arvada, sixty miles away, with shots fired and a car damaged by gunfire. Startled, Baker had to remind himself to route his follow-up inquiry through a different server, using the old laptop he called Eunice. Sure enough, the Hills' house had been targeted, and the news reported that the intruder hadn't gotten further than the front porch before being warned off. A neighbor, housesitting, had sent rock salt into the intruder and then a deer slug into his car. *You don't mess around, Adam Hill,* Baker smiled. Baker decided he'd start monitoring the trail cams on the third computer, a desktop with a larger monitor he called Dave.

"Well, thanks for using rock salt," Adam laughed, looking at the shredded screen door. "I thought there'd be more damage. I can re-screen it in half an hour."

"Yeah, I actually used only a half-load of powder, too. Sorry about the screen. When I was reloading after last season's pheasant hunting, I thought I might make up some 'anti-personnel' loads. That scene in *Kill Bill* where Michael Madsen shoots Uma Thurman as she comes through the door always struck me as hugely funny. I did try it a couple of months ago, just shooting at my barn, from a distance of ten or fifteen feet. Bob made me repaint the door. He didn't think it was funny, or at least not very funny. The deer slug was just a common Remington Vital-Shock." Marcia hugged Allison as she went out the door.

"I thought Bob was staying," Allison laughed at Adam.

"Well, he did the first part of the night, and then Marcia traded off with him. She's the one who got lucky."

"Where did she hit the car with the deer slug?"

"Well, when the guy was blown back from the door and down the steps, she turned on the light in the yard, then put a round through the driver's side door. I think it might have gone clear through, but who knows where the slug went. It was close to 50 yards away, and one door might be all you could hope for at that range. Then she turned off the light while the guy ran away." They walked out into the yard toward the spot where Marcia had seen the car. "No markings, no visible license plate, no tire tracks on the asphalt. She didn't come out into the yard, because she figured she'd have to shoot him if she did."

"Smart."

"Yeah. Remind me to make sure the menfolk know their wives can shoot pretty well. Like they need reminding. Any word on the Christmas letter?"

"Just starting to come in."

Adam smiled again. "Well, let's have a cocktail hour tonight and spend some time with the responses. I don't think it likely we'll be troubled again."

NOVEMBER 2021

CHAPTER 22: ABSENCE

Wednesday, November 3
Washington, D.C.

Cook was acutely conscious of time passing. The previous weekend's "package," covering Alabama, had focused more on racial issues than had Alaska's, but it wasn't the only topic. Again, the January 6th insurrection had shown up, as well as more papers focused on the former administration.

Her team's meeting this morning needed to see a breakthrough, he figured. She was aware that Fritz Elder and Nicole Watson had met with the "personnel" group, and were checking to see if any patterns emerged. They were likely to be the center point of this meeting.

As they sat down together, she began. "Let's hold off on Alabama for the moment, unless you have something dramatic. I'd like to hear from Fritz and Nicole about their part of the project."

Nicole began. "Here's what we did. Right now, we have seven 'packages' from the states, five from the initial upload, and then Alaska and Alabama. We coded every document by authorship and by receiver. Then sorted that down further and focused on governmental employees, particularly the staffs of the senate and house members for those states.

"We played with two contrasting assumptions. The first was that some staff member had deliberately collected data from his or her office computer and the computers of others in the office. If you think about it, that doesn't get you very far—one office's data. So perhaps the better way to think about it was to consider if he or she had introduced a virus or malware of some sort that spread itself out onto other computers—in fact, maybe even to every computer that came in contact with the first one. Even though we have strong network protections and strong anti-virus programs, something introduced from the *inside* might be able to avoid a lot of the network protection.

"You remember *Neuromancer*, Gibson's book from 1984? Case the hacker eases up against the firewall, and 'interfaces with the ice so slow, the ice doesn't feel it.' That's what we might have here.

"We're betting that this is what happened. Since the first announcement of the MOS project, IT and cyber specialists have been looking at every computer and every element of the network to verify firewalls and external protection. They've also looked at hundreds of computers to determine whether there's anything on the hard drive that looks suspicious.

"And they haven't found anything. Now what Fritz and I are speculating is that whoever did this not only found a way to get something on the network that would spread, they also figured out a way to erase their tracks so completely that we can't find anything about how they did it."

"Do we have any idea on when this actually happened?" Cook asked. There were nods around the table.

"No," Fritz answered, "we don't. And as far as we know, it might have happened a number of times, so that we have something like a multi-step process. Someone introduces the virus; it spreads to all neighboring computers through innocuous emails or file transfers; someone commands a download; then someone orders the programs to erase themselves. And he or she or they might have done this several different times, so at the end of the file transfer there's nothing left behind."

"Do you have any evidence of this? This 'multiple hack' you say might have happened?"

"No," said Nicole. "But given the fact that our cyber staff is always looking at the network and overseeing computer upgrades, repairs, and so forth—and given the assumption that these people are *smart*—they wouldn't leave either files or programs out there for very long."

"Devon, has anyone tried to get access to the non-governmental computers whose data MOS collected? I mean like the DNC or the RNC, or some of the lobbyists? Have we asked to examine them physically?"

Michael Life from New York had a good point, Devon nodded. "We have tried to get permission to get some of them. Since we can't document that those computers were used for any intrusions, we're getting stonewalled. It's their data that got hacked, but we can't demonstrate to a judge that they did the hacking. So far, no one's willing to let us look at them. I think we can see why," she said, with one corner of her mouth in a half-smile.

Cook began again. "Fritz and Nicole, what patterns did you see—if any—with the government staff who created, or edited, or distributed the documents that have showed up in MOS?"

Fritz took it up. "You know I had a hot idea about whether it might be the interns who were responsible. Now, that assumes either that some one intern was *extremely smart* or that he or she or they might not know anything, but inadvertently let some bad guy in. Well, I realized we can't really know if the interns were involved or not, because we can't see the whole picture. Even while I'm saying that, I want to point out something very, very odd.

"Nowhere in this stack of things is there a document with an intern's name or initials on it. And we don't know exactly what that means, but I still think it's suspicious. Hundreds of documents, dozens of interns *so far* in these offices, and nothing with an intern's name on it. And they network all the time, in the office and out. Is this the dog that didn't bark? The fact that there's *nothing* there, does it mean something?"

"Nicole and Fritz, follow that up, please. Patrick and Adrian, work with them. Get the computers on which the interns worked, and go over them carefully. And then look at any system backups." She looked at Fritz for a second. "How many interns are we talking about, in any one season?"

"The last number we had, Devon, was nearly 3900 in any six-month period."

"*Shit*," Cook said in disgust. A couple of her team looked a little surprised at the profanity. "Okay. Start with the states that have already had documents out there. If we have to expand, then we will. And we probably will." She stopped. "Okay, you four—Patrick, Adrian, Nichole, Fritz—I want you to look *just at the backups* for the next several days. Find out if *at some point* unexplained files either appear or disappear."

CHAPTER 23: SCHOOL OF FISH

Thursday, November 4
Pullman, Washington

Just after eight in the morning, Baker drove the old Mitsubishi pickup out of the garage and down off the mountain, into Newport. The truck had come with the estate, 120,000 miles on it, 33 years old, "totaled" in some long-ago minor accident, thanks to the vagaries of insurance companies, and perfectly drivable, as long as you didn't need air conditioning, which it hadn't had in the first place.

He had thought a fair amount about how to mix things up on delivering the state packages of documents. *The more options you have,* he had thought, *the more likely you can complete the job.* Even though he believed he had good security at his cabin, today's excursion would take him to Pullman, Washington, home to his alma mater, Washington State.

He could have driven straight into Spokane and south, but was skirting big towns and indeed, planned to avoid every traffic camera in northern Idaho and eastern Washington. Down 41 to Rathdrum and then into Coeur d'Alene. Cross under I-90, pick up Idaho 95 along the lake, through the wheat country of the Palouse, go past half a dozen little towns, and then from Potlatch Junction into Palouse. And then Pullman. He smiled in anticipation, and told himself to be on guard at inevitable disappointment. Full of memories and history. It would be like returning home, and finding home wasn't there any longer.

This morning, he was dressed a little better than his normal jeans and flannel shirt. He still had jeans on, but a button-down Land's End oxford shirt, a thin black tie, and a jacket. On the seat next to him was a herringbone tweed sport jacket and a backpack. The only thing he really needed from this "visiting academic" getup was his laptop, safely stowed.

He loved the drive. As he remembered it, the road down had some of his favorite country—mountains, the lake country, the Palouse wheatfields, and finally, Pullman, perched on its hills.

Crossing the bridge from Idaho and into Washington, he drove the line on State Avenue, one side of the street in Idaho, one in Washington. Soon, once he was out of the timber and into the mile-wide, flat valley, it'd all be recent-growth timber where the loggers had cleaned out mile after mile. A little deeper away from the road, he knew, cattle would be grazing on grassland that had been timber a generation or more ago. And even with the snowfall and the forest fires to dissuade them, people were building subdivisions out there, five-acre properties under the shadow of Hoodoo Mountain to the east and some unnamed Washington range to the west.

Coming out of Blanchard, no more than a wide space in the road, three streets wide, a mile long, and a speed-limit sign, he felt the valley open up as he swung south to Spirit Lake. From here south, the mountains surrounded the wide flood plain of what must have been a huge prehistoric riverbed, the remnant of which underlay Coeur d'Alene, Post Falls, and Spokane itself to the west. Wide, dry grasslands, wheat country, with the mountains around Spokane in the distance, Mica Peak over all. He turned south at Rathdrum, crossing the railroad tracks, a reminder of what had held the West together and even what had made it possible.

Post Falls reminded him of every small town in western Montana or northern Idaho. A good road, some of it four-lane, every kind of shop and store and lumber yard known in the West, and just a little further back, grazing country and mountains framing everything. There might or might not be stoplights, or an overpass leading to the freeway, but you'd always be among pines, or fir, or spruce, crowding up against the shoulder of the road. *These towns are outposts, beads on a road through wilderness*, he thought, not for the first time. *They're trading stations, like Conrad's Congo stations in 'Heart of Darkness.'*

It wasn't very different, in its peculiar way, from northern Minnesota or northern Wisconsin or the UP of Michigan. City folks didn't get it. And the whole pace and culture of life in these places was different from the rest of the country. And so were the politics.

As he skirted downtown Coeur d'Alene on Northwest Boulevard—*a mile down, and then right on 95*, he reminded

152

himself—he thought about how so many towns in this area had peaked with the Boomers, or even earlier, and now were trying to reinvent themselves, even in the face of the Aryan Nation cultists at Hayden Lake, a few miles away, or the anti-intellectual and terrified conservatism that haunted the colleges here. *There are always frightened, corrupt people in power*, he thought. *Small towns and large.*

It'd be fun to drive down to campus, he'd thought. He hadn't been there for more than 20 years, and the alumni magazine, he knew, wouldn't have prepared him. Outside of Coeur d'Alene, along the lake, the road bent through stands of pines and blue spruce. On the lake side, small family cabins and docks had been replaced over the years by nightmare five-thousand-square foot compounds with four and five-car garages, multiple boat lifts and docks at the waterline, and California-licensed SUVs in the driveway.

And then suddenly he was out of the lake valley, and the mounded hills of the Palouse surrounded him. The wheat had been harvested months ago, and plowing was done, and green, sprouting winter wheat, he knew, would be visible if he stopped and walked into a field. He was surprised. What he remembered as a good two-lane road was four lanes now, and cars moved at 75 rather than 50. *Everything put together, sooner or later falls apart*, he hummed.

He slowed down for Worley, and suddenly the road was bordered by the Coeur d'Alene Reservation, home of cheap, untaxed cigarettes and cheap, untaxed gasoline. *Oh, and a fair number of angry native people systematically cheated by a lot of us. Maybe gas up at the casino on the way back tonight,* he thought, glancing at the gauge, *and do my bit for tax avoidance. If there's no camera.* As he swept by the casino, parking lot filled, he thought about how the Coeur d'Alene tribe was winning this battle over the white invaders, one hand of blackjack at a time.

He kept on, through wheat fields and grassland, and eventually down to Potlatch, where a little later he turned west on 6 and into Washington, where suddenly it was highway 272. Then Palouse, then left onto 27, "The Palouse Highway," at Granny's Quilting Shop, and on to Pullman, 15 miles away.

Every mile or two, in the middle of endless wheat fields, a house sat two hundred yards off the highway, surrounded by a windbreak of fifty or a hundred pines, with maples and oaks thrown in for variety and color. A tidy square of lawn fifty feet wide around the main house, and outbuildings big enough for the tractors and the combines. If the house was old, it was a foursquare two-story, usually white, with a front porch the width of the building. If new, it was a brick ranch with picture windows facing southeast or northwest, and sheltered by maples against summer heat. If the farm was making money, the driveway was asphalt, and if not, gravel. You could tell who was making money. Almost everywhere, small "Trump/Pence" red-white-and-blue signs sat at the end of the driveways, even almost a year after the election. *People with conviction,* he acknowledged. Occasionally, he saw those signs decorating semi-trailers posted at the edge of a wheat field. He smiled, and shook his head. *Oh friends, get*

154

used to disappointment, he thought, and remembered the Dread Pirate Roberts.

As he drove into town, he turned left onto Stadium Way, parked out by the street in front of the Supercuts, slipped on his jacket, hat, and backpack, and started to walk up the hill. He would cut across through the Greek area, pick up Colorado Street, and end at Holland Library. He figured getting onto the campus network on a guest account would be a matter of a few minutes, and from there, it'd take less than a minute to execute the next delivery.

With the November sun, a day in the fifties, still some leaves on the oaks, but the maple leaves everywhere, he remembered how a college town had felt back in his teens. *Admit it, you were clueless and terrified most of the time,* he told himself. *Out of your league and desperate.* He turned up Monroe, remembering how overgrown everything was in this town, old streets, old sidewalks, houses a hundred years old full of faculty and students.

Baker's first years in college had been in the late 1960's, as the Vietnam War reached a climax of American involvement. His first spring semester had been the Tet offensive of 1968, in which—thanks to American media—Americans began to believe that America had been defeated. His second roommate had been expelled, eventually drafted, and ended up in Nam, kept out of the infantry by a high school typing class that won him a post in Saigon. Years later, Baker knew that Tet had nearly crushed the North Vietnamese, but he also knew what at the time only a few believed, that the war had been about old men's decisions and that it had been soaked in fear and corruption on every side. He wondered sometimes if that was what had led him into Political Science as a discipline and had contributed to his current adventure.

Skirting Bryan Hall, he glanced up at the clock tower and crossed the pedestrian mall to the library. He didn't even go in, but sat outside on the concrete benches on the roof of the Terrell Library, looking over the Student Union and toward the football stadium in the distance. Twenty minutes later, he was up and gone, past Kimbrough and what had been the Bookie, back the way he'd come. Yes, heretical, but he wasn't going to go to Ferdinand's for a cone today.

A little over three hours, and he'd be home for a drink and supper, he figured. On a campus with 16,000 students, and looking to anyone like a grad student, he was invisible. To his knowledge, he hadn't walked past or driven past a single camera all day. With commands issued for release of the next set of documents, a little over three days from now, his watchers would hardly know where to look, let alone at whom. *How do you pick one fish out of the school?*

By the time he reached the pickup, he was musing about what Arizonans would be thinking on Sunday afternoon. And he would begin to execute his "alternate narrative."

CHAPTER 24: INTERVIEWS I

Friday, November 5
Washington, D.C.

On Friday, now 15 days after the first MOS drop, 50 FBI agents from the "Personnel" team began interviewing House and Senate staff members in teams of two, working from lists covering the last three years. It had taken much longer than Cook had hoped, mostly because sorting the documents and assigning authorship had been complicated. Each of the staff members interviewed was presented with documents originating from his or her legislator's office, occasionally over his or her initials indicating authorship or preparation.

Although the documents had been available to the public for days—Alabama's the most recent—representatives and senators from multiple states had letters in the packages. As an example, while Alaska's package had been delivered on the 24th, letters from Minnesota and West Virginia legislators regarding Alaskan natural resource use and environmentalism had been in the package. Some of them clearly wanted to influence Alaskans. So, in the first round of interviews, staff who had worked in the five key states had been most prominent, but

Alabama and Alaska office people were there as well. Cook figured that the "personnel" people would likely spend all day interviewing the hundred or so permanent staff.

The investigators had ordered the same battery of questions be asked everyone. Each would be handed a document that he or she was likely to have created or edited, and asked if he or she remembered it. From there, each would be asked about the circumstances around it, including who prepared it, who reviewed it, and who signed off on it. One agent would ask the question, another would take notes and do follow-up questions that might occur. Their goal was to recreate the web of access that might have existed that led to distribution.

While the investigation focused on technical means as well as people, Cook wanted to understand the climate that existed in some of the legislative offices, aware that virtually anyone might have been responsible. Consequently, the questions were open enough to encourage expansion.

She sat in front of a monitor, one of several connected to different rooms, watching the live video and audio feed of one interview. After a cordial opening which included a review of the legal issues at play here, a woman interviewer began.

"Now, our records show that you worked for the senator from Alabama for eight years, correct?"

"Yes, that's right. Because he's a 'Class 3' senator, the position will open up in 2022, next year, and he's announced his retirement. But he's served for quite a long time, and I'm relatively 'new' in the office." Mrs. Evans didn't sound particularly 'Southern,' but she'd been in Washington for quite a while, and smiled as she answered. "It may be time for me to retire, too."

"On the third page of the handout I gave you, there's a list of people who worked with you in the office. Could you look at it and see if it's complete?"

Mrs. Evans pulled reading glasses from her purse, slipped them on, and began. After a minute, she looked up. "Well, this looks pretty complete, but you've missed some." She seemed surprised.

"Who else worked in the office at this time?" the interviewer asked. "What were their responsibilities? Did you give them materials to prepare?"

Mrs. Evans smiled, "Well, you don't have a lot of the interns on this sheet. We had some great ones, and they did a lot in the office—copying, answering the phone, sometimes polishing up documents when we got overloaded." She paused. "Well, I have to say we always reviewed things they'd worked on. The Senator was very particular about that."

"Can you tell me who I've missed—names, I mean? We haven't focused on the interns, because we thought they'd be harder to reach."

"They do move around a lot, at that age," Mrs. Evans laughed. "But I actually have tried to keep track of them, especially if they're from Alabama, or if they moved there. Constituents, you know! I've got some of them on my Christmas card list."

"Can you send the names to me later today?"

"Of course."

"Now, let's look at a couple of these papers that showed up in that email."

"Oh my, yes. Wasn't that awful?!"

Cook turned away. *Moving in the right direction, then.*

By the end of the day, the interviewers met with Cook and others to summarize what they'd found. Almost everyone agreed that the day had been productive, and yet with few breakthroughs. Some of the staff were very unhappy about the document release, particularly where "their" senator or representative looked bad, the interviewers commented.

"I had a couple of them who were furious," a younger agent reported. "They'd never seen any of the 'corporate' or 'lobbyist' correspondence—but others in their office had. The ones in the know seemed pretty embarrassed."

Others agreed—so it seemed to suggest that there were concentric rings of staff in most legislative offices, with some on the inside, and others not. Cook, for one, wasn't surprised at the compartmentalization. "Did the staff seem to understand that their legislator might be breaking the law?"

One woman held up her hand. "I had at least one person who seemed to expect that she'd be arrested today, or at least charged and held. She brought extra clothes, and said she'd told her husband she might not be home tonight." She smiled sympathetically.

Cook didn't smile. "If we continue down this road, it could come to that," she nodded back to her. "She's not wrong. But we're not at that point."

As they finished it seemed to Cook that everyone had stumbled on the intern issue—the staff databases or office lists didn't list them consistently, even though the 'regulars' had a lot to say about them. Some of the interns, it turned out, were now on staff themselves. Cook made a note to talk to some of them herself. The staff interviews were continuing for the next several days, even over the weekend.

Saturday, Cook and Angela Hall, who'd made the first Alaska report, shuffled the interview list, and by the afternoon were interviewing the first of a dozen former interns who were now working full time as legislative staff.

"Good afternoon, Mr. Jacobsen, and thank you for coming in on Saturday. We know we weren't scheduled to talk until Monday, so I appreciate your flexibility." Hall began, taking the role of the senior interviewer while Cook took notes. They sat in a well-lit interview room, one with a view Cook had asked for. Jacobsen faced them across a table, and had stood to shake hands when they entered. Hall gestured to him to sit, and they settled themselves, Cook off to one side.

"Well," Jacobsen, in his late twenties, blond, almost crewcut, athletic, smiled back, "it's November, and it's not my favorite month, and it's cloudy to boot. Might as well be inside today."

"Thanks! Now, you're working for a Wisconsin legislator now, but when you interned, you were working for an Alabama senator, weren't you? We got your name from Mrs. Evans, who was a senior assistant in that office, just yesterday."

"Yes, that's right," Jacobsen replied with a smile. "She was a nice person to work for, and even though I'm from Wisconsin she never called me a Yankee. No Civil War hard feelings. And she was a good help to all of us who were interns."

"Good to hear," Hall replied. "Now I wonder if you can tell us about some of these things," she said, handing him some of the Alabama papers that had so upset Mrs. Evans.

Jacobsen studied them for a couple of minutes, and Cook watched his eyes widen as he turned the page. "I worked on this one," he said. "Those are my initials at the end of the letter. I expect Mrs. Evans reviewed it, but I remember typing it up. This showed up in the Alabama 'Month of Sundays' files? Wow!"

"Did you ever talk with anyone about the materials you were working on? Ever share anything with other interns, for instance? Swap files?" Her voice was a little harder-edged, Cook noticed.

Jacobsen sat up a little straighter, and put the papers back down on the table. "No. Never. We had some pretty straight talk from Mrs. Evans and others in the office. It's not just secrecy. Some of the things we worked on were actually competitive against other states, and they told us Alabama could lose out on funding if we didn't keep things 'close to the vest.' That's how the Senator described it."

"Did you have intern friends outside your office?"

A Month of Sundays

"Sure. I had others from my university working there—
we were in the same program back in Wisconsin, and we'd
talk together about how the office work fit with the classes
we'd had. But we all got the same message—don't share
the stuff from the office."

Cook spoke up for the first time, shifting the momentum
and pace of the interview. "So, how many Wisconsin
students were there during your semester? Was it a big
group?"

Jacobsen looked surprised, and eased back into the chair.
"Well, the University of Wisconsin has one of the biggest
political science programs in the country. If you look at
their website, you can see the internship offerings. I look at
it from time to time, just to see who might be out here. This
year there are some big foundations—The Heritage
Foundation, the American Enterprise Institute and a bunch
of others—and the NSA, the FBI, and of course legislators.
You can pretty much cover what's here in DC, left and
right. When I was an intern, I think there were two dozen
of us. But a lot of smaller colleges had three or four
students every semester. And we all networked."

He sat forward again. "I haven't been following this
'Month of Sundays' stuff, because, frankly, we're busy. All
the COVID stuff, and the 'election fraud' stuff, and a lot of
local constituent meetings. And Alabama is years in the
past for me. Why do you think the document I worked on
was in there?"

Hall passed him two pages clipped together. "Look at
this and then look at your paper." Jacobsen glanced at the
letterhead, then laid it next to the page he'd worked on. He

suddenly pursed his lips, and started to say something, and stopped. He looked up at Hall and Cook. "So, you're telling me that my Alabama senator was adopting word-for-word the legislative language of a Washington pressure group, working to get a law passed that would give them a huge financial windfall? Well, I'm not surprised. I never thought of him as particularly principled or smart. But I am *damned* angry about it."

"Okay," said Hall. "That's about all we've got for today. We're going to talk to some other interns who are now full-time staff. We're still trying to get a picture of how this happened. I don't think I have to tell you that this whole thing is confidential. Don't talk about it, even in the office."

"One thing," Jacobsen said, as he stood up. "You might talk with some others who were interns about the same time. Connie Peterson was one. Paul Hamilton, another. Justin Ross—he was an intern about the same time I was, and he's been in DC a couple of years longer. He's working for one of the Minnesota senators. I think any one of them could give you an earful."

"Thanks," Hall said, jotting a note, as Cook did the same thing.

CHAPTER 25: INTERVIEWS IA

Friday, November 5
Washington, D.C.

Flores and Myers had a lot fewer people to interview, nearly all working for their employers.

They had started a day or two earlier, and had run into the problem Flores had expected. They couldn't get a sense of where it all started. But they did have a much better sense of the process of work in the office.

"When you worked on a project like this, Becky, what was your process of keeping drafts or revisions clear of the final document? Did you, for instance, renumber the versions, or have a 'version control' approach?" Myers was treating her very gently, Flores saw.

"We numbered and dated every version as part of the header and file title. We also kept documents segregated in folders and subfolders."

"Okay, what was your response when you saw the 'Month of Sundays' things coming out?"

"I was mildly curious. Then I started hearing some things on the news, and downloaded some of them. I was shocked when I found things I'd worked on included in the packages."

"Did you compare them against your own versions, on your computer?"

"Yes," she said. She looked pained. "They didn't have the most recent versions, in some cases."

Though Flores thought Myers knew the answer, Myers continued. "How recent were some of those versions? Months, weeks?"

"I think the most recent versions I could identify were from the end of May of this year, so a few months ago. I noticed that some of the versions didn't reflect updating since then."

"And how did you do that?"

"We use Microsoft Word for a lot of our letters and memos and reports, and there's a 'compare files' option that will show you the differences."

"The files online were in pdf format. Did you change them back into Word?"

"Oh no, nothing like that. I just found the original file in Word that matched the one sent out, and then compared it to more recent ones. I'm an exceptionally good proofreader, so I didn't have much difficulty."

Where is this going, Myers? Flores thought to himself.

"Now, I have a good idea who on the Hill got this particular report. Was the office in contact with him much? A lot of email and so forth going on?"

"This congressman seemed to need a lot of ammunition, a lot of evidence, to convince his state senate and house to go where the office wanted them to go. So, yes, we had a fair amount of email."

"One thing." Myers shifted direction. "How often did you make backups of files or hard drives in the office?"

"Pretty much once a week," Becky said. "We have an IT guy who does that, Randy, and then stores the backups off-site."

"We've talked with Randy. It seems like he knows his business. What exactly did he back up—everything, just correspondence, reports and so forth?"

Becky looked a little uncertain. "Well, I think everything. He even backed up photos on our machines, and backed up software pretty often. I think he wanted a snapshot of every system just for safety."

Get to it, Myers, Flores thought.

"How often did you physically trade out computers, Becky? Were we updating our systems every year or so?"

"Yes," she said with a smile. "I got a brand-new desktop—and a new monitor—back in April, when the old one slowed down for some reason. Wow! Was it fast!"

Myers and Flores looked at each other. "Do you know what happened to the old one, Becky?" Flores finally spoke.

"Not a clue," she said. "But Randy would know."

With that, they were done. Myers ushered her out.

Flores got on the system, asked Randy to come upstairs to the conference room, and wondered if there'd been other system slowdowns like Becky's before.

Randy arrived a few minutes later. Forties, tall, thinning short blond hair with a lot of scalp showing through, almost cadaverous, bright eyes, the natural confidence that borders on arrogance as Keeper of the Secrets.

"You know what we're working on, right?" Flores began.

"Month of Sundays," Randy nodded.

"Tell me about Becky's new computer last April. Why did she need a new one?"

"Good question. It looked to me like the hard drive had been damaged somehow. When I booted it up, it ran fine, but I needed to defragment the drive, something we don't have to do very often any more. It was like there'd been a lot of disk use, or high levels of storage, and then like those files had gone away. The result was a very slow drive, relatively speaking. About fifteen minutes of hard work, and it ran fine again. We use a lot of SSD storage now, but hers had one of the older mechanical hard drives—you know, spinning platters, all that. But her computer was getting near the end of its cycle, anyway. A new one was not a problem. After I wiped the drive, we sold it."

"Do you keep any backups from before April? Like January through March?"

"Sure. You want me to look at those and compare them with the April version?"

"Yes, and I'll go with you right now and watch."

Bingo, thought Flores. Randy had a complete backup made at the end of March, and he had copied it to a small hard drive so they could download it to his desktop computer. Flores had been insistent that the backup be loaded on to a computer isolated from the network, and

Randy had shrugged his shoulders and complied. The download showed a very large compressed file, although not as big as Flores would have expected, and stored in what might have seemed like an out of the way location, in the system folder. It wasn't there in the April backup. "Is there any way to open this folder and extract the files, or even see what's in them?"

Randy looked up from his keyboard. "Let's have a look. If it's password protected, it'll take longer. We'll know in a second."

It was, but it didn't take long to defeat the password. In a couple of moments Flores, with Myers standing over his shoulder, was looking at several months' worth of documents, emails, and even videos of video calls that were almost all internal.

If Randy's thinning blond hair could have been standing on end, it would have been. Already pale, he was now sweating.

Myers looked down at him. "You've done a good job here, and you're not fired. If the federal government can't keep these guys out, I'm not going to believe you could. Now check every damned one of these backups for the last five years and see if you can find when this started. How fast can you do that?"

"I'll be at it until tomorrow morning. You'll have a report then."

"Now, I have a question for you that's a little different. Do we back documents up to 'the cloud,' Randy?"

"No, Mr. Myers, we don't."

"Why not—I mean, every company in the world has some sort of cloud backup, don't they?"

"No, Mr. Myers, they don't. I was specifically directed to turn off cloud access for our work, because the kinds of things we work on have high enough security that we didn't want them stored anywhere else. 'The cloud' really means 'someone else's computer.' And do we want what we work on out there on 'someone else's computer'? I don't think so."

Absolutely right, Randy. Let's keep it that way, thought Flores. He nodded.

Flores called his counterparts at two conservative foundations in Washington, and they agreed to meet for a drink at the end of the day. He laid out for them what Randy had found, and suggested that they might talk with their IT people.

"Our guy Randy is pretty good, and he didn't tumble to what was happening—why a staffer's computer slowed down significantly, for instance, or the fact that somewhere some enormous file had disappeared—had, in fact been transferred. You might check with your people." They were sitting in a booth, and both of them pulled out cell phones on the spot. Flores listened—or pretended not to—politely, and then continued.

"We still don't know who did it, but we're starting to develop a profile. We've also got ears out to listen to what the "Official Sources" might be finding. Can we agree to share information if we hear anything?"

The other two nodded, lifted their drinks, finished them, and left. Flores went back to the office to wait for Randy.

CHAPTER 26 CONCLUSIONS

Saturday, November 6
Washington, D.C.

Devon Cook thought about her life and tried to stay awake. FBI, cybercrime specialist, transplanted from the West Coast, married with children, tired to the bone, and she was wondering what the Month of Sundays group really wanted to accomplish. She had been home enjoying the Saturday morning and her children, and now was headed for an interview at the office.

Motives, she said to herself, recalling herself to focus on the job. She wouldn't be sure, of course, that any Bureau reports would actually reveal what the motives of the Month of Sundays people were, because the Bureau had to deal with politics, just like everyone else in this year. Some things just could not be said. That was one of the reasons she really wanted to be in on the capture and interrogation of whoever might have done it. First hand might make a difference.

In the meantime, she was going to interview Justin Ross, the third of the interns Jacobsen had mentioned. He was a graduate of a midwestern religious college, Masters in Government (Democracy and Governance) from

Georgetown, almost three years working for a senator from his home state of Minnesota after a similar stint working for a senator from Texas. She began there.

"Thanks for meeting with us," gesturing to her partner today, Nicole Watson, like Cook, assigned to DC. "You've had more than six years working in senate offices, first Texas, then Minnesota. You know we're working on this Month of Sundays thing. What's your take on it?"

Ross didn't hesitate. "I know whoever did it broke the law, but actually, I think it's about time something like this happened." He looked as though he were aware he'd just stepped on a land mine.

Cook paused just a second. "Tell me why. You know it's clearly wrong, but why do you think these folks did it?"

"I've been here for a few years—you know that—and from time to time, I felt like I was working for a huge criminal enterprise." He air-quoted the last three words. "It's what led me to quit the job for Texas when someone I admired got elected in Minnesota. It's not just 'home' that led me to work for her. It's that the other office was just morally bankrupt."

Watson snorted, almost choking. Ross smiled.

Cook began again. "You're a conservative—I know this from your own writing in job reviews and reports—and you graduated from what I'd guess is a conservative college. Do you feel like you might be over-reacting because of those experiences?"

Ross nearly laughed. "No, ma'am, I don't. Let's consider some of the things I was supposed to overlook when I worked for Texas."

The next fifteen minutes were...*revelatory*, Cook thought later. Ross obviously had a list well-prepared, and it had been *grinding* at him awhile.

"Well, *that* was interesting," Watson said at the end. "I guess we don't have to ask why you left."

"Did you ever discuss these issues with others?" Cook asked. "Because this sounds a lot like some of the things the MOS documents highlight."

Ross squirmed for a second, Cook noticed. "Well, I did, once," he answered after a moment. "Back in late 2019, I met with one of my college professors. Dr. Baker created a program for our college, the Washington Studies Program, an internship opportunity for all of us in Political Science. One night in November, every year, he meets here in DC with the new people and any alums who can attend. Back in 2019, I had dinner with the group. I was trying to make up my mind what to do, and we talked about it in a general way. There were probably forty of us there, new people and a bunch of alums. I was one of the few who was actually working full-time in a legislative office."

"Who was there? Can you give us a list of names?" Watson asked.

"I think so, although you could also ask Dr. Baker. He usually had someone take notes, because he asked us about how our experiences ought to change the course the next time he taught it." He stopped. "Actually, I don't know if that'll work. When I said that there were things going on, he made everyone turn off their phones, and the notetaker was told to shut off his computer. So, none of that maybe got written down."

Cook made herself sit still, and told herself to step back. "Do you think anyone in this group could have done this Month of Sundays stuff?"

"Well, I've asked myself that off and on. Most of the PoliSci students wouldn't have the skills, or the access. Quite a number are working for nonprofits outside the government or working for lobbying organizations—the ACLU, voter registration groups, or compassionate groups like Feed My Starving Children or the International Justice Mission. I'd guess only half a dozen or so are still here in DC working in government."

Cook raised a finger. "Again, can you give us names?" Ross nodded.

"What did Dr. Baker suggest you do?"

"He quoted something he used to use in class. He said that the most important reason to leave your job wasn't whether or not you could get paid better elsewhere, or advance faster. It was when your job forced you to be unethical or compromised your core values. 'What does it profit a man to gain the whole world and lose his own soul,' he said. Matthew 8:36. That made it easier."

"And that's how you viewed it?" Watson asked.

"Oh, *hell* yeah," laughed Ross.

"And what happened afterwards?"

"We never talked about it again," said Ross. "He keeps in touch, sent me a Christmas card this year, and congratulated me on supporting a senator he really likes. He just retired this year."

"Mr. Ross, thank you for your information. Please send us those names by tomorrow, would you? We will start exploring them. And best wishes working with the senator from Minnesota. I like her, too." They stood, shook hands, and Watson walked Ross out.

When she returned, she looked at Cook. "That bunch jumps to the top of the pile?"

Cook laughed. "Well, maybe, but we have a lot of angry candidates to look at, too. It'd be pleasant if we could put the professor at the top of the list. And premature. At least for now. How about you get that list from Ross and get those interns scheduled in for interviews? I'm heading home."

Flores and Myers were waiting for Randy in their conference room. When he knocked and entered, he was still wearing clothes from the day before, needed a shave, and had lost some of his confidence. Flores was glad to see that his attitude had been scuffed up a bit. He'd likely be better at the job from here on.

"Coffee?" Myers offered.

"Lots, thanks, and buffer it with everything." Randy set up his laptop and searched for an outlet. "This thing's just about out of juice."

"Is your wifi turned off?" Myers asked quickly. "I don't want anything about this on a network."

"Yes, of *course* it is," the tech came back. "Give me some credit."

Maybe not scuffed up enough, Flores thought. "Let's have it."

"Okay, I went through several years' worth of backups for ten computers in the office. We generally make a backup once a month, automatically, and we dump stuff to a server-connected hard drive. Then we take the drive offline. We actually re-use the drive the next month, which I'm thinking isn't as smart as I thought it was, so by the end of the year we maybe have three drives that have all the backups for that year. When we fill one up, we actually do unplug it, package it, seal that up, label it, and put it off-site in a secure location. So that's where I've been. I went back five years, so I went through fifteen hard drives, 3 backups each. I can tell you that the first compressed file with our documents or files on it came from March of 2020. But that file grew and grew and then suddenly disappeared at the end of May 2020."

"Transferred," Myers breathed.

"Exactly. Then in the fall of 2020 and the spring of 2021 there are also compressed files in the backups, but they're much smaller. And they look like they only cover from the last 'dump' to the present. The last one is the one in April or May of 2021, just a few months ago."

"So the first one, fall 2020, was a lot bigger?"

"It was huge," the tech replied. "And it went back ten years, at least. It sucked everything off the hard drive it was on, including stuff downloaded from elsewhere, and then, I think, it somehow sucked stuff off other people's computers as well."

"Can you tell how it was done?"

Randy sat for a moment. *He was already shaking his head,* Flores thought. "No, I can't. The program's not on the computer, not even on the backup. And neither is the 'send' program that would let someone download the files."

CHAPTER 27: EAST AND WEST

Tuesday, November 9
Wisconsin, Wyoming, and Boston

In Wisconsin, Morris Watson, "social chairman" of the Iron County Rangers, had sat on the Wisconsin material for two weeks, perplexed about what to do. Watson, in his early 60's, owned one of the three grocery stores in Hurley, Wisconsin, nestled up against the Montreal River and one bridge away from Ironwood, Michigan, in the Upper Peninsula of Michigan. Ironwood was two-and-a-half times the size of Hurley, and Watson nourished that as a grudge against it. And he had to go up against the Walmart Supercenter on the other end of Ironwood.

Fifteen miles from Lake Superior, atop the Gogebic Range of low bedrock mountains, Hurley, Montreal, and several other small towns were the remnant of the iron mining that ran across the whole of the area south of Lake Superior. The county now boasted "300 pristine lakes" on its website, and "34,000 acres of pure water." *It was also dying*, Watson thought, with fewer than 6,000 people and a grand total of 34 new children born in the county a year or so earlier, a third of them to unmarried women. He could see that families were dying, or dying out. Gogebic

Taconite had closed its office in town in 2015, six years before, finally acknowledging that the cost of exploration for more iron wasn't worth it. *But damn,* Watson would tell visitors, *do we have snow. A hundred sixty inches in a good year.*

Watson had been part of the shift in politics in northern Wisconsin. Iron County had been reliably Democratic for a century, up until "W" in 2000, and then wavered to Kerry in the face of what Watson thought was Bush's floundering. In 2008, despite being 97% white, the county went 55% for Obama, and in the face of 2012, went for Romney, the neighbor from Michigan. And then the county became increasingly Republican until Trump won handily against Clinton in 2016 and then did even better with 60% of the vote in 2020. Watson was sure the collapse of iron mining and unionism and the dramatic shift to capture the urban vote were behind the deepening red in his part of the state, and he had done his part. He had honestly believed the unions and the Democrats cared about the little guys in his area, and had honestly believed Trump would fight the coastal elites and the billionaires and bring back mining and the economy of states like Wisconsin. He resonated when Billy Joel sang about how "the union people crawled away." His wife had been more sensible than he, Watson mused, voting against Trump in the 2020 election. It had been the cause for some straight talk in the house, of which he was now ashamed. He had been man enough to sit down with her after dinner and show her the Wisconsin documents, and she had been kind enough to be shocked and not do an "I told you so" dance on his head.

Once he had read the Wisconsin package from "Month of Sundays," he was on the road from Deeply Depressed to Load Your Guns. *And what can you do in a town of 1500 people?* He had been asking himself that for a week, watching people in the seven states that everyone knew about coming to terms with the way they'd been deceived. *And then there's us in Wisconsin and Wyoming, and no one knows about us yet.*

So, like the Hills, he called his friends together, beginning with the mayor and the local parish priest of his Catholic church and the Baptist pastor of the little church a block away from his store. All of them were "Rangers," enjoying hunting in the county and coffee together to talk over politics and world issues. Watson also realized that they were connected to the wider community. He asked them to come over to the house on Thursday evening, two days away, and to bring their spouses. The priest would laugh, but he'd come for the coffee and the apple pie.

The Hills were further down the road than Watson. The "Christmas letter" Allison had sent out on the 26th was reverberating around Wyoming. Everyone knew about the five-state document dump, and hundreds of Wyoming voters, ranging from Cody and Powell and Jackson in the west right through to Casper, Rawlins, Laramie, and Cheyenne had read what was going on under the covers in Wyoming politics. Adam's professionalism and recognition across Wyoming ranching, plus his unwavering affiliation to the state, resulted in an extensive network of leaders across towns small and large. It wasn't just the "social chairman" role of a "social club," but his steadiness and groundedness in his conservative values that people liked. Allison was right: his credibility mattered.

But what can you do when 500,000 people are spread out across the tenth-largest state? *Well,* Adam had figured, *you use the internet to organize, just like the MOS group.* And that's what the Hills were doing. People were hot.

That night, with Allison's help, Adam sent emails to the Casper Star-Tribune and the Wyoming Tribune-Eagle, published in Cheyenne. He invited reporters to call, but he also included a dozen memos or letters from the Month of Sundays package, as well as the cover email he'd received. By ten the next morning, he had a reporter from each paper in the yard.

Lorraine, Bruce, and Amanda were the slowest of the three groups. They had met with a House member, and after the initial shock, it had gone nowhere. They had talked about this three times since and still were struggling with what to do. Finally, Amanda had called them on it. The three of them knew that one of their senators would be in Boston on Thursday, November 11, for a Veteran's Day memorial ceremony, but they also knew that her afternoon was relatively free. They emailed her office with a sample of the Massachusetts package, identified themselves and the source, and were still surprised when an hour after they'd hit "SEND" that they got a call.

The meeting had not gone as well as they'd hoped. The senator was outraged when the group presented her with materials from her office, but she was horrified when she reviewed documents between the national party and some of the lobbyists who had supported her. The senator had asked for copies to review, to which they'd agreed, then had pointedly not answered their follow-up calls.

The next step—as they'd advised her—was the newspaper. When the Massachusetts narrative broke in the Boston paper on Sunday, she suddenly became insistent on a conversation. They met her in Amanda's law office in Boston Monday morning. As the three of them reviewed their notes, Amanda's assistant knocked and brought the senator in.

"Thank you for agreeing to meet with me again," she began, an immediate take-charge expression of energy. After she shook hands all around, Amanda gestured her to a chair, and moved to sit down at her desk while Lorraine and Bruce sat on a couch facing her. The senator's chair completed the circle, the just-let's-keep-this-between-us message obvious. *Wow, Amanda, way to go with the non-threatening nonverbals*, Lorraine thought to herself.

Hands folded in her lap, the picture of contrition, the senator began. "I want to apologize for my attitude in our first meeting. I felt like I'd been ambushed, betrayed, and even that I was being blackmailed. My response was over the top, and I regret it. That's the first thing. The second thing is that I'd like to understand how *you* understand the materials that you got from the Month of Sundays group. You've seen what *The Globe* has to say. They felt like I betrayed Massachusetts in dealing with the Antifa and BLM stuff, and the *Globe* and the *Herald* are all over my tax and economy proposals.

"The fact is, I don't trust my advisers right now—because they look to me like they were in on things that they expected me to front for them. I'm trying to get a handle on how local activists like you see this."

Amanda took the lead. Sitting behind her desk, her black-woman-attorney-mother-firebrand face on, wearing her going-to-court armor, she still was impressed by the senator's strategy. *Enlist your critics with your humility, and ask how you could be better. I'll give it to her. That's memorable. Just a little icky.* Aloud, she said, "We think you and nearly every other legislator got caught with your hand in the cookie jar, senator." Out of the corner of her eye, Amanda could see Lorraine sit back and Bruce wince. "We know you need to make deals to get things done—and you have, in the past, and it's clearly been beneficial. But some of this stuff makes you look like you got played. And maybe like you played along."

She got down to business, looking at the single sheet in front of her on her desk. "You might start by getting the broom out, and cleaning house. The internal letters show that some of your advisers had a double game on. Some of your financial backers did, too. I think a lot of us would expect you to firing-squad some of these people. You want to add insult to injury? Take their money and then publicly swear not to do what they want. No *quid* for the *pro quo.*

"You might be pretty public about stepping back from the most violent parts of the BLM, for instance, and meeting with the FBI and the House committee that's going to do the Antifa research and report.

"And you might start working with your colleagues— and your colleagues across the aisle—to deal with the *fundamental* issues, like financial discrimination in housing and infrastructure. The President has already talked about this—why aren't you by his side on this?"

The senator, for all her candor in public and her fiery rhetoric, was frozen in her chair. *Clearly not used to getting a talking-to from another liberal activist,* Bruce thought. He brought his left hand up to cover his mouth, the picture of reflection and consideration, because he knew he'd be smiling otherwise.

"I can do those things," the senator said quietly. "And I'll start today."

"That's great!" Amanda smiled. "We'll be watching!" And she stood up to move around the desk.

The senator, seeming a little stunned, picked up her purse, stood, and moved to shake hands. Instead, Amanda enveloped her in a hug, and then leaned back to say, "We'll be watching, right?"

Bruce moved to open the door, and like that, the meeting ended.

Lorraine stepped to the window, looking down at the street. When the senator emerged, the press they'd notified moved in, cameras and recorders on. The three looked down from the window, and Bruce commented almost under his breath, "Feeding frenzy. Mm, mm, mm. Tasty."

Amanda's smile was about as wide as it could be. "There is nothing quite like seeing a sitting United States senator at a surprise party, is there?"

CHAPTER 28: AMERICANS

Wednesday, November 10
Newport, Washington

Baker had wanted to be a teacher since he'd been in ninth grade. He'd wanted to be a college professor since his sophomore year in college. The world of politics had fascinated him since Kennedy had been elected in 1960, his parents bitterly opposed to a Catholic from Massachusetts—which Baker's father had been. Baker still remembered the Johnson-Goldwater race, though he'd only been fifteen.

He thought about all of that, as he ran the chainsaw Wednesday morning. He had a fair amount of wood for the fireplace, but it'd be nice to have some more in the wood shelter, and he had downed several dead pines that needed limbing, sectioning, and splitting. *Sometime this week*, he thought, *I'd better burn the junk branches, the slash pile. It's almost wet enough so the DNR will let me have a fire.*

When he thought back, he realized later that his childhood had been spent in one of the few periods in which Americans seemed generally in agreement about most issues that involved "politics." The Eisenhower years, though turbulent internationally, had focused on the

186

growth of the postwar nation, and Eisenhower himself had seemed a benevolent and paternal figure to a nine-year-old. *It's a lot easier to be collaborative when there seems like plenty to go around,* he remembered. *Harder if it seems like there's not enough.* Baker's parents had done their best to keep the worst issues of the day away from him, particularly the civil rights issues that dominated the east and south of the country. The whole anti-communism crusade of the early fifties was invisible to a seven-year-old. In the Pacific Northwest, DC's concerns were easily overlooked. The bigger threats, though remote, were the Russian missiles and bombs targeted on Fairchild Air Force Base thirty miles away, where the brand-new B-52s were hangared. *Oh, and unity is easier if you've got a deadly external enemy,* he reminded himself.

He remembered his first dose of anger at a "political" issue. Baker's high school civics teacher had quietly ridiculed the Republican perspective in class, putting a hand up an inch from his nose and his other hand an inch from the back of his head, and then explaining that the Republican consensus depended on ignoring the past and failing to foresee the consequences of actions for the future. He'd probably said something equally offensive about Democrats, but it hadn't stuck. Natural teenage rebellion, as well as affection for his parents, guaranteed at that moment that Baker would be a Republican. Baker remembered that frozen moment in the classroom. Over the years, he had tried to be more compassionate and thoughtful in characterizing America's diversity.

He had lived through the slow-motion collision of values that reached back at least to McCarthy in the 50's, resurfaced in Goldwater, and had sprung up again with Reagan and come to flower in Newt Gingrich. In every case except Reagan's, he suspected that some bright, ruthless person had seen an opportunity and seized it. Reagan he would excuse for some things, not because he thought Reagan was right, but because he actually thought Reagan was clueless, bright about many things, with strong convictions, and really ignorant about the economy and consequences. About "race," though, Reagan was simply played by those around him. He seemed to have no idea that minority suffering was real, and that the political system he led had contributed to it. He also suspected that Reagan was increasingly influenced by his donors and the conservative foundations that supported him. *California,* Baker mused, *was not the real world.*

Baker had been trying to find "the big picture" for most of his career in teaching. Every college professor does. Was there a perspective from which you could see how movements, people, ideas made sense and fit together? Or is there always too much happening for any set of claims to make sense, to be honest, to fit the facts?

As Baker had been analyzing the data over several months, he had been thinking hard about what the big picture was here. What was it that the parties—and behind them, the lobbyists and donors—really wanted? How did they see the world, and how did they want the American public to see the world? He thought he might be on to something with the issue of "identity politics," which so many conservatives had attacked the last two decades. "Identity politics" as the conservative fountainheads defined it or the liberals demonstrated it, was not what he meant, though.

In college he had roomed with an African-American a year younger than he, and he realized he had no frame of reference for understanding his roomie's life. But he watched him insulted, threatened, and bullied until he fought back. And then his roomie had been jailed, together with his friends, because in Whitman County white fraternity boys prevailed over angry black kids from Seattle.

Baker recognized that the increased tribalism of the last decades had originated in part as more and more Americans discovered that in very specific ways they were not included in "the larger America," not valued as citizens or honored. In fact, certain "tribes" had pushed hard for recognition and status, upsetting a conventional balance, the conventional thinking that America's riches were finite and shifts in allocation were a zero-sum exercise. Tribes like LGBTQ citizens argued not necessarily for a bigger piece of the pie, but for a chance to help make the pie bigger. Citizens of color objected to being frozen out of the economy, when their participation might well make the economy larger and more robust.

But Baker was concerned about a larger issue than the just division of power or resources.

He thought about this, taking a break from the chainsaw for another cup of coffee. *If it gets any colder,* he thought, *I'll have to get the chairs in off the porch.* As he sipped, he thought more about what he'd taught.

Who is an American? Who are we being told is or can be an American? Baker had asked his students. *That's what's being contested here. And we're being directed to think in particular ways about others by people interested in dividing us, rather than working together. Are we going to face up to our history as a country, or deny it? Will we embrace that history in which we picked and chose who qualified as American? Are the Irish in or out? The Chinese? The Italians?*

Do we believe you have to be a Christian to be an 'American'? Do we believe you have to be white, or English-speaking?

Who do we think we are? Who do we imagine ourselves to be? Who are we really? And most of all, for me, Baker thought, *who is telling us these things?*

CHAPTER 29: WISCONSIN

Wednesday, November 17
Newport, Washington
Madison, Wisconsin

Baker sat with his laptop at his kitchen table, looking over the meadow through the living room windows to the west. Cloudy, 26 degrees and damp, but no snow yet. High of 34 today, and it felt like a typical November. Not encouraging. He was looking for tracks from the Wyoming, Wisconsin, and Massachusetts folks, in particular.

He had relished the impromptu press conference and confrontation with the Massachusetts senator the week before, watching her wide-eyed and stunned as she came out of an attorney's office. He had to admit she had grit, however. She'd spoken to the camera from the second step on the porch, and had told the reporters that she'd just met with three supporters who had helped her clarify how they felt about her political decisions. When one reporter pointed out that Amanda Ellis, whose office she'd just come from, had released some of the Month of Sundays material to the papers, she smiled, and added, "And Amanda and two friends have just given me a good talking-to. We got the air clear, and I'm headed back to the office." The next day, she'd announced the departure of three senior staff members, and made an offer to Amanda to join her office.

At this point, Baker was a distant observer, but certainly interested.

Wisconsin, he sensed, had to be about to break. He couldn't follow what Morris Watson and his friends were doing, but he was willing to bet it would be a splash. *Ah well*, he thought, *we do what we can*. And then Clov's rejoinder came to mind. *We shouldn't*. Baker winced. *Too true. Beckett's* Endgame *should* not *be on my mind*.

Indeed, Watson and two others had been "deputized" by their friends to drive down to Madison, and on Wednesday, they were preparing for a meeting. They'd had a lot of time to think during the four-hour drive, and knew they were about to take a major step into a corral of manure. The threesome might have looked a little disparate to an onlooker, but they were firmly agreed about their course of action.

Watson had with him the parish priest from his Catholic church and the Baptist pastor, both men about as level-headed as anyone could want, and pretty much the most peaceable people he could find. Watson would not have described himself as "peaceable," but "hot," about the MOS materials.

Watson had gotten them hotel rooms at the Madison Inn and Suites, just off I-94 and Washington Road, the first one he could find with a meeting room he could rent for a couple of hours. They'd stayed overnight, and had breakfast together, talking idly about the world and its craziness. At least Watson had. Neither of his two religious friends would admit to "crazy." "Lost," maybe, but not "crazy."

About 1:00 p.m., the first guests arrived. Others had been invited for 1:15, and the first group didn't know about the second.

The "WisDems" and the "WISGOP" members included, for Republicans, the state chair and the National Committeewoman and National Committeeman; the Democrats, organized somewhat differently, included the state chair and two vice-chairs. Watson had been able, through some miracle, to get the president of the State Senate, a Democrat, and the Speaker of the Assembly, a Republican, in the same room. The parish priest was at the door of the meeting room, welcoming the guests in. After a few moments, Watson asked them to take seats around the conference table, and he sat at one end, a pastor on one side and a priest on the other.

Watson was fine as a local businessman, but he knew he would struggle with a meeting like this. And he was playing for a little bit of time, just five minutes or so.

"Thank you for coming to meet with us. We promised you something important for the upcoming few months from Iron County, and we'll get to that. I'm Morris Watson, and I'll let my friends here introduce themselves."

As the Baptist pastor finished, the priest heard a knock at the door, got up, and welcomed in the executive editor of the *Wisconsin State Journal,* a senior reporter, and a reporter from the Madison FOX News station.

The atmosphere in the room changed instantly.

The media people made their way in, and sat at the far end of the table, the politicians opposite each other, and the Iron County folks nearest the door.

Watson cleared his throat, nodded to the media, and began. "A month ago, I got an electronic package of documents from the Month of Sundays group. Only about a dozen people know about this, and only the three of us have seen all of the files and read them."

You could have heard a feather touch down on the floor.

"Yes, that's right. About the same time the 'big' papers got a five-state package, several of us around the country got things just about our state. Wyoming was another one. And I'm going to give them to you today. I sent this information to the FBI this morning, because, after all, the President said federal laws were broken. And I know, I've sat on it a long time, because I didn't want to believe it. But I'm putting it out now.

"We all know that this year one of our Senators is up for re-election, as well as House members. So, *we* know"—he gestured to his companions—this is pretty high stakes. We decided that all of you should get this stuff at the same time—Republicans, Democrats, party leaders—and the news media. I think you'll see why when you look at them.

"I don't know that anyone will trust any of you politicians from here on."

With that, the priest and the pastor reached under the table and pulled out labeled manila envelopes. Each had a chunky USB drive like a piece of candy lumping it up. The men walked down the table, looking at the labels and then making sure each went into the right hands.

"In case you're wondering—it's the whole package on each of those USB drives. Everyone got everything the Month of Sundays group sent me."

He looked down for a second at a sheet of paper in front of him. "Now, my friends and I are going home. You'd better make the best use of this stuff that you can. Just remember these are copies, and we can send them to other people if you don't make good use of them. We're done."

Watson, the pastor, and the priest walked out.

They walked through the parking lot a few minutes later, and down the sidewalk, headed for the Perkins across the street. They walked in, side by side, found a booth, ordered coffee and water, and laid the menus down. Morris suddenly started chuckling, and in another ten seconds all three of them were belly-laughing so hard they were almost in tears. The server rushed back to the table. Folks even a few booths away were smiling and trying not to look.

Watson, gasping, finally could say, "Glory be to God! I am done with that and off the hook!" The clerics looked at him, and at each other, and began laughing again.

Finally, the priest got himself under control enough to say, "Morris, you poor, benighted idiot! The fun is just starting!"

They were just finishing their second breakfast of the day when a woman and a man in suits came in, glanced around, and headed their way. "Mr. Watson?" The African-American woman, the older of the two, asked him. "And friends? Could we join you for a few moments?" The two unobtrusively revealed photo identification that was marked in large blue letters *FBI*. "My name is Devon Cook."

CHAPTER 30: REPERCEPTION

Friday, November 26
Newport, Washington

Baker's Thanksgiving the day before had been cool, cloudy, and a little threatening. Any time you got to a low of 29 in November, things might happen. So far, light wind on Friday, and they'd had snow overnight. He figured he was ready, well provisioned. He already had the V-blade on the pickup, and chains on. The pickup was rear-wheel drive, which meant he'd needed to throw some firewood in the back and some sandbags. If the snow didn't get ahead of him, he'd be fine.

Thanksgiving had been lonelier than in the past, with a call to his daughter and grandchildren in Minnesota, a VOIP call routed through a server in Arizona. The teen boys had wanted to talk about the end of the soccer season, and his granddaughter about the newest book she was reading. The kids thought that he was in Arizona for the winter, and asked for pictures from one of his hikes. They envied him the warmer weather, they said. Despite his solitude, he'd done up a turkey breast in the oven, made his traditional cranberry-orange relish, baked a couple of potatoes, done up some green vegetables, and slipped in a frozen pie to bake at the end. Apple, because frozen pumpkin was awful. Lots of leftovers at the end of the day. God bless turkey sandwiches, provolone, and Hellman's mayo.

Baker's closest National Public Radio station was in Spokane, and depending on the weather, he might or might not have a clear broadcast signal. Today, he was listening to KPBX over his internet connection on Leroy, piped in from some TOR server in Scotland. The stock market was dropping like a rock, as he listened at mid-day, because of fears of the new COVID variant. Black Friday sales were still pushing limits, even though most people had shopped online for the whole month.

And then at noon his time, 3 p.m. Eastern, the Republican National Committee announced that the chair and several senior leaders were resigning. Baker exited the KPBX site and shifted to the main NPR site out of Washington, D.C., to pick up *All Things Considered* as it started at 3:00 Eastern. The first ten minutes after the news discussed the pressure the RNC chair had been under since October. Donations to the party were down a stunning 90% during the month, and Republican state committees were floundering under public scrutiny. The former president exploited the debacle by encouraging people to join him in remaking the party as an "America First" organization, returning to "the values of our founders." He was demanding RNC funds be turned over to his organization as the legitimate inheritors of what it meant to be Republican.

Baker wasn't surprised, because he'd imagined this as one outcome. From here on, though, he didn't have a sense of what would be next.

He wondered if what had really done in the RNC chair was Arizona, whose package had gone out on Sunday the 14th. The Arizona state party had bought in wholeheartedly to the "election fraud" scenario, and the extreme conservatism of some prominent Arizona politicians, especially those hinting at a run for office, would have been evident in some of the claims they were making. *Claims*, he thought, w*holly supported by the state and national committees. And revealed to be false, and which the parties knew to be false.* He'd listened to some of the chatter on KJZZ, the public radio station out of Phoenix, and read some of the *Arizona Republic* editorials and letters over the last ten days, and citizens who'd supported the party were halfway between embarrassment and rage. *Maybe*, he mused, *just maybe they'll end up with better candidates next year.* NPR continued:

In other news, California politics are still shaken by the Month of Sundays release this last weekend. Both Republican and Democratic officeholders have been affected by publication of internal correspondence. In Orange County, a stronghold for conservatives for generations but which now has a majority of Democrats as congressional representatives, and which supported Biden in 2020, the remaining Republican representatives who voted against impeachment in 2021 have issued a statement of apology to their supporters.

In the Bay area, by contrast, charges of financial corruption have been made about the Democratic State Central Committee and the Democratic National Committee.....

Well, we tried to be even-handed, Baker smiled.

DECEMBER 2021

CHAPTER 31: RECKONINGS

Wednesday, December 1
Washington, D.C.

Baker had expected that, at some point in the document production process, some Senators and Representatives were likely to be recalled by their states, be expelled from office by the Senate or House, or would simply resign.

But even he was astonished when the House Committee on Ethics received a resolution from the House on December 1 regarding four House members, two from each party. The House committee, taking advantage of the Month of Sundays momentum, completed an investigation within a week, returning a recommendation to expel these members from the House.

Warp speed, Baker thought to himself. *Someone is terrified.*

Expulsion needed to meet a high bar, with two-thirds of the House voting to approve. Instead, with the eyes of the country upon them, thanks to C-SPAN, the House voted at an 80% rate to approve expulsion. Baker was focused on the hearings, watching from his cabin in the woods. The states immediately announced special elections to occur early in the new year.

Within the next two weeks, leading up to Christmas, four Republican senators resigned, effective at the end of the calendar year. None of the states they represented had yet received the public Month of Sundays package, although they were on the list. One was from Wisconsin, where Baker had limited distribution to the Iron County folks before the general campaign began. The other three senators were one each from Pennsylvania, North Carolina, and Virginia. Since three of the four states had a Democratic governor with the statutory power to name a replacement to fill out the term, the second session of the 177th Congress, to begin in early January 2022, had suddenly swung to favor Democrats, 53-47. *The Senate minority leader must be looking to gut some of these guys with a dull knife,* Baker thought. *In my wildest dreams, I didn't expect that level of change.*

The senator from Wisconsin had been on the telephone to the President. "Mr. President, please," he opened blandly enough, "I'm asking you to call off the dogs. You know this whole thing is nonsense. I'm up for election this year, and I don't care what this 'Month of Sundays' stuff is, you're not going to force me out of office. The people of Wisconsin elected me, and I'm going to serve until they say other-wise." His voice had steadily risen in volume, and the President had the sense that he had been biting off every word.

"My friend, I don't have anything to do with what's been going out in the press. The materials that are showing up in the papers were generated from your office, by your staff, and by the people you wrote to. I haven't a thing to do with it. The FBI still has very few clues about who is sending out these documents, or how." He paused. "In your case, it's some of your own conservatives from up in Iron County who got the documents, and they're the ones who gave them to your state legislators. Again, I had nothing to do with it. Now, you and I know that what's in those letters is true, and that you've steadily lied to your Wisconsin people about election fraud, about COVID, and about the economy. It's the chickens coming home to roost, man. I think you're lucky that the Iron County Rangers didn't just publish the whole package instead of giving it to the parties and the reporters. The documents demonstrate that you knew you were lying, and that you had agreed with the former president and with your party leaders to use your position to slow down legislation and hinder the work of government. The hearings you chaired, for instance, led to outrageous misinformation."

"But, Mr. President, that's what politics is all about. We need to use our best judgment to protect our people—"

The President cut him off. "And to protect your power, right, Senator? But you can't protect anything when you have to carry on business in the open, right? Well, it's in the open. Your legislature has it now, and the papers as well."

The President continued quickly before the senator could respond. "Look, I want to be honest about this. I took your call because I know you're under pressure. But you haven't seen pressure yet. You know Article V, Section 1, I'm sure. Well, let me tell you, with this stuff in public—

which it will be, it's not up to me—it won't be difficult to get two-thirds of your Senate colleagues to vote to expel you. So, it seems to me that you can go quietly, or you can go noisily. Noisily, trust me, will not help your Republican colleagues, and it will make it that much harder to elect a Republican to succeed you. I'm not involved in this—it is the Senate that must discipline its own. Good afternoon, Senator." He put the phone down, and for a change in the last three weeks, actually looked satisfied.

A few minutes later, after reviewing his notes, he called the Senate Majority Leader. "How are things shaking out since Thanksgiving?"

"Mr. President, so far there have been no surprises. We expected the losses in the House on both sides. I think people are pretty gun-shy right now. I have heard that a number of senators on both sides are combing through their correspondence to see what might be coming out about them.

"I will say, Mr. President, that this seems like a time when we might focus on legislation that can be clearly moderate and centered on the well-being of the American people. If senators and House members can point to accomplishments outside of their ideological fences, we might actually get some things done."

"I want to be clear about this, Senator. You recognize this has to be bipartisan. We can still be filibustered out of accomplishing anything if it's too radical. So put a couple of your best people on it, and meet with moderate Republicans and the minority leader.

"Let's push on the voting rights bill, first, and then on the domestic policies, okay?" The President knew the Majority Leader actually viewed the voting rights bill as the more difficult. He explained. "Because this MOS stuff is likely to put front and center how some in the Senate have capitulated to white nationalists. I want to get them on record about this. And I encourage you to give a little—like the photo identification issue—and then include dramatically increased funding to accomplish that. It'll cut them off at the knees. Talk with the Speaker of the House about this."

"Yes, sir. Sir, are you telling me there's more stuff coming? Have you seen it?"

"Yes, Senator, and No, Senator. I think we can count on more, and I haven't seen it. But I think we both know what'll be there."

A few minutes later, the President called a Democratic senator. His tone was friendlier, but still pointed. "Mr. Senator, up until today we have needed every Democratic vote in the Senate. That's given a lot of folks the sense that their voice needed to be heard, and that they had an outsized importance, because I needed them. Now, you've certainly identified with our agenda, and you have for ten years now. But I anticipate, with these resignations, that our party will have maybe a year where we will actually be in the clear majority. I'm giving you a heads-up on this. I hope you will work with us to pass legislation this session. I don't want to leave you out or leave you behind. But come Monday, you won't have the leverage you do now.

So, I'd like to see Build Back Better get through soon, and smoothly. It'll be better for all of us if that happens." He waited. "I know. I feel like a Mafia guy sounding like that, and I don't like it either. But the facts are what the facts are. Thanks. I hope I can count on you." He listened. "Thanks, Senator. Good afternoon."

CHAPTER 32: ASSIGNMENT

Friday, December 17
McLean, Virginia

Myers and Flores were now eight weeks into the project. They'd been through every document drop, analyzing patterns of collection, as far as they could see them, patterns of arrangement, and patterns of distribution. They'd presented several reports to "management," as Myers called it, Gray and the people he reported to at the US Conservative Conference, and had proposed several alternative scenarios on how all of this had happened.

With their "connection" to the FBI task force, they thought they had a handle on what their primary competitor had, as well. The FBI group was meeting on a slower schedule than they had been, since they had been sending their team members into the field and into other task force groups to share information. Cook now had them assembling by videoconference weekly, rather than two or three times a week.

And today Myers and Flores had received clearance to do some on-the-ground research. Flores had a team of three "investigators"—his "intrusion" specialists--he kept on retainer, men he'd used for years around the country.

They were flexible enough to pick up and go when he needed, and specialized in careful, quiet breaking and entering. When necessary, they could also be relied upon for discreet and absolutely effective intimidation. They'd never gotten as far as broken bones or fatalities, but their success rate was pretty close to perfect. They always got clearance, and they always kept to the limits of the contract.

Flores met with them in a strip-mall office in McLean, Virginia, just over the freeway from Tyson's Corners, and near enough to Dulles International to get anywhere. He'd bought the building years before, and rented it out to a Pilates studio, a pizza delivery service, and a barbershop, keeping one office for himself. The office was a lot larger than the frontage would suggest, the security better than the location warranted, and it served as an equipment base for fieldwork.

Ed Clement, Jimmy Davis, and Mark Goldhammer were ex-military, trained in security and equally adept at negotiation and research. Ed was nearing retirement, in his mid-50's, still fit but slowed by increasing arthritis and joint damage. Jimmy, in his late thirties, was the "cracksman," the lock-picker and computer hacker, and gentle-looking Mark was actually the muscle of the trio. All of them had experience with breaking, entering, evasion, and escape, although none of their targets in quite a while had required much skill.

Flores welcomed the trio at the parking lot door, waving them past him. He smiled, and began. "Nice to see you guys after a couple of months rest. Come on in, and let me show you our project." They took seats around a conference table, and each opened a manila folder at his place.

"Wow!" Jimmy said, scanning the first page. "The Outfit is involved with this?"

"We're not the mob, Jimmy," Flores smiled. "But yes, we're involved. Have you looked at this stuff as it's been coming out?"

Ed and Mark nodded, but Jimmy shook his head. "Been working on other projects. Not this one!" he added quickly.

"No, I don't think so, Jimmy. No disrespect, but you know better. Nope, this one pretty clearly has stuff from our office—or things derived from our office—going out from us to members of Congress, to state and national political parties, and to interest groups. There are people who are starting to nose around and connect the dots, and the FBI is doing that, too.

"Here's the deal: we think we've identified the kind of person or group of people who might have been responsible for putting this together, but we have no first-hand, on-the-ground evidence. We've identified six or seven possibilities, ranging from Tennessee up to Michigan, someone in Colorado, someone in Utah, someone we think is in Washington but whose home is in Minnesota, and then two in California. We think we know how they did it, but we're looking for evidence of that, too. All of them are academics, political science teachers, or activists. They've had sustained contact with congressional offices over time, sometimes supervising interns. And we thank the FBI for their help in narrowing the field," he laughed. "Let's see if we can beat them to our source.

"I want you to pay each of them a visit. You don't have to speak with them, and in fact it'd be best if you did your best get-in-and-get-out-no-contact with them. Download what's on their computers, scope out their libraries, hack their email, read their social media, and find out any connections to this Month of Sundays group."

He flipped a page over, and the others followed him in their own folders. "As far as I can tell," he said, "none of them has the technical skill or interest in setting up the computer side. That's still a wide-open question. But you might find out something when you look." He lifted a hand, indicating a suitcase against the wall near the door. "Here's sixty grand for expenses—fly, stay in hotels, rent cars, the usual—and also lockpick and computer intrusion tools. Don't use your own, as much as you like them. Don't use plastic for any payments. I want this insulated from us as much as possible. Ed, there's a 92FS Beretta, three magazines, and 300 rounds of 9mm in there as well. It's as clean as we can make it." I take it you each have clean ID, including drivers' licenses?" They nodded. "How about vaccinations linked to your ID—are you up to date for COVID? I do *not* want you getting sick on the road, so watch yourselves."

"I think we have, at most, a month to do this. We need to get this leak stopped, we need to recover our data, and we need to put the fear of God into whoever's doing it or has done it. Finding out how this happened is important—specifics—but getting it stopped has priority. When you think you've found the person, report in, and we'll discuss a response. And yes, this is a case of 'the horse is already out of the barn,' but there are other horses in the barn we'd like to stay there. If we can turn these people over to the FBI and make examples of them, it's less likely ever to happen again."

"Well, so much for Christmas," Ed shook his head. "But what happens if we can't find whoever this is within the month?"

"You keep looking. The stakes go up with every release. Take a couple of days off at Christmas and New Year's," Flores said. "Do your planning, and Jimmy, maybe do your hacking. You don't have to be on-site for that. You can be sure there's a bonus in this if you're quick and effective. And you know the One Rule: don't get caught."

JANUARY-FEBRUARY 2022

CHAPTER 33: HAPPY NEW YEAR!

Saturday, January 1, 2022
The Press

On New Year's Day, sometime after the Rose Parade, Baker had scheduled what he thought might be the most interesting non-state package delivery. Thanks to people in the White House who just couldn't keep their hands out of the cookie jar, the package consisted of all the correspondence between the previous president and President Vladimir Putin, stretching back to 2013, some of which had appeared in print in 2020. And as a bonus, Baker had thrown in the correspondence between the previous president and Supreme Leader Kim Jong-un of North Korea. The two or three dozen exchanges were lit up by a sort of "fan-boy" excitement on the part of the American president.

Baker figured that somebody in the White House, wanting to show off his or her access, had scanned the letters and then sent them to a friend or family member. As a package, they were on the edge of embarrassing. He had no doubt they were authentic. He expected the next few days to be pretty interesting. For this drop, he'd limited distribution to his original newspapers and to the Director of the FBI. Bold, and maybe stupid, he thought. On the other hand, the drop came through a computer in a coffee shop in New York City, sent there from a TOR server in Norway.

As he'd expected, by the next day the story was in the papers, being broadcast with downloads available of the letters. The furor from Florida stretched across the country.

"The Big Six," as they called themselves, the editors of the *Seattle P-I*, the *Denver Post*, the *LA Times*, the *New York Times*, the *Wall Street Journal*, and the *Washington Post*, had planned a little ceremonial video call on the afternoon of New Year's Day. Everyone needed a little breather, even if it was a Saturday. The Denver editor was distracted by unseasonal wind-driven wildfires in the area that had already burned 1000 houses; the LA editor was musing over the impact of more than 700 new laws that were taking effect, including a huge jump in the minimum wage and changes in vote-by-mail regulations; the WSJ was looking at the spike in COVID in Europe and its implications; the New York paper offered a sentimental retrospective of Betty White amid harder things. The Washington paper, though, was already beginning to ramp up for its story on the January 6, 2021, insurrection.

The video call began at 3 p.m. Eastern, so in Seattle and LA the editors were grabbing lunch while the others were well into an adult beverage or two. The New York editor greeted everyone, then proposed a toast. "To the Month of Sundays group," he offered, holding a champagne glass up to the screen. "Responsible for the best increases in circulation in half a century." The others laughed and lifted schooners, martini glasses, and a couple of Old-Fashioned glasses up. "Hear, hear!" came as a chorus.

"Do we actually know anything more about the Month of Sundays group now than in October?" the *P-I* editor asked. "We haven't found anything, and the FBI isn't talking."

The others confirmed it—not a word. "And yet," the *Wall Street Journal* editor added, "you have to admit that whoever it is or was, they've given us material to last a decade. I'm waiting to see what the legislation will be like coming out of the new session of Congress. Voters are seriously up in arms about this."

"What are you going to do with this package today—the Putin-Trump-Kim Jong-un letters?" came from Denver. "Let me put my cards on the table. We're not going to waste newsprint on them, but we're putting them in full on our website. I've asked the international editors and a couple of political scientists to write analyses and opinion pieces on them for tomorrow."

The Washington and New York editors nodded, and New York said, "We're going to do the same, and probably the only thing that will differentiate our story from yours is who we get to do the analysis. We do have a former Secretary of State in the wings—you know, the one who ran for President. She said she can hardly wait."

At least three of the editors were laughing so hard they were in danger of spilling their drinks.

The *P-I* editor, as the end of their time approached, smiled, held up her glass again, and called out, "Let's hear it for the Month of Sundays!" With a cheer, the others responded, gave a salute, and signed off.

CHAPTER 34: ANNIVERSARY

Thursday, January 6
Washington, D.C.

On January 6, the first anniversary of the attack on the Capitol, Baker's six favorite newspapers received a special "dump" of documents. The House committee had already been releasing documents through its hearings, but Baker's package contained a few surprises. Among these were "revisionist" position papers from the national political parties, showing internal discussions on how to exploit or to control the damage from rioting and arrests. They showed committee staff members in both parties in a panic throughout the first two days, and then a refocusing on shifting audience perceptions.

Legislators didn't look good, either. And neither did commentators at some of the broadcast venues, whose emails and text messages Baker's program had swept up. With a little work, Baker had paralleled the House committee in setting up a timeline over several days showing the evolution of the messaging emerging from the White House and from the media.

When he included directions from the national political party offices down to the state offices, though, he touched on new ground. To see how a Wyoming, or Colorado, or Arizona state political staff—Democratic or Republican--was encouraged to frame January 6th was eye-opening. Democrats might be directed to condemn the Republican Party as a whole—guilt by association—Republicans might be urged to see the frame of "a fight for liberty" defending the rioters.

For fun, Baker included something not at all secret. He inserted a half-dozen fund-raising letters from the Republican and Democratic national and state committees. And he added the famous document "Language: A Key Mechanism of Control," distributed to Republican candidates back in 1996. In the process, he highlighted every example of the "loaded" language in each.

One of the keys to understanding political messaging, Baker knew, was to address and appeal to basic, widely shared emotions. In the list of words "to define your campaign and your vision of public service" were touchstones like "courage," "crusade," "dream," "duty."

Among his favorites was the Trump/Pence letter from just before the 2020 election, which he highlighted, then fact-checked for his audience. Using an "italic" font for those "approving" words Newt Gingrich might have recommended—show yourself strong, and creative, he could hear leadership say—and "UNDERLINED SMALL CAPS" for those benighted liberals who deserved contempt, he showed visually how the campaign worked the audience. *Stunningly inept,* he thought, *and impoverished to the degree that even the writers must be embarrassed.*

Dear XXXXX,

Last night's debate between our *wonderful* Vice President and <u>PHONY</u> Kamala proved one thing: the <u>RADICAL LEFT</u> would <u>DESTROY</u> America if they win in November and **<u>THEY CANNOT BE TRUSTED.</u>**

Mike Pence was *incredible* and <u>EXPOSED</u> the <u>RADICAL LEFT</u> for their <u>LIES</u> and <u>DECEPTIONS</u>.

He did a great job *fighting* for America. He reminded the American People just *how far we've come* in the last three and a half years. We've *lowered taxes* for the middle class, we've *protected* pre-existing conditions, we've fought for the unborn, we've *strengthened* our military, we've *defended* our *great* law enforcement and we are quickly *developing* a vaccine.

CONTRIBUTE NOW FOR AN 850%-MATCH. >>

Meanwhile, Kamala RAMBLED and REFUSED to answer a single question HONESTLY. Since she wouldn't give you the *truth*, I WILL:

Democrats would PACK THE COURTS

They'd RAISE YOUR TAXES by $4 TRILLION

They would encourage Americans NOT to take a coronavirus vaccine

Joe Biden's mental state is DECLINING

The Left would reinstate the TERRIBLE Iran Deal

Joe is WEAK on China

They would DESTROY the economy

The Democrats are threatening to take away everything YOU stand for and we cannot let them GET AWAY WITH IT. I need you to *step up* and show them this is YOUR COUNTRY NOT THEIRS.

STEP UP IN THE NEXT HOUR AND YOUR GIFT WILL BE 850%-MATCHED.

The Election is less than 4 weeks away. We can't take a day off. I need you to *step up* right now for the sake of *America's future*. My team will send me a list of every Patriot who *steps up* at this critical moment.

Please contribute ANY AMOUNT RIGHT NOW to *fight for America* and your gift will be 850%-MATCHED. >>

DONOR FILE

SUPPORTER:

ACCOUNT NUMBER: 34826505 - 2020

850%-MATCH: ACTIVATED

DEADLINE: 1 HOUR

CONTRIBUTE $45 = $428

CONTRIBUTE $250 = $2375
CONTRIBUTE $100 = $950
CONTRIBUTE $50 = $475
CONTRIBUTE $45 = $428
CONTRIBUTE ANY AMOUNT
I need you right now, XXXXXX

I've requested a list of ALL *Patriots* who *step up* right now to *fight* with Vice President Pence and me. Will I see your name?

Please contribute $45 IMMEDIATELY to get on the list and your gift will be 850%-MATCHED.

Thank you,
Donald J. Trump
President of the United States
CONTRIBUTE $45 = $428

Baker didn't have to comment on the untruths of emails like this. He added enough documentation from others to make the point, including the poll data that showed almost 60% of voters had believed the Democratic candidate had won the debate.

For all his planning, things often surprised Baker. The biggest unexpected impact from this set of documents would come several months away, and shift the media landscape. He might have called it "not-exactly-unintended consequences."

CHAPTER 35: LUNCH AT DAVIE'S

Tuesday January 19
Newport, Washington

Baker thought his luck had been way better than he had hoped. He felt at times like he was walking blindfolded, since all his data collection sources were shut off. He was watching the news, listening to the television, and cautiously exchanging emails around the country with friends. This was all part of his "alternate narrative" of the New Sabbatical Project, as he called it. At the same time, he thought it likely that any day the FBI or someone else might show up at the front door.

He'd made some preparations, but didn't want them to hamper the work he was doing now that the "real work" was mostly done. In the last month, Indiana, Iowa, Kansas, Kentucky, and Louisiana documents had been published, mostly from overseas servers, but not all. Thanks to a lucky break, the largest Louisiana employer had published the state's documents from its own website, and Baker had smiled while others had grimaced. Some of the most appalling documents—in terms of attempts to influence—

had come initially from that company to House and Senate members. Insult added to injury, he supposed.

Seasonal Affective Disorder troubled him some in this dark January. And he was lonely. He had worked hard to lay aside his wife's loss three years before. He intended to make a certain Minnesota legislator pay dearly for the way he'd bribed his son's way out of responsibility for Jean's death. The son, drunk and on his way back from the lake, had fallen asleep and drifted across the road, striking Jean as she walked in their neighborhood in the twilight. She was thrown into bushes on the side of the road, and he drove back onto the pavement, thinking he'd hit a deer. She'd bled to death before anyone could find her, and no one might have known except for the tire tracks across the grass. The young man had the car in the body shop the next morning, and the investigation went nowhere.

But Baker had found other things going on, the revelation of which wouldn't point to Baker himself, that would almost certainly end the congressman's career. And they'd be in a Minnesota packet all by themselves.

He was still lonely. At his age, he knew a number of attractive single women who'd outlived their husbands, women he'd enjoy getting to know. And right now, he thought, he'd like to enjoy a relationship that had no danger in it. He didn't fancy getting arrested in the middle of a courtship, though. *Better wait until November*, he thought. And sighed.

As he reviewed the last six months, he thought, *This wouldn't make a very good novel*, and laughed to himself. *No car chases, no assassins showing up in the middle of the night, no scenes of torture.* He squirmed for a moment at the thought of Sean Connery or Daniel Craig or someone similar. *On the other hand,* he admitted, *I'm not Gerard Butler working as a 'law-abiding citizen,' either. No power tools. For which some people ought to be glad. Ah, but no romance.*

And he thought to himself, *Am I telling the American people a good story? What's the debate like out there?*

And with that, he decided to go down to Spokane and find out. Maybe swing over to Seattle and see family, too.

Spokane's weather throughout the winter tends toward gray and chill, and Tuesday was no different. A high of 41, which meant that whatever snow there was would be slushy and a mess. Baker took the more direct route to Spokane, down highway 2 to the "Y" and then down Division to find a restaurant where he could listen. The road was full of memories for him, some of them the Boy Scout camp on Diamond Lake, or a holiday dinner in the Country Homes neighborhood. He drove by the family's earliest home in Spokane, a few blocks off Division, from the first years of the twentieth century.

And all of this now, he thought, was profoundly Trump/Pence neighborhood, anti-vaxxers, anti-maskers, people who read the latest conspiracy stories, whose news was All-FOX-all-the-time, or the One America News Network. How did these profoundly skeptical, thoughtful people he'd grown up with take this path? These pragmatists, hard-headed, tempered by hot, dry summers and winters that wavered between 40 below and a melt-the-whole-thing *chinook* wind sweeping in off the Pacific.

By lunchtime, he was back in the Valley, where he'd grown up, and less than a mile from the junior high he'd attended. His destination was Davie's Bar and Grill, going for the Flame-Broiled Chicken Sandwich, with all the fixings of bacon and swiss *on a sesame seed bun,* he hummed to himself. They were just newly reopened after mask mandates went down, and only one table in the two rows of tables was open. *And the best,* he reckoned, *in the back corner where I can watch everything.* He waved to the server, and took the seat in the back corner, looking out. Once he'd ordered, he took out a pad and pen and began listening.

The Spokane Valley was a mix of older and younger folks, the whites of his generation being supplanted by California couples coming in, or transplants from the Coast, more often multi-racial. Davie's, in part because of location and in part because of the insularity of Opportunity, Washington, was small, familiar, and uninteresting to new people. Baker expected to find the more conservative voices here, and he wasn't disappointed.

"At this rate, they're projecting we won't see anything until the end of *June,*" a woman said to her friend across the table. They were finishing pie and coffee, and Baker guessed they met regularly from the way they'd been talking about grandchildren and church. "I'm annoyed by the pace. Most of us just want to understand what's going on in our state."

Her companion nodded. "We can't do much about Idaho or Oregon—Washington's the one we can do something about." She took another sip of coffee.

Baker's server came over, and he ordered, got coffee to hold him while the sandwich was prepped, and kept listening. "I am so tired of this racial nonsense," the other woman replied. "Of course, we've got problems here, but they're not Seattle's problem with the blacks, or Yakima's problem with Hispanics. But I don't dare go downtown at night without Mace in my pocket, and my hand on the trigger."

"I'm carrying a 9mm in my purse," the first woman said. "I have for years, every time I go to town. The homeless."

"I don't go *that* far," her friend laughed.

"I don't understand why the west side of the state can't seem to understand what we're up against over here. Again and again, the laws that get passed benefit Seattle, and never the farmers here."

"Over there is where the money is," the Mace woman said. "Seattle is booming. Microsoft, Amazon, all the banks, all the shipping, all the trade."

"Yes, and over here is all the food and most of the land. What gets me is the idiots and the gas tax. Don't they realize we can't run farms or trucking or transportation with electric cars? Do they ever try driving across the state in a Tesla? And running out of power along about Cheney?" Both of them laughed.

The server came to their table with the check, and the two women smiled and asked for a final cup of coffee. "What do you think about this talk about getting rid of the dams on the Columbia?" the first one asked. "Don't these people have a clue about where our electricity comes from?"

"Damned if I know," the second one said, shaking her head. "But I tell you, everything on the internet these days makes me afraid. I wish I knew who to trust. Somebody keeps telling us that if we want to save the salmon, we've got to get rid of the dams, so they can get upstream to spawn. If we don't, they'll die out. Well, if we don't have power, we will too! These internet stories make you wonder. Where's the truth in any of this?"

"Yeah, I read that article, too. Then I clicked on the author's name, and found that all he writes about is "big government," "conspiracy," "the deep state," "treason," "traitors," and "false flag" stuff. He specializes in making people feel afraid. The hell with him." She set the now-empty coffee cup down, picked up the check, and took her coat in her other hand.

Mace woman moved to join her. "Have you heard the latest about President Alzheimer's?" she laughed.

Nine-millimeter woman smiled. "Which one?"

Even Baker smiled at that, as his sandwich platter arrived. *Will what I'm doing help people be less afraid, or more?* He wondered.

He'd have supper somewhere a little more left-leaning, he thought. Maybe Bar-High's Restaurant at Liberty Lake, which his brother Terry had suggested. And, he smiled, where his Subaru would fit right in, although on the low end with the Audis, Mercedes, and Porsches of the "new age" Liberty Lake folks. He'd heard they had great food. *Better check to see if I've got a mask in the car,* he thought, remembering Terry's story. *Don't want to give offense.*

CHAPTER 36: HUNTERS 3

Wednesday, February 2
Washington, D.C.
Newport, Washington

Some people were definitely not finding the project boring. The technology people working with the FBI and Randy, working with Myers and Flores, had pretty well figured out the strategy the Month of Sundays group—whoever they were—had been using for delivery. They were scouring European servers, looking for access points almost in real time, so they hoped to track when the MOS established an account and sent materials back to US. They knew they were up against a deadline every Saturday and Sunday, and while the FBI wasn't ready to interfere with the document releases, Flores and Myers certainly were. They had arranged to have Randy pulled from everything else he was doing.

The mystery of how the MOS had gotten the materials and gained access in the first place was still out there. Both groups of hunters thought it likely that some sort of intrusion software had been loaded into a government system and had spread from there. They still didn't know how, although some of the FBI cyber people were actually quite close to the truth.

Baker didn't know any of this, and so continued as low-profile as he could.

Baker, working with his Minnesota IT friend, had added code to the campus pictures he included with every email to his students. Technically, it was called "steganography," and involved a "hide in plain sight" addition to each picture. His friend had actually developed not only the program for the document collection, but also a program to conceal the code and upload it. Every few days, Baker had emailed his students, always enclosing a campus picture or two, and the program wrote itself onto their computers. They'd read the email, so it was present both on their laptops and their phones; at the office, the cell phones would dump the email on to the office computers...and so it went, week after week until the program was ready.

He was hoping to keep the hunters on a wild goose chase for at least a little longer.

Iowa and Kansas had come out on the previous two Sundays, and he was sure people were doing both "content analysis" and "method of delivery" analysis. These deliveries had been a little different, because even though the commands came in from overseas, the documents themselves had been stored the U.S., on the websites of three different newspapers. That did not please the newspapers involved, as they didn't know anything about it. Baker's point was to keep the delivery locations or storage as unpredictable as possible. He had a long month ahead, and wanted to keep one jump away from trouble.

In the meantime, in the world at large, things were happening. The President was struggling to get legislation considered by Congress, and although even with resignations and expulsions Democrats retained the House, the balance in the Senate gave the President almost no room. Several Senators had resigned, stemming from their own writing revealed in the MOS documents, but while Democrats now held a majority thanks to governors naming their successors, they could not break the filibuster. They knew they had a brief window until the fall elections, but seemed unable to follow through on the President's vow to seek bipartisan solutions. Baker was agnostic on some of the legislation—he wasn't an economist—but the rhetoric used by conservatives continued to be unprincipled nonsense, and that used by progressives dreamily unrealistic.

Cook and her team had a clue. They'd interviewed some of Baker's interns, even going so far as to meet with some who'd been in D.C. well before the MOS "collections" in 2020. Baker wasn't the only one on their list, of course, and along the way the team had found things that they'd handed off to other investigators, including the Securities and Exchange Commission, the Food and Drug Administration, the ATF and the FCC. The Month of Sundays folks had handed them everybody's safety deposit box, indeed.

But Michael, Nicole, and Fritz had pushed a little harder on the interns than anyone else. They'd gotten lucky when one of Baker's women students had given them her old HP laptop, one that had failed in the middle of a semester and that she'd never discarded. She said it might have some of her notes and things from her internship, and they were welcome to it.

They pulled the hard drive, and hooked it up to an adapter to download the files. In an hour, they had everything. For the first time, they had samples of Baker's emails and notes to the students. Fritz was the first one to point out the number of photos—at least two—Baker sent his students in every email. "Did you ever get email like this from an instructor?" he asked Nicole.

"When I went to college, half the faculty didn't know how to *use* email," she laughed. "It was too long ago."

"What if we take a *really* close look at this," Fritz suggested. "Not as in 'zoom in on it,' but break it down to the level of code. We've got a suite of programs to determine if there's something unusual about these emails."

They ran several of the programs in sequence, scanning a USB drive where they'd dumped the emails, and carefully keeping the original drive disconnected from any network access.

Anomalies began to show up. Over about eight weeks, half the semester, more and more of them appeared. Scanning the hard drive fully, they located a segment of the Windows system subdirectory where they appeared to be collected.

But they only got half the semester.

On Friday, having recovered everything they could, they reported in to Cook and the rest of the team. Cook paid for dinner for the three of them, and sent them all home for the weekend. She had to figure out what to do next.

At the end of Friday evening, kids in bed, sitting with her wife on the couch in the living room, they watched the television shift from news into an especially irritating pundit. Elise turned to her, and with that mocking voice she used when she was especially annoyed, said, "Devon, are you going to spend any time at all with this arrogant white boy? Honey, he may be a city boy, but he has barnyard up to his knees."

"No," Devon laughed, "he has barnyard coming out of his mouth. Listen."

The smooth, carefully made-up, sneering face on the screen paused a moment. He began again. "Funny that we're hearing all this dirt on our elected representatives and senators and a big move to find out who is responsible, but we hear nothing but crickets from the Epstein case and all those people on the Lolita Express. Where's the justice there? These people are only out for their own skins."

Devon muted the screen.

"Well," Elise breathed, "yes, he has a point. But it's also a red herring, isn't it? Sure, we'd all like to see justice on those rich white people—and the Ay-rabs—but that doesn't have much to do with the Month of Sundays, does it?"

"I think you'd be surprised," Devon side-eyed her. "It may turn out badly for them. Think about it. What are the senators and representatives, really, the way the rich people play the game? They're the tools these people use. Well-compensated, but tools. Take the tools away, and

233

what happens next? We'll see. We may have people standing in line to testify, if only to save their own skins. This guy is right about that, and wrong at the same time."

"Mmmm," Elise leaned over and kissed her cheek. "And I get to watch."

CHAPTER 37: CIRCLING

Monday, February 7
Washington, D.C.

"Has it occurred to you, Devon, that we could profit from this problem in a number of ways?" They were at a conference table in Ed Collins' office in the FBI building. *And what a depressing building to be in,* Cook thought for the dozenth time.

Cook sat a little straighter in her chair, facing her boss. Head slightly tipped to the right, putting on her best disarming smile, she asked Collins, "Ed, can you tell me exactly what you're suggesting?"

"Where are you exactly in this investigation, Devon? Lay it out for me."

"Okay, we are now four months in. First, we are working with documents from 21 states—Kentucky yesterday—and possibly a couple of others we're just hearing about, including Wyoming, Wisconsin, and Massachusetts, that have been released to just a few activists. You know we're handing off some of this to other federal agencies, when we find suggestions that a crime's been committed. I think some state governments are getting involved, too. Second, we think we're closing in on some of the distribution methods. Third, we don't have any examples of the 'collection program' or the 'transfer program' or the 'distribution program' that the MOS group used, although we're looking at what we got from that intern's computer. Fourth, we have at least one or two examples of how the collected data was stored on computers, tucking in a new file into a system subfolder.

"And we finally have a suspect, although we literally have nothing beyond some altered emails to tie him to the data collection. At best, we have some 'unusual' code. And we don't know for sure if there's anyone else beyond him. This whole Month of Sundays group might be just one person, but we have no idea if this guy has the computer knowledge to do the hack that was necessary. And my team tells me that this is not off-the-shelf intrusion software. This is custom, and it's elegant, even the fragment that we have."

"Now, what I've heard you say is that you're noticing, but not spending time on a whole set of secondary sketchy behavior. If not criminal. Right? So, there's a lot of progress on *the main thing*, but you still have a way to go, right?"

Cook had to nod. Then she shook her head a fraction. "So, what did you mean by 'profiting from the problem'?"

Collins waved that off. "Devon, how is our competition doing? I know you've been monitoring some of the foundations and lobbying groups, because they want these MOS people nearly as much as we do. What do we know?"

Cook sat for a moment. She hadn't briefed Collins on this yet. "Well, I'm not hearing a lot. We do have a source in the USCC, the United States Conservative Conference offices. They have a task group headed by two people focused on finding out who is behind the MOS and how they can stop distribution. And they have a source inside us, and they don't think we know it."

Collins leaned back, cupping his chin with one hand. "And would you mind telling me how you accomplished that?"

Cook laid her hands flat on the conference table. "It wasn't as dramatic as it sounds. One of *our* people got a call from them with the offer of some considerable cash if she would keep them informed about our progress. She came to me immediately, and I told her to get from them as good as she gave, and to clear with me what she'd tell them. We're keeping an eye on them. They have more cash to throw at a problem than we do, and fewer ethical hesitations. And I don't ignore the fact that they hire smart people and give them room to work. We're ahead of them so far. Oh, and their influence goes further, into other organizations."

"Do they have a source inside us that *we* don't know about?"

"Actually, I think they do have another source, and it's someone in the main task group. I'm not convinced about it, and so I'm watching carefully. Our *actual* source tells me things that our team are discussing or working on that I *haven't* told her to release. So, maybe. I haven't told our working group that we're releasing information to the USCC, so I'm trying to keep this stuff compartmented."

"And I'd like you to cover your backside. Send me a report on this tomorrow, and detail what the USCC is *supposed* to know from us and what we *think* they know that they shouldn't. Include the name of our 'official' liaison in a copy to me only. She needs cover, too. I'll write you an authorization to proceed further. And if you have suspicions about who their mole is in your task group, I'd like something about that, too.

"Okay, back to Professor Baker. I want you to proceed deliberately on this. Keep trying to collect information about what you think he did and how he did it. It sounds like you got lucky on the crashed computer, and your team did well to keep pushing on it. Hand it to them and tell them to do it again. What do we really know about him?"

"Right. What about the Professor himself? We don't know a lot—but mostly because we haven't asked. We're looking at him, but it's like looking at a black hole. He's almost suspicious because he's keeping himself invisible."

"One of my favorite novels has a line about a professor on vacation between terms." Collins leaned back and quoted from memory. "'A don in the middle of long vacation is almost a non-existent creature, as you ought to remember. College neither knows nor cares where he is, and certainly no one else does.' And that's Baker, now he's retired. But I want you to keep an eye on him, metaphorically. Find a way to watch him, maybe with the help of local authorities. Unobtrusive. And maybe interview a few more of his students, quietly."

CHAPTER 38: WATCHING BAKER

Wednesday, February 9
Brooklyn Center, Minnesota

Cook had assigned two agents from the task force to fly to Minnesota and interview three of Baker's students who had been in the program, two who had interned in 2019. They'd all been present when Ross had shared his concerns, that night in November. The field office in Brooklyn Center had invited the students in, and Cook had taken some pains to make the invitation both positive and vague at the same time. Before they were done, they'd do their best to keep the students from contacting Baker, they hoped.

Angela Hall, based in Los Angeles, and David Harstad from Denver met with the students.

Luis Reyes, now 24, had been the "note-taker" at the November 2019 meeting in Washington. Summer Morgan was in the same class. Both were now working in the Twin Cities, Reyes in Minneapolis for a non-profit involved in low-income housing solutions, and Morgan in St. Paul with a program for single mothers that highlighted education and empowerment.

Hall and Harstad had also arranged to meet with Patrick Bennett, now 26, who'd been in the program two years earlier than the others, and had served as an undergraduate teaching assistant for Baker in his senior year.

Hall began the interview with Reyes and Morgan. "Thank you for coming today. We appreciate your making the time to meet with us. We mentioned that we've been asked to look into Dr. Baker's background, as he is about to be involved in some work with the government. Some of it is involves national security and legal issues. We got your names from Justin Ross"—they both looked up, smiling—"who suggested you could help us."

"Could you tell us a bit about yourselves, first?" Hall eased into the first question smoothly, Harstad thought. "We're not from around here—he's Denver, I'm Los Angeles—so we may ask you to explain things we don't know."

Luis looked at Summer and gracefully gestured that she should take the lead. She laughed, and began.

"Luis is always the gentleman," she laughed. "I'm Summer Morgan, originally from Denver. Agent Harstad, welcome to Minnesota! I came to the Twin Cities for college, and found a job here with a program helping single mothers and children to get an education. I've been with them since I graduated from college, and work with the program as an advocate for women with the state government. Dr. Baker helped me think through my skills and values, and helped me make initial contacts with this organization. It's worked out very well." She turned to Luis.

"I'm from western Minnesota, out near Worthington. I'm what you might call a 'Minnesotano,'" he said with a smile. "Hispanics are about 5 percent of the Minnesota population, but there are a lot more of us down in the southwest, in agriculture. I'm a 'first-generation' college student, though I'm a third-generation American citizen. Dr. Baker was a terrific help to me, too. I met him when I visited campus as a high school student, and we talked about how a Latino in public service could make a difference. I'm working with a non-profit that tries to help get people into housing and to develop housing alternatives. So I get to work on policy and also swing a hammer when I need to. It's called Urban Homes. Dr. Baker took me with him once on a work crew with them, and I was hooked. We did demo all day getting ready to rehab a house that later became three apartments." He smiled. "I live in one of them now."

Harstad stopped taking notes. *Impressive*, he thought. "We know from Justin Ross that you were doing internships in fall 2019, and that you met with him for dinner. Can you tell us about that conversation? We know already from Mr. Ross that there were some difficult things discussed, and we know what they were. How did this affect Dr. Baker?"

The two alums looked at each other for a moment, and Luis raised one eyebrow fleetingly. "Well, I think we were all surprised," he said. "Justin was sort of a model for a lot of us, working in the Senate after a terrific college career.

I'm glad he's back in the Cities working with one of our senators." He paused. "We had already talked a little about how divisive the atmosphere in DC was—somebody said that even Minnesota legislators couldn't sit down easily to talk. We had a hint of that going in. But what Justin told us was much worse than that. In the Texas offices there seemed to be a lot of hypocrisy and everything. He mentioned a couple of things that were worse than unethical, that bordered on fraud or finance violations. He honestly seemed sick about it."

Summer picked it up. "Dr. Baker was very careful about getting all of that on the table. You probably have heard we turned off our phones and Luis, here, shut off the computer from note-taking. Dr. Baker got Justin talking, and sort of helped him problem-solve right there about what his next steps might be. He was very patient about it. I think the rest of us were sort of fascinated—and not by the awful things going on. Prof was doing this terrific job of counseling right there, and I think a lot of us were taking mental notes about 'What questions should I be asking?' and 'What should I do if....?'" She stopped, sat up a little straighter, and stretched at the memory. "By the end of it, Justin summarized what he thought he ought to do, and three weeks later he was working in a different office."

Luis laughed. "And a bunch of us in the room decided that we would never work at the federal level. Ever."

Hall moved in on the key question. "Tell us about how Dr. Baker regarded all of this stuff Mr. Ross was talking about, can you?"

Harstad felt himself focusing more. Luis began. "He was very concerned. I think he was concerned as much as anything for Justin. I think—would you agree, Summer?—that Prof thought that Justin could be damaged by all this stuff. Not just 'caught up in' it, but actually *damaged* by it. You know, morally, psychologically."

Summer was nodding. "Yes, exactly." Her lips narrowed a bit, and Hall could see she was thinking hard about this. "I think Prof was angry about it, too. You could tell when he'd get real quiet and sort of slow down. He was very upset. He didn't like what he was hearing, for a lot of reasons, but maybe the most evident was what it was doing to Justin. He has always loved students."

The interview continued for a few more moments, and Hall and Harstad wrapped it up by asking the two alums *not* to talk with Dr. Baker about this. They'd be communicating with him themselves. And they did their best to make Luis and Summer feel that they'd contributed very helpfully.

And they had.

The third interview, with Patrick Bennett, began late in the day. Bennett was working in the office of the governor, which seemed an unusually prominent position for a 26-year-old, and he had worked a full day before he could meet them. When he sat down with them at the field office, he was clearly tired.

They began as they had with Reyes and Morgan, and worked their way to the November 2019 meeting. Bennett confirmed what the others had suggested, Baker's concern for Ross and his barely suppressed anger.

"Was he an angry person, typically?" Harstad asked. "Emotional?"

"No, not at all. He was often sort of…measured, if you know what I mean. He was hardly ever negative, even when discussing political issues where he disagreed. He tried to give alternative positions the benefit of the doubt, you know."

"Would you call him patriotic?"

"Very much so. In fact, I think he bleeds red, white, and blue. He's in love with this country. The only time I've ever seen him seriously angry was when his wife was killed."

"Angry? Not grieving? What happened?"

"Oh, he grieved plenty. And so did all of us. Jean was a wonderful person, and as much as people loved him as a teacher and a friend, they loved her even more. We were all stunned when she was killed."

"Can you tell us about this? We haven't heard anything about it."

"Sure." And he did, commenting on how Baker had seemed more withdrawn after her death, and then had come back strong in the fall. And that was the fall of 2019.

Harstad tried a different gambit. Almost casually, he asked, "How do you think Prof Baker feels about what's going on with this 'Month of Sundays' stuff? Really something, eh?"

Bennett shook his head. "I'm sure he's upset about what's coming out. He's an idealist, you know, about what government *can* do. He has high expectations, just as he did for all of us. And he warned us about exactly the kind of stuff that's showing up—the intrusion of money into policy-making, for instance.

"He taught us not to be naïve about this sort of thing. And still, it's disappointing. Some people need to go to jail."

"What about the whistleblower?"

"Well, I know you all want them for lawbreaking. But anybody who had Baker for class probably wants to pin a medal on these people."

A Month of Sundays

MARCH 2022

CHAPTER 39: ACCOUNTING

Tuesday, March 1
Washington, D.C.

On March 1, the President gave his State of the Union address to a packed, although mostly quiet Congress. At the top of his concerns, not surprisingly, was the Russian invasion of Ukraine, in its sixth day. After speaking forcefully about Russian intentions and the destruction already evident, and about Ukrainian courage in the face of massed forces against them, he reported that he intended to ask the Congress for aid to support these fighters. For once, he advocated something that got a standing ovation.

He moved to describe the change in the nation in the last fourteen months, including the difficulty he had faced bring legislation that could be passed with bipartisan support. As usual, he presented his hopes and a vision for the future.

And then he addressed directly the Month of Sundays group. "We still don't know who you are," he said, looking right at the cameras, "and we know what you did was wrong. You broke the law—several of them, in fact—and your example is not one we want to follow. We are still looking for you, and when we find you, we will prosecute you.

"But we also owe you a debt. Your work, whoever you are, has brought to light behavior in government, in industry and lobbying, in the whole of our political institutions, that deserves correction, and for some people, probably merits jail time. This body," he extended both hands to include the whole of the legislative audience, "has had to face up to the conduct of some members that has deserved censure. Some of our colleagues have left government in shame because we now know who bought and paid for them. Out there in state governments, similar things have happened.

"Theodore Roosevelt said in 1883 that 'The first duty of an American citizen, then, is that he shall work in politics; his second duty is that he shall do that work in a practical manner; and his third is that it shall be done in accord with the highest principles of honor and justice.' Some of our colleagues and supporters, on both sides of the aisle, have forgotten the 'practical' part. That's the part that develops laws and policies that truly benefit people. But some others have forgotten the 'honor and justice' part. Month of Sundays, thanks for reminding us.

"That doesn't mean we will stop looking for you."

The next morning, American broadcasting was jolted as several networks fired senior commentators. The chairman of the board of one network spoke on the midday news of his anger that his company had been complicit in the Russian aggression, if only passively, by its critique of

European and American support for Ukraine as it had attempted to maintain its independence.

"We have allowed ourselves, in our attempt to support a former administration and to win audience share, to become isolationist, with a mistaken belief that 'America First' meant 'America Only'. We are reluctantly admitting the truth of Dr. King's observation that 'Injustice anywhere is a threat to justice everywhere.' Dr. King went on to say that 'We are caught in an inescapable network of mutuality, tied in a single garment of destiny. Whatever affects one directly, affects all indirectly.'

"And we at our network believe that is true today. Since the January 6, 2022, documents emerged from the Month of Sundays, the board has conducted an investigation into our editorial and broadcasting practices. The investigation concluded last week with a report to the board. As a result, we have terminated the contracts of five senior commentators and several executive officers whose editorials or policies have directly or indirectly supported this aggression by Russia by their attacks on the administration. At a later time, we will provide documentary evidence that reveals that they knew full well what they were doing, and further, that they had agreed together to present a partisan perspective, rather than an accurate one. They have attempted to stir up fear and anxiety about this conflict and have downplayed issues of justice, democracy, and a country's sovereignty."

He looked down at his notes. "As a result of these actions, our network will re-commit itself to a focus on accurate news reporting over the next weeks. While we will work to rebuild our staff of commentators, we commit to a focus on intellectual and journalistic integrity that is balanced and bipartisan."

He looked up directly into the camera and the reporters in front of him. "I have no further comments on the individuals whose employment we have terminated. I expect that you should interview them."

The crowd clearly believed this was the end of the statement. A buzz was beginning when someone in the front realized that the board members with the chair, and the chair himself, hadn't moved.

"I also want to add that we are terminating the contracts of staff and the programming of several afternoon 'talk' programs, particularly those which have specialized in political advocacy. We no longer wish our network to be associated with the inaccurate and damaging characterizations of a range of political causes."

He turned a page in the folder he'd brought in. "I am also announcing today that our network will discontinue advertising for a number of companies which have supported causes supportive of Russian aggression. We are prepared to provide documentary evidence of this support in the next few days. Here are the companies whose products we will no longer advertise. We have already taken steps to return any money remaining in our accounts to these companies as of tomorrow morning. We have billed them for costs of advertising through yesterday, the last day their products will be featured on our network."

He smiled a very thin smile. "Nearly all of these companies believe in the right of corporations to decline to do business with those who do not hold their core values. We are claiming that right for ourselves, and encouraging them to sell their products through other means. They won't be doing it with us. We are prepared to go to court if necessary."

A few blocks away, a similar set of announcements was being made. Another network board chair announced termination of three commentators. "We've determined that these individuals have supported—in a couple of cases, pretty directly—domestic violence that has led to anarchy, to bloodshed, to serious injuries, and to property damage. They have helped create a climate in which such behavior was tolerated, and they have excused the perpetrators. There'll be a news story about this handled by our news division beginning on Monday of next week. We are also terminating our relationship with five advertisers who funded groups that have been associated with 'anti-fascist'"—he air-quoted this—"groups in several states. In some cases, their funding was directly linked to actions that resulted in property destruction and personal injury. These actions will also be part of our documentary next week, and we will provide internal memos and emails confirming what they did. We are also forwarding all of this to the Department of Justice." Reporters in the room were looking around at each other, and whispering was rising in volume.

"Some of our senior executive officers are also leaving their positions, effective tomorrow morning." The room suddenly got very quiet. "I'll have a list for you in the morning. We have determined that they and the commentators involved have been inappropriately seeking to manipulate public perception of the clashes going on over the last eighteen months in several cities. Much of this was calculated to create audience interest and strengthen market share; some of it was deliberately planned to polarize Americans in the interest of increased revenue from advertisers."

"Once upon a time the great networks of our country identified with that country. ABC was the *American Broadcasting Company;* CBS was the *Columbia Broadcasting System;* NBC was the *National Broadcasting Company.* But some of our networks have failed to represent our nation honestly and faithfully either to ourselves or to others."

He took his reading glasses off, standing at the podium, and looked right into the cameras. "I don't know who you are, Month of Sundays group, but we appreciate what you have done to call our people and our network to account. It's never pleasant being wrong, but we have a chance to do better. Thank you. Good afternoon, friends." And he walked away.

CHAPTER 40: INTRUSION

Monday, March 7
Eastern Washington

Flores and Myers' team showed up at Baker's cabin at 6 in the morning, March 7th, a Monday. They had been long delayed, but getting COVID in the middle of the assignment was just part of the delay. For Jimmy, his case had meant his whole family was quarantined, and once the school-aged kids were done, his wife felt comfortable getting sick herself. The month they were out hadn't been wasted. Jimmy had been online looking at everyone's accounts, finding a way in, assessing the homes and work networks of each of them.

They had already been at Baker's Minneapolis home, been through it, and had found nothing beyond information about where he was, near Newport, Washington.

At Baker's cabin, they had made their way in quietly from the road, leaving their car fifty feet up the dirt and gravel inside the middle gate after cutting the lock and closing the gate again. They hiked in through the dawn-lit woods. Jimmy had sent a small drone ahead—they could see Baker's house, however well concealed, on recent satellite photos—and ten minutes of looking made them think Baker wasn't home. In fact, Baker had spent the weekend in Spokane with family, and this seemed ideal. They intended an invisible break-in, a quiet opportunity to go through the house, and an equally noiseless departure. Their goal was anonymity.

They were used to the eastern and northern forests, not the Pacific Northwest. Their Colorado "visit" had actually been suburban, in Colorado Springs. The last four break-ins they'd done, spread out across the country, had gotten them nothing, and they had two more after Baker's place, and nowhere had they run into obstacles. This was certainly different, though. They weren't sneaking through a neighborhood or blending in on a college campus. Baker's property had been logged a century earlier, and then the new growth had suffered a forest fire, decades ago. That meant the underbrush, on the west side of a range of the Rockies, was a tangle of bushes, half-grown pine and spruce, and impenetrable for someone wanting to be quiet. Baker liked it that way. His visitors didn't. The damp ground from snowmelt packed sand and mud onto their boots, and they'd leave tracks everywhere.

There was another difference from the other "intrusions." For a change, Jimmy had gotten nowhere with hacking Baker's accounts, because they weren't there or they were very well concealed. They knew he had a fiber optic line, because they'd hacked the utility companies, including his security system with its connection to the sheriff's office. Jimmy had a workaround for that. They could see Baker's wireless setup because his router was clearly visible on his network. Because they didn't want to hack the line physically, Mark was carrying a small laptop, Jimmy's gear, and a range of cameras and microphones with which they could seed the house. A day or two, and they'd have the take from Baker's computers, as well as the chance to download directly from what he had in the house itself.

They decided to approach the cabin with more discipline than it might have warranted on the surface. The "missing" internet traffic was a puzzle. They'd split up a hundred yards before the meadow, one going north down into the track along the marsh, below the level of the meadow and so invisible, one cutting across the middle road to come in from the western woods, and one approaching through the trees across the meadow.

Ed, coming in from the west, glanced into the garage, and saw that Baker's Subaru was gone. He gestured to the others. Jimmy confirmed with an infrared scanner that no one appeared to be home—everything showed "cool"— and then they gathered near the front door. They smiled at the security system labels on the front and back door, although they took seriously the magnetic sensors on the windows and doors. Jimmy could prevent any notification to the outside, but they'd prefer not to have sirens or alarms going off. Even with the nearest neighbor a half-mile away, it might be heard.

They weren't suspecting the trail cameras Baker had set up under the branches of several spruce, nor the computerized notification that meant he'd know someone was there, and that he could see them. And they didn't know that Baker's network was hardwired ethernet on a separate line and not connected to the wireless router at all.

"We'll be out of here before anyone can get here," Ed said. "We're a couple of miles from town, and no sheriff is going to want to get up here through the gate, if it's locked. Jimmy, open the door, please."

Jimmy stripped off his gloves, unzipped his coat pocket, and pulled out a powered lock pick, a Multipick "Kronos," something like a silver light saber with a three-inch probe replacing the blade. He began to kneel down on the mat, one hand holding a tensioner, one the power tool. As his right knee touched the mat, he cried out as though stung, dropped the pick on the concrete, and fell over, clutching his knee with both hands. He lay on the concrete porch, holding his bent leg rigidly. The older man hovered over him.

"What happened?"

"Ed, something was on the mat—it's like a knife, right into my knee!" He held himself protectively, and the older man couldn't get near enough to look.

"Are you bleeding?"

"No, but the damn thing is in my knee—what'll happen if I straighten out my leg?"

The older man stood up and cursed violently and steadily for twenty seconds. Mark had started to think about how they were going to get him down the hill. He was carefully kneeling next to the locksmith.

Lights on the porch flicked on, and the older man flipped open his coat with one hand, the other hand holding the Beretta. He looked outward into the trees. Suddenly a blue-white light flashed on from the door.

"This is the owner," they heard. And just inside the front door, one of the sidelights had a live picture on a small screen. "I'm not home. We're live, so I can see you. I'm sorry about your injury. You were warned. I want you to know that I've notified the sheriff in Newport, and he'll be there in a few minutes. You've been on hard-wired trail cameras for the past half hour. Jimmy, I don't recommend straightening out the leg, because the needle I embedded in the rug will break. That'll mean that surgery will last longer, and your ability to walk normally will be compromised. And there's one other thing," he added, face close to the screen. "Close your eyes, please—that's a recommendation." The older man looked around, alarmed, head swiveling to find a threat. "Hey, I mean it! Shut your eyes!"

The older man stepped off the porch, out of the line of sight of the camera. A series of small "pop!" sounds, lasting five seconds or so, filled the air. Jimmy felt something wet on his face and hands, where he held his knee. Instantly, his skin was burning. Mark, kneeling over him, by having his face down had missed most of it, but was starting to cough with every breath. The older man was swearing again, wiping his face, blinded by tears.

"About half of that was pepper spray in paintballs," the voice said. "The other half was a fluorescent green dye that will show up under blacklight. It'll wash off your clothes, if you use the right chemicals. In the meantime, the sheriff won't have any trouble identifying you. Hang tight. He'll be there soon, and I've notified him that Jimmy will need a hospital visit."

"So why are you here, guys? And who do you work for?" He didn't really expect a response, though it was only polite to ask.

Ten long minutes later the Newport police appeared, in a year-old Ford Police Interceptor Sedan and a newer Ford Police Interceptor Utility, lights bouncing along the west drive up to the meadow, and then sweeping across the three of them, nearly immobilized by the pepper spray.

"Let's go, gentlemen," Deputy Sheriff Jesus Castillo said. "Hands out. Jimmy Davis?" Jimmy grunted, swearing. "We heard you need the hospital, and I'll let you keep your cuffs on in front of you. Mr. Clement and Mr. Goldhammer, turn around, hands behind your back. I think you know the drill." His partner, standing behind the open door of the Utility, had been covering them with a shotgun as they complied. Once they'd been cuffed, Castillo searched them carefully, bagging items as he went. Ed's Beretta and a spare magazine went in a bag by themselves, as did the knives each one carried. The lockpick and attachments were carefully bagged. Mark's backpack slid into an oversize garbage bag and went in the trunk. Jimmy was still on the ground as the deputy searched him, turning him over gently to pull a handgun from his belt holster in the small of his back. Ed looked at him, surprised. One of the other two deputies had padded and tied Jimmy's lower leg so it couldn't move, and the two officers got him into the back seat of the Utility.

Castillo noticed that none of them carried identification or cell phones.

"We'll talk when we get to the station, and you can make your telephone calls." He pointed them to the Interceptor Sedan, and shut the door carefully when they were in. He glanced at Ellen, his partner and a few years senior to him. "What do you think? Check the car at the gate?"

And so, without much trouble, they came upon the team's wallets, cell phones, and contact information. And cash. Lots of it. After some discussion, they called a wrecker from town, loaded it on the back, and parked it in the city garage behind a chain-link fence at the police station. She and Castillo would spend some time on it later. They would also call the FBI, because that much cash probably meant something.

CHAPTER 41: CATCH AND RELEASE

Tuesday, March 8
Newport, Washington

Baker had returned to the cabin from Spokane, late in the day of the attempted break-in, and with the permission of the sheriff's office had cleaned up the front porch. He had mixed up some heavy-duty cleaner in a spray bottle, pulled out the hose from the garage winter storage, hooked it up to his outside faucet, screwed the spray bottle on, and had gone at it for a half hour, scrubbing the concrete porch slab as well as the siding, soffit, and fascia. *The paintballs had really done the job*, he thought, satisfied. A final rinse, drying the windows off with some clean shop rags, and he was done. Since the trio had never gotten into the building, the sheriff's office figured they didn't need to, either.

Now on Tuesday morning, the three men weren't saying much at all, beyond calling a Spokane lawyer who'd be there in the afternoon when they were arraigned. They were facing misdemeanor charges, first for criminal trespass in the second degree and then a gross misdemeanor for possession of burglary tools. Depending on the way the investigation came out, a conspiracy charge might be added. Because Ed had drawn a handgun when the lights went on, the pistol would be confiscated, and since he couldn't show that he had a carry pistol license, he faced an automatic fine.

Weeks ago, Baker had finished his plan to welcome visitors, and had executed it over the last three days before the weekend. There seemed to be more electronic surveillance out there, he thought. A little thoroughgoing ruthlessness was in order. He was down to one phone, for instance, and while Dave, Eunice, and Leroy were still in the basement, their hard drives had actually been changed out and were innocuous. Dave still watched over the trail cameras, but Eunice and Leroy now had book and article manuscripts that appeared when he booted up. Of course, Leroy's manuscript was his research on the "Month of Sundays" project and its impact on American politics, which he figured was reason enough for people like Ed, Jimmy, and Mark to come after him. But the manuscript began with the release of the first package to the newspapers, and was carefully constructed to reflect actual distribution. Back in November, he'd even applied to his dean for permission to change the announced sabbatical project to this one, and had the confirmation letter filed. The email exchange was impeccable.

His trip to Spokane had been an opportunity to shred, torch, crush, and discard pretty much everything related to the project. USB drives and SSD cards from the computers had literally been shredded in an industrial recycler. The hard drives had been disassembled and crushed. Paper had been shredded and then used to start a fire in his brother's shop stove, warming the building for an hour or so. Once the ashes were stirred and the fire renewed, there was nothing left. What remained were a half dozen telephone numbers, URLs he'd memorized, and a dozen or so passwords. And they were all in his head, and nowhere else.

Even all the distribution computers he'd used out there, spread out across the country, had been reformatted down to bare operating systems, and the drives scrubbed. *This message will self-destruct in five seconds, Mr. Phelps,* he thought.

As requested, Baker showed up at the District Court building in the southwest corner of Newport, at 1 p.m. Deputy Sheriff Castillo met him in the waiting area of the office, and escorted him to an interview room for questioning and for a statement.

"Thank you for coming in, Professor," Castillo began. "We were pretty surprised to get your call yesterday, but I have to say you really handed us what we needed to make a good arrest. And how the *hell* did you come up with that stuff?"

"Well," Baker began, "I intended to use my trail cameras more for watching for deer and turkeys, but my brother-in-law used to own the property, and every fall and spring he had problems with break-ins and poaching. I thought they might help, especially since I was going to live out there."

"They did help, didn't they? And you were set up to monitor them remotely?"

"I didn't plan to be on the property all the time, but with the house, the garage, and another vehicle up there I wanted to watch out for theft. I've never been satisfied with wireless networks by themselves, so I actually hardwired the trail cameras with ethernet cable. The 'anti-theft deterrent' paintballs were a later addition—you know the Pepperball ads? I made sure they were legal before I installed them. I broke them down, took out the powder, and made up my own launcher. I tried to give people fair warning—don't approach my house.

"Is there anything you can tell me about the three guys who tried to break in?" Baker finished. "And how is the guy who was injured? I can't imagine what they wanted. I'm a retired college professor working on a book, after all."

Castillo grimaced. "They aren't saying much of anything, and they'll have a lawyer coming up from Spokane in"—he glanced at his watch—"another hour. We plan to arraign them pretty quick after that. Once we got 'Jimmy' into the hospital, the doctor got the needle out in one piece, so he'll be sore, but he'll walk okay. They are all a little hot at your defense system. That man-trap *might* have been a little extreme on your part, by the way. Just sayin'." He smiled, then glanced down at his notes. "It's not a secret that what we have are misdemeanors, here. Unless there's a serious problem, they'll be offered bail, and they could be out by suppertime. They could even plead guilty, agree to pay a fine, and be on their way. The judge can decide that. They didn't actually break in, so there's no felony. They had burglary tools, which is the more serious charge, a gross misdemeanor. Because all their wallets were down in their car, the guy named Ed didn't have a pistol carry license on him, and so that's another charge. We've confiscated the two handguns."

He looked up at Baker. "We also found about $40,000 in cash in their trunk. And they won't talk about it. That got us wondering if these were guys hired by someone else to break in to your place, which would make it conspiracy. They won't talk about that, either. We'll see." He shuffled his notes together. "Are you planning to be around? This might go to trial, and if it does, we'll need your testimony, as well as the video you sent us."

"I'm not planning to go anywhere for several months, except maybe down to Spokane to visit family and get groceries. I just retired, and I have this book project I'm trying to finish."

Castillo nodded, and stood up. He paused. "There are some other folks here who'd like to talk with you. Can I send them in?"

Baker looked up at him, raised his eyebrows, spread his hands, and said, "Sure." Castillo nodded, and moved to the door.

Devon Cook stepped into the interview room, with Adrian Davis behind him. Castillo gestured to the chairs opposite Baker at the interview table, then waved to Baker and left the room.

Cook, still standing, reached across the table to shake Baker's hand, and Baker stood up. "Professor, I'm Devon Cook, a special agent of the Federal Bureau of Investigation, specializing in cybercrime. This is my associate from Seattle, special agent Adrian Davis." Baker shook hands with each as they sat down.

"I'm curious about why you're here," Baker said, "just like I'm curious about why three guys tried to break in to my house. I assume they're related?"

"Yes, they are," Davis said. "We've actually been watching these guys for the last two months. They've broken into other houses scattered across the country, and we've kept tabs on them." He was watching Baker's attention shift and his eyes widen as he leaned back a little.

"Can you tell me what this is about, or is this the point at which you say, 'We're asking the questions here'?" Baker smiled.

Cook responded with an answering smile. "Can you tell us about your research project, what you're working on? Because we think that's their interest."

Baker considered for a minute, then began. "Oh, I get it. The 'Month of Sundays' thing. That explains your cybercrime connection. Well, I moved into retirement this year, and started what they call a 'terminal sabbatical.' That means the college will pay me for a year to work on a project, and I don't have to teach. They decided it was a good way to ease me off the payroll with a bonus. Who wouldn't want free time while getting paid? They save some money, get a newer, younger, *cheaper* faculty member, and I get a good going-away present." They could see he was smiling, and Cook thought, *Okay, looks like no sting in that line. Maybe not bitter.*

"When all of this 'Month of Sundays' stuff started, I was fascinated. I had a lot of my students in political science serve as interns in D.C. over the last ten years or so. The 'Washington Study Program,' I called it. They were right in the middle of the 'Washington underworld,' I guess you'd say. So, I was more than interested when all of this stuff started coming out. I wondered what the public would think." *Increasingly animated,* Cook thought. *Yeah, he's a teacher.*

"Once the President did that press conference, I thought about shifting my focus, and making that my sabbatical project. The dean agreed, so I got permission to resubmit my proposal, and it was approved. As a result, I've been watching things pretty carefully and starting to work on a first draft based on the last few months. Naturally, I can't finish it until sometime this fall. I expect the real effects won't be known until after the election in November, right? Anyway, that's it."

"Are you researching who might be responsible?" Davis asked. "Any clues on that?"

"Not a one," said Baker. "And I don't care, really," he shrugged. "I'm a political scientist, and it looks to me like someone with a lot more technical skills than I have is responsible. I do people, not machines." He paused, and then said, "I will say that whoever *put the packages together* must be pretty interesting as a researcher. I'm looking at the effect of the documents on people, in particular what they'll mean for democracy. In fact, I did wonder if this was some sort of social psychology experiment."

Davis smiled. "That seems a little too academic for us. We're more concerned with enforcing the law, and whoever did it broke a bunch of them. How have you been gathering your information?"

"Well, I've worked from what the newspapers put out, first. I put some feelers out to friends in some of the states who got packages, and they sent me the zipped files they'd gotten. It looks like I haven't gotten all of them, though—I heard about that uproar in Wyoming, but haven't seen anything about why. Now that the papers are assembling all the state mailings on a website, I hope I can look at them all."

"Who did you contact to get some of the documents? Can you give us some names?"

"Sure," Baker said. "I'll have to get them from home. I don't have a list in my head or on my phone."

"Can you get that to us today?" Cook asked. Baker nodded. "Email it to us, can you? Here's my card."

"By the way," Davis chuckled, "I don't know if we're happy with you catching these guys or not. We think they've got a list of people they're looking at, and you may have put a stop to it. We're sort of exploiting them to see if we can find who the 'MOS Group'"—he air-quoted—"really are."

"Sorry about stopping them, but not really," smiled Baker. "Nobody needs a break-in. Good luck. Glad it's your problem and not mine." He cocked his head, looked at Davis, and said, "Well, you know, I'm from Minnesota, and you could do like we do up there." Davis's eyebrows went up. "Catch and release, you know. Take the barb off the hook, and put them back in the lake." He smiled and sat back.

Cook glanced at Davis, and they stood, as did Baker, and shook hands again. "Wish you well, Professor," Cook said, "and I'm looking forward to your book." As they opened the door and stepped out, Castillo waved to Baker.

"Time to go, Prof. Stick around, eh?"

"Sure," said Baker. He walked to the door, stretched in the spring sunshine, and headed back to the cabin in the Subaru.

And then used a scanner casually to walk through the barn, and then to go over the Subaru very carefully once it was in the garage. And check the whole house for wired and wireless transmitters, cameras, and recording devices. At night, he'd look for infrared. He wondered if, like Ed, Jimmy, and Mark, he was being given just enough line, and then Cook or someone like her would reel him in.

CHAPTER 42: THINGS UNSEEN

Moments later

Davis looked at Cook as they watched Baker drive away. "So, he thinks we ought to look for someone *'with a lot more technical skills,'* huh?"

Cook smiled a little crookedly. "Noticed that, did you? I think the professor might have had some help, but he is a seriously good candidate for the 'bomb-maker,' isn't he? I wonder if he realized that that elaborate a man-trap is like a neon sign turned on. You don't go to that much trouble unless there's something there. Still, I'd prefer not to have to get a search warrant for a place that I bet is now spotless. He strikes me as pretty careful. I think we might take him up on his 'catch and release,' though, don't you? And then monitor our three stooges and what they say to their bosses in D.C. Enough of that. Tell me your impressions of the good Dr Baker."

Davis nodded in agreement. "I don't want you to duck my question. What you haven't told me yet is how you knew they'd be coming here, and who they'd be after. How did we find out about them in the first place?"

"Later," Cook nodded, as they headed toward Castillo. "Deputy, what is the plan for our out-of-town folks here?"

"Well, there's a hearing with the judge in less than half an hour. We'll present evidence, and then see what the judge has to say. Depending on how eager they are to be out of town, or how stubborn they are, we could be done in an hour. They're going to pay some fines, if nothing else, but if they can do that in cash, we can escort them out of town by nightfall."

"Is there a way to watch the courtroom without being present?" Cook asked.

"Yes, we had to put in a streaming camera and microphones when the COVID thing hit. We just went back to live hearings a week or so ago. You don't want them to know the FBI is looking at them?"

"Exactly, and Agent Davis and I sort of stand out in this company."

"You're not alone. A Mexican-American deputy and two black FBI agents aren't exactly your typical Pend Oreille County residents. Well, let me show you to a room where you can watch." He gestured down the hall. They got coffee on the way.

"Okay, Agent Davis," he said as they shared the half-and-half into the to-go cups. "Baker. Talk."

"Did you notice his wedding ring? Hall and Harstad said his wife died three years ago. Does he have kids? Where are they? What's his specialty in Political Science? And why aren't we asking these questions? Are we so focused on our own problem that we're missing things about people?"

Cook blinked at the rapid-fire questions. "Uh. Well, you're right. Go get the answers. Talk with Harstad and Hall. They met with his students. I think they know what punches his buttons."

Their attorney is smooth, Cook reflected, as she watched the video feed. *Appropriately deferential, and their hangdog looks don't hurt. Neither do Jimmy's bandages and crutches.*

The hearing ended after a half hour, with a five-minute tongue-lashing from the magistrate, fines paid in cash, and directions to be out of the county by sunset. Cook was pleased that the magistrate and the Pend Oreille police went along with their request. What the trio didn't know, although Cook thought they might have suspected, was that Cook and Davis had a team plant tracking devices in their rental car, hacked the electronics to install a video feed in the rear-view mirror, and planted small trackers in their luggage. All of it was passive, for now. The video feed went to a recorder-on-a-chip installed under the car's battery and powered by a tap so dusty it looked like OEM equipment.

Cook wasn't surprised to see the attorney walk out with the threesome and, once away from the building, hand Ed an oversize envelope. The attorney turned, waved his hand to them as he walked away, and climbed into his car, headed for Spokane. As the three gathered together, Ed opened the envelope, looked at the contents, shook his head, and clearly looked defeated. One of the deputies had parked their car close to the building, and Ed got his keys out, gesturing to the others. They checked the trunk, verified the contents, and climbed in, giving Jimmy the back so he could stretch out.

"Well, that was just dandy," Cook heard Ed begin. "Okay, phones off. Strip them. We'll talk later."

Ed started the car, and they headed south to Spokane in silence.

"About what you expected?" Davis asked, next to Cook. "Yeah, they're professionals. Dump the phones, regroup, plan for the next one."

"I don't think so, Adrian. I think they're pretty sure it's the Professor, and that's my guess what gets reported. We'll see what happens next."

"Okay, but let's go back to my question. How did you guess they'd turn up here? How do we even know about them in the first place?"

Cook tossed her empty coffee cup in the trash, gestured to the door, and they walked out together. "We have someone feeding them information, someone in our group that they think is working for them. That person's actually working for us, a double agent, if you will. That someone came to me months ago and told me she was being recruited, and I told her to go ahead. This way, we get their take and we feed them what we want them to know from our side. And we get to hear about their findings, too."

"And you kept this quiet from all of us?" Davis's voice sounded a little irritated.

"Yes, and you're only the fourth person who knows about it," Cook answered. She could see that the steam was going out of him as he realized that he was really on the deep inside of whatever Cook was doing.

Cook had a team monitoring the take from the car, all the way to Spokane. In fact, she had two teams, one in a U-Haul cargo van that kept up with Ed's car, and one that met them near the city limits, passing the van and Ed and staying just above the speed limit all the way to town. The trio turned in the rental at the airport and picked up another, driving back into Spokane and stopping for the evening at a hotel on the west side of town. A team of two technicians dressed as company mechanics at the airport stripped the electronics out of the rental in twenty minutes, and they were gone.

Ed, Jimmy, and Mark might have been invisible, electronically. They had supper at The Old Spaghetti Factory, where the background buzz was loud enough to conceal any conversation. After dinner, with Jimmy still on crutches, they went back to their motel, and were clearly getting ready to leave the next day. Cook's airport observer saw them board a Delta flight for Seattle, on their way to Washington, D.C., at 5:30 in the morning; they would arrive at 4:30 or so that night. *God,* Cook marveled, *Spokane does suck as a place to fly out of. Long, long day.*

CHAPTER 43: WATERFALL

Friday, March 11
Newport, Washington

Early Friday morning, Baker sent an email to what looked like a friend in Newberg, Oregon, a historian who worked at another small religious college. He'd also copied another friend, someone who worked at a similar college in Pennsylvania. The message was innocuous enough, a greeting and a request for their perspective on the current Month of Sundays response around the country. Totally legitimate.

The email triggered an automated response in each of his friends' computers, however, and both of the computers sent a command to *other* computers, one in Fresno, California, and one in Toccoa, Georgia—where other religious colleges were located. These contacted computers at other such colleges in every region of the country. It was like nuclear fission: a couple of lone neutrons out there, wholly innocent, striking an atom in just the right way, and suddenly, a cascade. A waterfall of documents suddenly began, so that every remaining state's files began going out to voters.

Baker had never intended to keep the leisurely pace he'd promised at the beginning. At some point, he knew he'd either be caught or his methods discovered. And while being arrested and "disappeared" wouldn't be good, he did intend to see the job through to the end. And so he'd figured, why not do the unexpected? Use his contacts as a faculty member and respected political science professor—and a network of friends developed over forty years—to upload documents and then send them on their way, emerging from an entirely unexpected direction. The most conservative educational institutions in the country were about to deliver the equivalent of a blind-side block to legislative corruption.

It had taken time, but he had managed to upload the documents and the address lists in compressed form to the institutional databases and records computers of the colleges involved. The college databases—Enterprise Resource Products, ERPs, were enormous, used for schedules, payroll, faculty contracts, student records, donor accounts, maintenance schedules, online catalogs and historical records and on and on. He had counted on no one actually noticing that the databases—Ellucian's Banner, Oracle's Student Cloud, Mentis, Einstein, STARS—were already enormously bloated. A little extra wouldn't even matter. He stuck the documents in with the older catalogs in the database. Having registrars as friends had made it easier to discover that most of the ERT systems had known "back doors" that could get you into the system. One email to a friend, and the friend's computer contacted the registrar's office, and they were off to the races.

And his "deposits" hadn't been noticed. He'd sent his email at midnight, and in two hours, MOS had done its job. He hoped Cook and her team were well rested. He had just dumped a load of ball bearings across the dance floor.

And he figured that he might as well do the "blow-off," the closing act of the strip-tease, like the end of the Fourth of July fireworks show. At the end, there'd be nothing left to find.

Across the country in D.C., the phones and emails were flooding in. Cook, still in Spokane, was convinced that the MOS group would be releasing the North Carolina files over the weekend, and had alerted agents and others in Charlotte to notify him. The cyber teams were gearing up to discover how MOS would do the release *this* time. Cook was paying special attention to anything radiating out of northeastern Washington, increasingly confident that Baker was her man. But they weren't prepared in the least for the waterfall.

Seventeen states: North Carolina, North Dakota, Nevada, New Hampshire, New York, Ohio, Oklahoma, Oregon, Pennsylvania, Rhode Island, South Carolina, South Dakota, Utah, Virginia, Vermont, Washington, and Wisconsin.

Of course, Cook had had the Wisconsin files since Watson had contacted them in November, but they hadn't been released generally. And now, everything *else* was out there.

CHAPTER 44: CONSEQUENCES

Saturday, March 12
The Dakotas, Ohio, Oregon, Pennsylvania

On the world scene, Baker observed, things were getting more difficult all the time. Russia's invasion of Ukraine was stalling, but it still looked as though Putin could bring overwhelming force to bear. COVID was still an enormous problem, with renewed cases in China, even as the United States seemed exhausted and unwilling to go further. Mask mandates were in disrepute. Leaked information from the January 6th hearings in the House continued to roil the water politically, even as House members and Senators threatened to ignore subpoenas. Americans were fighting higher gas prices. Inflation was ramping up. And the Republican and Democratic National Committees were stuck on the same messages they had been for two years, in the vain hope that someone would overlook the name-calling, the fear-mongering, the anger and the outrage.

And then the document dump increased the tempo. Protests began Saturday morning in half a dozen states. In South Dakota, where the electorate was heavily influenced by the former president, the only senator standing for re-election was a Trump opponent. Members of the party had attacked him in January when he announced a re-election campaign. Suddenly in Sioux Falls there was a rally for him Saturday evening as *Argus-Leader* subscribers discovered how they'd been lied to by the state and national party leaders. The governor, who opposed statewide mandates on the COVID shutdowns, quietly retracted some of her statements when interviewed, acknowledging that she had been influenced by her party's leaders, and had not pressed South Dakotans for vaccinations. By March, fewer than two-thirds had completed their vaccinations, and only 50% of the 18-64 population had gotten the free medication. Infection rates were rising again.

North Dakota wasn't a lot different. The 2020 explosion of COVID across the state, thanks to the state leadership failures regarding contact tracing, stay-at-home orders, or mask mandates, resulted in hospitalizations and deaths. The state's trust in "personal responsibility," in the face of known facts about the disease, had failed. And now it was becoming clear that Dakotans had been lied to and misled. Farmers just starting their plowing-planting cycle took time off to write their legislators. On Monday, some in the middle of the state drove into Bismarck, walked into government offices, and demanded to talk to their representatives. Some were pretty hot, and since North Dakota is a "constitutional carry" state, and many of these visitors wore openly visible holsters, office workers responded. With caution and politeness.

Baker wondered how "Ms. Mace" and "Ms. Nine Millimeter" would respond when they read about how the former president's trade policies had damaged American agriculture in Washington State, and how *the administration had known that this would happen.*

In Ohio, he noticed, a prominent conservative congressman had been awakened at 2 a.m. Saturday after the documents had been dumped, to find his house surrounded by hundreds of his constituents. Some of them were carrying firearms, and many more were carrying signs demanding his resignation. The mayor of the town was in the crowd, and once he'd seen the bedroom light come on had politely knocked at the front door. The congressman greeted him in robe and slippers.

From that point, the television version, shot with a long lens and a shotgun microphone, Baker guessed, filled in the rest.

"Good morning, sir," the mayor began, politely taking off his hat as he stepped onto the porch. He did not go into the house, though the congressman waved him in. The mayor held the storm door open as the congressman peered around the edge of the front door in the hard light of cameras. "We're sorry to wake you up, but the police and I figured we'd better get here as soon as we could."

"The police! Can you tell me what this is about?" the congressman asked, eyes focused over the mayor's shoulder at the crowd, just a few yards outside his front hedge.

"Well, that Month of Sundays group dumped the Ohio state documents—with a bunch of others—at midnight. We've been reading your interactions with the former president and with some others in Congress. Looks a little shady there, sir. You might be thinking about a statement, come morning. I've asked the police to stay throughout the night, in case something gets out of hand."

The congressman's eyes noticeably widened, Baker saw, even though the television camera was at the other end of the sidewalk. His smile, responding to the mayor, seemed a little uncertain. "Well," the microphone picked up, and what sounded like a forced laugh, "thanks! I guess I'd better go have a look at my email! I appreciate your concern!"

"Just don't look for my vote ever again, sir. You're a bloody idiot," the mayor said, putting his hat back on. He turned his back, stepped away from the storm door, and walked down the steps out to the street. He picked up a bullhorn from the police chief, and addressed the crowd.

Late in the day, the congressman posted his resignation on his official website. Although he was among the most combative representatives in the House, the published materials left him no choice. You don't ask for a pardon if you're not guilty of something.

Oregon had been a different story. The state was seriously divided between the very conservative "drylands" of interior Oregon and the very liberal coastal counties. Nonetheless, the failure of legislative leadership in Oregon on both sides of the state had given "unaffiliated" voters—the largest group, larger even than Democrats from the populous "wetlands" west of the Cascades—a bump in membership. Revelations of the cowardice of state and national leaders about the Portland riots, and revelations of the racism driving Republicans in the east meant everyone was on edge. When the roots of the "Greater Idaho Movement" were examined—the proposal to have conservative eastern Oregon counties join Idaho—hard questions were being asked. Baker, watching from Newport on Leroy, expected the legislature to be called back into session within a week.

Pennsylvania, one of the most contested states in the country in 2020, was ramping up a Republican primary for the Senate seat held by a retiring Republican. The former president had already made his pick, and was actively sponsoring someone. After the Pennsylvania document release, several candidates withdrew their names, and the Trump-endorsed candidate was among them. *Pretty much only moderates and crazy people left,* Baker realized. *Well, that'll be interesting.*

Time to pack it up, Baker thought. *Someone's likely to come looking. If you push them, they push back.* He took two hours, packed three coolers with the rest of the food in the fridge and freezer, made sure his files were backed up to a portable drive, and closed up the house. Shut off the hot water heater, flip the breaker for the well, draw the curtains. On the way out, he put a slow charger on the battery on the pickup, safely stowed in the garage, and activated all the security systems with a half-hour delay to get him out the gate and locked up.

When he got to Newport, he called Deputy Castillo to let him know he was headed for Spokane, and gave him a contact number. He also told him where he might find a key.

Castillo called someone else afterward.

CHAPTER 45: DEBRIEF

Monday-Thursday, March 14-17
Washington, D.C.
Newport, Washington

Back in Washington, Flores and Myers at the USCC found themselves as overwhelmed as the men and women at Justice. In his worst dreams, Flores had thought it might all come down at once. He and Myers were both pretty sure by now that Baker, out there in northeastern Washington, was their guy. The anomalies just made him stand out. *Here's a guy who's a college professor who just drops off the map,* Flores had argued, *somebody who's used email and web searches and web publication for years, and he's suddenly not there. Here's a guy who moves without notice from Minneapolis to the North Woods, to a house no one knows is there, and who boobytraps it so intruders end up sore and sorry. And who has the police practically on call when intruders show up. And he's a guy who has had access for years, through his interns, to representatives and senators.*

Flores's debrief of Ed, Jimmy, and Mark had been thorough, professional, and reassuring. He was giving them three months off, he said, because they needed it. They'd done the job he'd hired them for, and some R and R was the right thing to do. And he told them they were still on the payroll, because he'd have other jobs. He'd talked them down with his quiet professionalism, talked them down from their fury at being caught by someone as innocuous as a political science professor on sabbatical.

And Flores told them there would be an accounting, and he would see to it. But he wanted them out of the way, and visibly alibied, when it happened.

When Myers and Flores reported in to "higher," they brought with them all they knew, and all they suspected.

The first question for them wasn't a surprise. "How exposed is our work with legislators?"

Myers responded honestly. "It may take a while for people to put it together, but if you look across all the state packages, and if you look at our organization's documents, pretty much everything we've recommended to legislators over the years is there."

Flores added, "It might not take any length of time at all. There are text-comparison programs out there for free. All you have to do is input a key text—like something from our office—and tell the program to find every one like it that's sitting on your hard drive—and it will give you page and line numbers. If that happens, it'll be pretty obvious."

"Higher" wasn't ready for that answer. "Do you have any recommendations from this investigation?"

Myers, glancing at Flores, took the lead. "We've already discussed recommendations about technology security with Mr. Gray, and had other discussions with the senior IT tech."

"One of our strengths, gentlemen," "Higher" commented, leaning on his elbows at the end of the conference table, "is that we've been able to use technology like this to our advantage. We're able to email people, to customize our appeals to them, to research the issues in their districts, to connect the strengths of our policies to their concerns. You know all this. Are you really telling us that we're going to have to reinvent ourselves *without* this technology? Because our effectiveness, as well as our ability to demonstrate to our supporters that we can make positive change, are both going to be affected."

"Yes, sir, that's exactly what we're saying. At least for now." Flores ran his hand through his hair, sweeping it back in frustration. "Sir, this is likely to change. People will get over this, because we and everyone else want to get beyond this and get back to business as usual. But right now, people are alarmed, and we don't want to get this stirred up any more than it is. If you could back away for six months from anything substantive—just maintain the relationships you have, and then sort it out after six months—you might be able to pick up exactly where we were."

"In six months," "Higher" growled, "the President will have his agenda passed, because the House and the Senate will swing his way. It'll be years before we can get the direction shifted."

"Yes, sir, probably so. But that's what Mr. Flores and I are recommending."

"Of course, sir," Flores followed up, "we are also recommending some consequences for the person who's responsible for all this. We'll need some authorizations."

"Talk with Mr. Gray on that."

In the end, they agreed that they'd burn him out to make a point.

It wasn't like fires hadn't happened before, Flores suggested. Back in 1973, the property had been blackened by an arsonist who, on a hot day, had pulled up to each of the three gates on the road and had tossed in what amounted to a Molotov cocktail. The fire had lasted for days, and burned most of the 120 acres. Very few trees had survived west of the marsh, and although the fire had burned partway up one of the hills, the backdrop to the cabin, the eastern mountain had been untouched. It became a footnote that year, because the arsonist had kept on firebombing through the county. The last big fire that had hit Pend Oreille County was in 1910, the Big One that had burned 3 million acres across northern Washington right into western Montana. Flores shared the story from *The Newport Miner*, a big story back in 1973, as the Forest Service was finally wrapping up the fire.

Just pure meanness, in 1973, lighting fires up along the road for several miles. They never caught the arsonist. It had taken Baker's in-laws five years to replant the forest, helped by volunteers from the Boy Scouts and thousands of free pine seedlings from the Forest Service.

Myers and Flores wanted to be much more targeted, sending a message to Baker that would hurt a lot and leave them entirely in the clear. Ed, Jimmy, and Mark's debriefing had made them aware of Baker's security, and Myers considered it a sporting challenge to find, disable, and evade his trail cameras and everything else. He didn't intend to go in the house, just firebomb it and the garage, coming in and going out over the northeastern hills, walking along Exposure Creek. He'd leave a pickup and a kayak at the landing at Marshall Lake, as though he were a fisherman out for the day. Myers would verify Baker's location, make sure he was gone, and then burn the place to the ground. "So much for a quiet retirement," Myers sneered. Flores just lifted an eyebrow. Myers left Washington that evening, flying to Atlanta, then roundabout through Los Angeles, Portland, and Seattle.

From Seattle he borrowed an old pickup from a friend and drove over the mountains to Spokane, where he went to Facebook Marketplace and bought an old $200 Coleman kayak and tiedowns to keep it on the truck. The seller threw in a paddle and a life jacket, and Myers spent the night in Post Falls. The next morning, he drove north, and was at Marshall Lake, just three miles beyond Baker's, by lunch. He spent the afternoon on the small lake, struggling a bit as he hadn't paddled a kayak in years. At dusk, he put it back on the rack and drove east to Sandpoint, to a Rodeway Inn. In the morning, he was back at Marshall Lake, parked at the landing, picked up a backpack, and walked south into the woods.

He had to hike up a ridge 1100 feet above the lake, and then down Exposure Creek to come in from the northeast, next to the marsh, and up behind Baker's cabin. He figured it for a full-day job, because he wanted to go out the same way he'd come in. Once away from the lake, he picked up a bulldozed Forest Service road that climbed the range of hills. Although it twisted him around to the southeast, he knew it'd take him to the top of the range, and he could make his way along the creek, skirting the edge of the marsh for the half-mile it'd take to get to the cabin. He'd be under cover of the trees from the time he topped the ridge. Under two miles to get there.

Just before noon, he could see the cabin, and he moved more slowly, from tree to tree, pausing to look around and wait for movement. He realized that spring was way behind the Northeast up here, and most of the underbrush was an impediment, rather than concealment. No leaves, and most of the trees along the creek were white-barked river birch. *So much for Google Earth.* Even with his typical hunter's camo jacket, he was a lot more visible than he wanted. *There are no cameras from this approach,* he thought, *because there are no trails in this direction. Still good to go,* he reassured himself.

In another twenty minutes he was within fifty feet of the cabin, and at the end of the trees, crouching down to see his next move. From here it was tufts of orchard grass, unmowed but beaten down by snow, the new growth not yet visible. It'd be a good place to start a fire, he supposed, but it might burn out before it got to the cabin. No, he'd have to go right up to the back door. *Should I focus on the barn, instead?* He wondered. No, no cover over there, either.

"Mister Myers, right here would be a good place to stop."

The voice came from a small speaker next to a light by the back door, he thought. He froze in place, crouched at the edge of the meadow, behind what he realized was very thin cover indeed.

"You are right on the edge of a Class A or B felony in Washington State," the man's voice said. "Arson or attempted arson, depending on what's in your backpack and what you do next. At a minimum, that's two years in jail. The maximum is life in prison. Why don't we stop and talk about this?"

I am more than a mile from my truck, he thought, *and if they can see me, then they probably have a camera on me. I am at the bottom of an eleven-hundred-foot ridge that I have to get up and then back down. I have been screwed from the moment I started this. What do they want from me that I can give them?*

He stood up, tossed the backpack in front of him, and walked into the meadow.

The back door of the house opened, and Deputy Castillo emerged, holding a shotgun carefully. From the side door of the garage, two black FBI agents, a man and a woman, emerged, handguns held low.

"I'm unarmed," Myers called out. He carefully got to his knees in the damp grass and stretched out, face down.

Castillo came up to him, handcuffed him, stood him up and patted him down, emptying his pockets. Myers looked steadily at the FBI agents in their blue windbreakers, and wondered what he was in for.

"If you would come along with me, Mister Myers," the deputy said, taking one arm. "We're going into town."

"Would you like us to bring your friend's truck along?" the woman agent asked.

Myers nodded, and Castillo tossed her the keys. "We'll see you in an hour, deputy," the male agent said. They opened the doors to the barn, and Castillo pulled his Ford out, stopping to ease Myers into the back seat. Behind him sat the FBI's plain gray Ford sedan. The black male agent started the car and drove it out, and the female agent took a moment to close and lock the barn door behind them. They eased down the west road to the landing, and after fiddling with the gate, Castillo set off for town, while the other car turned north, headed for Myers' pickup.

Back in Newport, Myers waited in a holding cell for nearly an hour, uncuffed. He hadn't been fingerprinted, hadn't been read his rights, hadn't been cautioned, and was beginning to be confused.

His backpack would do him in, he knew. He'd made up almost the lowest technology he could think of, lots of sawdust and wood shavings embedded in candle wax, formed up around a candle at the center that held the wick. The device pretty much guaranteed a hot fire and would leave virtually no trace. He had a half-dozen of the 4-inch cubes wrapped in foil, as well as two butane lighters.

Finally, Castillo came to bring him to an interview room. The two FBI agents were there, as well. Castillo sat him down, under the watchful eyes of the agents, who moved to take seats across from him.

"Mister Myers, my name is Devon Cook, and this is a fellow agent, Adrian Davis." Cook noticed that Myers was fractionally quieter when he said Davis's name. Myers looked at him. "You'll notice you haven't been fingerprinted, been cautioned, been Mirandized, or anything else. That's because we'd like to make all of this go away, and you can make that happen."

What did I tell myself? Myers thought. *The issue is what I can give them.*

CHAPTER 46: UNRAVEL

Monday, March 28
Washington, D.C.

On the last Monday in March, with Baker's waterfall two weeks behind them, Cook met Collins with a report in hand.

"Good to see this in front of me, and good to see you. Lay it out," Collins smiled.

"I have good news, and I have bad news," Cook smiled back. "The good news is that as far as we know all the mailings are done. It's been two weeks, and federal and state prosecutors are notifying us of grand jury hearings from around the country. Some of them involve legislators, and a couple of them involve judges, and quite a lot of them involve corporate executives and foundation directors.

"The bad news. We have a pretty good idea of who and how. We're pretty sure that Dr. Baker, a college professor, ran this whole operation. It's pretty certain he didn't arrange the programming that got into emails he sent to his interns. He just doesn't have the skills. What he does have are the analytical skills that put together the packages. You could argue that he's just the middleman, and that someone else made all this possible, ranging from collection to storage to distribution. But while we might have a couple of ideas about who—it's in the report—there's absolutely no way we can take this to court.

"As far as we can tell, while he worked through his interns, none of them had a clue about what he was doing, and he evidently went to some pains to insulate them.

"On the distribution side—if we could prove it was him, we'd have him for major violations of federal and state information technology laws. The last document dump—the 'Waterfall,' we called it—went through two dozen college campuses spread around the country. And when it was done, we couldn't find any evidence anywhere that the data had ever been there."

Collins looked at Cook across the table, brow furrowed. "What about his computers? Can you do a Hunter Biden on him, and analyze the hard drives? Right down to deleted files and fragments?"

"We haven't asked him for the drives, or his phones, or anything yet. I can do that if you want. But here's the thing: we won't find any evidence. This guy isn't stupid. If it's him—and I'm virtually certain it was—he was rigorously disciplined about setting up and taking down stuff. He's the kind of guy who actually would physically destroy a hard drive. He would overwrite everything on the drive a half-dozen times, and then shred it. He'd flush SIM cards down the toilet after breaking them in half."

"What about his use of overseas servers and VPNs?"

"Absolutely consistent. I bet he never used a server more than once, and only through VPNs. He probably used TOR browsers for every stage."

"Do we have any leverage at all on him? Are there any 'hooks' we can use?"

"We could pressure him through his interns, but again, I'm as certain as I can be that none of them knew a thing, and we can't demonstrate that any of them participated in any willing way."

"I'll review your report," Collins said, closing the cover, "and I'll take it to the Attorney General. The President wants to see it, too—and not just a summary. Did you include the reconstruction—the *imaginative reconstruction*—of how he might have done this? The one I asked you for?

"Pages, uh, 30-45."

"Now what about the other part of your assignment? The more recent one?"

"You'll get a notice about that later today, in a separate and *entirely unrelated* document. Adrian Davis has been reassigned."

"You talked to him?"

"Yes, and after some pushing, he admitted to being the conduit—the *unofficial* conduit—to the USCC. Flores is a family friend, and he got over his head, and there's no excuse. He's smart, and with this in his file, he knows we have him by the throat. He asked to be reassigned to Rome, and I'm recommending it."

"Reason? Why not fire him?"

"It's as far from what the USCC cares about as anything going. He knows I could have forced his assignment to

Africa or Southeast Asia, or terminated him. That'd be a waste of a good agent. And with the other thing, he knows *I'll* know if he contacts USCC again. If we fire him, he will go to them. Here's a chance at redemption."

"And that?"

"Yes, we own Myers now, and he's inside the USCC. If we ever feel the need to turn them inside out, he will be the key."

"Well, Devon, I'd say that's *entirely* satisfying. My compliments to your team. Draft me up some commendation letters, and the Director and I—and maybe the President—will sign them.

"And does Dr. Baker have a clue about what we know? Is he behaving any differently? Are you keeping tabs? And do we have any idea *why* he did this, other than idealism?"

"No, sir, as you suggested—in fact, as *he* suggested—this might be a catch and release strategy. I think he's likely to be very careful after this. I had a clue about the motive, but it took a long look to figure out what might be going on. Loss, sir."

"Really? Loss of what?"

"His wife, Jean, was killed back in 2019. Hit and run, and it looks like it was a congressman's son who did it. And pretty much got away with it, as the congressman called in some favors. Oh, and the congressman resigned last week when some of the Month of Sundays documents turned up. Insurance fraud of some sort. He may go to jail, and he's certainly out of Congress. Democrat, as it turned out."

"Fair and balanced again, eh?"

CHAPTER 47: CONVERSATION

"So, that's the story. And the ending so far is about the best news I could have," Baker said to his youngest brother. They were standing in Terry's shop and garage, out back of the main house in Spokane. "I hoped the networks would get the job done before the Department of Justice, and it looks like the punchline to that lawyer joke. 'A good start.' Let's hope it continues." He and Terry toasted the good news with mugs of coffee, standing next to the small wood stove that heated the shop. The ounce of Jameson just added more smoothness and character. Miles had brought the coffee from Seattle.

"So, what did you accomplish?" Miles asked Baker. Miles, the middle brother six years older than Terry, hadn't agreed with Terry on political issues for twenty years. He held up one hand, and began ticking off items on his fingers. "You initially made American voters suspicious of the government. That's a mixed result, isn't it? Second, you brought 'fringe' people in out of the cold and actually got them mobilized in the same direction—a 'centrist' direction. That's a huge plus. Third, you revealed some

295

deeply hidden shenanigans with corporations that stretched outside the US. Massive success. Fourth, you helped people see that the most radicalized groups were being led that way by people in power at all levels. Your rocked that one. Fifth, you truth-bombed the broadcasters into starting to make changes. Amen to that, with applause. And sixth, you did it without melting down the stock market, which Terry and I both appreciate, since we're close to retirement. Although that was a close thing. Give you propers on that one. And Terry didn't have to get the guns out of the gun safe once."

"Better and better," said Terry.

For a change, the two of them laughed with Baker. *Nice to have their support now, even if they hadn't known what was going on at the time,* Baker thought.

"I'd like to add an eighth," said Terry. "You focused on the importance of individuals and their membership in a society. One side sort of forgot one, and the other side forgot the other. Individual integrity matters, and so does the common good."

Baker nodded. "Yeah, that one's important. I think there's one other, and I'm hopeful it will last. For the last hundred years, the people in charge haven't been accountable. It's like the curtains have been drawn, so everything gets looked at except the actions of our leaders. Oh, Presidents get x-rayed, but not Congress. And now Congress will have to deal with that. You remember that "xenon decontamination" scene in *The Andromeda Strain*,' back in '71? 'This is the outer epithelial layers of your skin that have been burned away.'" Well, I think that's what it'll be like for a while. Leaders will be naked, whether they're in business or in public office. It will be uncomfortable. It will itch. They will feel 'thin-skinned.'"

Miles asked him, "So what happened to the sabbatical project? Are you turning this one in?"

Baker looked at them both. "As it happens, probably. I still have to find a way to put this together so that I don't go to jail, but yes, I'm thinking about it. I'll have some research ahead, especially on the small groups out there. Interviews, maybe. I actually thought about turning it into an oral history, sort of like the print version of *World War Z*. There will be no Brad Pitt." The phone rang in his pocket, and he pulled it out. "Excuse me, guys, I've gotta take a call here."

He stepped outside, flicking the screen to accept the call. "Yes, this is Baker." He listened to the voice on the other end. "Thank you, Mister President. It's been an honor to work with you on this project. Yes, sir, the sabbatical project is wrapping up, and it'll be published in early December, I think. Oh, yes, sir, not a word until after the elections in November. Congratulations on that recent legislation, sir. You're welcome!"

He listened, as the voice began again. "Oh, really, sir. That's very interesting. An attempt to overturn *Roe v. Wade*. Well, I haven't looked at the Court deliberations at all, sir, but yes, they're in there, as recently as two weeks ago. Separate project. When do you think it should be released?"

"Yes, Mr. President, I think that's possible. End of the month, maybe five weeks?"

A Month of Sundays

A Month of Sundays

Afterword

Although they might disclaim any support of this book, I would like to thank four remarkable people whose lives and conversation flow into it. Dr. Bill Johnson, Dr. G.W. Carlson, Dr. Stacey Hunter Hecht, and Professor John Lawyer, historians and political scientists, have informed, as much as they could without knowing it, my Dr. Baker. The first three, in their careers and in their lives, were the kind of people Baker himself might aspire to be. Beloved by their students, deeply in love with America, sharp-eyed and witty, generous, and wise. They are all gone, now, as Henry Vaughan wrote in 1655, "into the world of light." John Lawyer, retired, still remains, in his modesty, professionalism, and thoughtfulness the kind of citizen that students admire and want to emulate.

And, for the first time, as this is my first novel, I get the chance to acknowledge the love, support, and critique of my wife, Marjorie Mathison Hance. As she wrote her third novel, I worked on this one, and our conversations taught us both.

Made in the USA
Middletown, DE
10 July 2022